"I'm a demon summoned from hell. This is St. Abigail. She's a Saint returned from the outskirts of heaven. We work for the Holy Roman Inquisition and are humanity's greatest, and perhaps only, hope for survival as we approach the coming apocalypse. Our primary job is protecting humans from evil, supernatural entities that grow stronger by the day. Oh yeah, and I'm also a singer in a rock and roll band that plays in a bar off Thirty-eighth. Maybe you've heard of me." Silas said.

Lily said nothing, her mouth wide open.

Silas smelled something rancid just before hearing the faint scurrying sound. "Quick, get into the tunnel."

"Why?" Abigail asked. Lily was still looking stunned.

"Goblins. A lot of them."

ALSO BY ERIK LYND

SILAS ROBB: OF SAINTS AND SINNERS

ERIK LYND

BROKEN GODS PRESS

Silas Robb: Of Saints and Sinners
by Erik Lynd
Copyright © 2018 Erik Lynd.
All rights reserved
Published 2018 by Broken Gods Press
www.brokengodspress.com
Cover design by Damonza Designs
ISBN-978-1-943069-16-3

To my family, both old and new.

1

Sometimes Silas just wanted to kill him. That's unfair though, Silas wanted to kill anybody, Mort was just the most convenient human.

He sat with his back to Silas at an outdoor table at the café. Although café might be too grand a name for the jumped-up sandwich shop that had expanded its stale bread and day old meaty reach onto the curb. Mort was hunched over his laptop, chubby fingers stabbing at the undersized keyboard. Silas had never seen him without his laptop, but he still typed with the hunt and peck method. He hadn't even looked up when Silas pulled up on his bike although the exhaust thundered loud enough to set off the alarm of a car parked along the street. He could not see Mort's face, but he knew that his glasses had slid down to the tip of his nose and he was squinting as though his sight was failing. All in all, he looked uncomfortable in front of the laptop, a quintessential Luddite. He was Silas's tech support, although Mort preferred the term handler.

Silas approached the table, his hands itching to choke the life out of him. They flexed open and closed with fury as though practicing. It was evening and his shadow reached the table before he did, his six foot five 275 pound frame cast a shadow large enough to cover the table. When the shadow touched him, Mort tensed.

The head splitting sound of a two thousand cc bike exhaust did not make him flinch, but he sensed the danger now. Silas's shadow was an extension of his demonic fury.

In two smooth strides Silas was at his side and placed a hand on his shoulder forcing him back into the chair. He squeezed the shoulder, harder than he probably should have and Mort winced.

Humans were so skittish.

"Relax. I won't kill you tonight," Silas said.

"Uh-huh," Mort said.

Silas sat across from him. As he expected, Mort's glasses had slid down his nose and perched at the tip.

"You have a way of sneaking up on people Silas," Mort said.

"I will take that as a compliment since I am not known for my subtlety."

Silas slid a cigar out of his jacket's inner pocket and said, "But it is an odd thing to say to someone who just pulled up on a loud ass bike." The cigar lit as he brought it to his lips. Being from hell meant never having to carry a lighter.

"Why the fuck did you call me out? I'm missing band practice," Silas asked.

"Ah, you are referring to that motley group of thugs as a band now?"

Silas slammed his fist on the table rattling the cups and plastic utensils and upturning Mort's coffee. A few patrons at another table looked nervously at him.

"Why am I here?" Silas yelled.

"Jesus Silas," Mort said as he grabbed some paper napkins and mopped up the coffee before it reached his laptop. "I didn't mean anything by it, I was just joking. You guys are actually quite good."

"Why. Am. I. Here," Silas repeated. He ignored the compliment, Mort might have heard his band a handful of times, but he was sure Mort never listened, he plucked slowly at his laptop at the gigs.

Besides, rock and roll didn't really suit Mort, he was more of a classical guy or maybe even country. That made Silas shudder.

Mort sighed and looked down at his laptop, after a few hunt and pecks at the keyboard he answered Silas.

"A fairy," Mort said.

Silas looked at him for a second trying to see if this was some sort of joke. Mort didn't blink.

"A fairy? You brought me out here to take care of a fairy?" Silas asked.

"It is an unseelie fairy."

"Of course it is, you wouldn't call out a demon to do battle with a nancy flittering about in tights, sprinkling happy dust on passersby. My point is why do you need me at all? I mean fairies can be annoying, but even one of your mortal agents can handle one."

"According to the report this one is especially difficult."

Silas grunted. This was going to be a long evening.

"Father Teager filed the report after he came for a wellness check on a woman named Martha Willamet. She lives in that apartment across the street," Mort said. "She missed church several Sundays in a row. According to Father Teager, she never missed a day and with the recent disappearances he thought he should go check on her."

"Disappearances? What disappearances?" Silas asked.

"Jesus Silas, what rock do you live under?"

Mort spun his laptop around, Silas saw the headline on the online newspaper. THIRD DISSAPEARANCE IN BROOKLYN

"I don't read the news much," Silas said.

He scanned the article. Three missing, two young men and an elderly woman.

"You think this is related to the fairy?"

"No, not necessarily, that was just the reason Father Teager went to check on her. According to the report she answered the door when he knocked and they had a pleasant conversation and she apologized that she had made him worry, but she had been sick."

Silas twirled his fingers in a hurry up gesture. Mort coughed and flipped the laptop back so he could read from the report.

"At some point Father Teager asked to use the toilet and when he was in there, that is when the incident happened."

"Incident?" Silas asked and smiled, this was getting interesting.

"Apparently, the Father heard noises coming from the toilet bowl and before he could investigate something clawed his ah... buttocks, painfully. He jumped up and saw a little head pop up from the bowl, like a wizened baby was how he described it. It spat and hissed at him. That made him think it was a little imp or demon."

"Of course it's always a demon, all the bad little things that go bump in the night are devil spawn..."

"If I may go on and be spared the rant?" Mort asked.

Cocky little shit, Silas thought, *I knew there was a reason I let him live*. Out loud he said, "Go on."

"Well apparently Father Teager quickly left the bathroom and tried to tell Mrs. Willamet that she had a monster in her bathroom and she needed to leave. That is when she laughed in his face and said it was her little pet then she spat and cursed at him. He fled with her cackling after him. As soon as he reached the church, he filed this report."

Mort reached into his laptop bag side pocket and pulled out a folder. He passed it to Silas. Silas did not accept it he stared at Mort and puffed his cigar. Mort shrugged and put the file back into the bag.

"Sorry I forgot you don't read," Mort said.

"I can read and I have read more books in my thousands of years of existence than you could even grasp. I don't like to read when I have a perfectly good mouthpiece spewing it for me. Besides I don't need the details, as they say, the devil is in the details," Silas flicked his ashes onto the table.

"Anyway, he wrote it up as a possible supernatural event, even went so far as to claim it might be an incarnation of Satan."

Silas barked a laugh, "If good old Lucy decided to incarnate here in New York it would be a little bit more noticeable than a shrunken imp body floating in the toilet like some satanic turd."

Mort ignored him and went on, "While the report was ignored by most of the Vatican, it of course was singled out for Father Moreales. He thought it was important enough for the Inquisition Project and here we are. Apparently, what makes this different is the control that the entity had on the woman. Not normal for a standard fairy."

Silas sat back in his chair and puffed for a moment.

"So what you are telling me Mort, is that it's a slow news day?" Silas asked.

"Yep, pretty much."

"I mean a fairy, really? They are a nuisance, but a threat? Hardly."

"All I know is that Father Moreales told us to personally take care of this and he is our boss. Unless, of course, you have found a way out of your contract? Then again you don't want to bother reading a ten page report, so I doubt you have even glanced at the thousand page Binding contract."

Silas glared at him, but the mortal was right. The contract was a monument to legalese that would drive the greatest legal minds in the world crazy. Silas would know, Hell is full of them. Demons have the greatest lawyers who have ever died create their infernal contracts, but the devious holy minds at the Vatican have them all beat.

And unfortunately he had signed it when he agreed to join the Inquisition Project. The Inquisition Project was a secret group within the Vatican charged with protecting humans from supernatural entities. The supernatural world, called the Pale, existed alongside the human one, separated by a thin metaphysical Veil. Whenever activity from the Pale threatened to spill into the human world, the Inquisition Project was called in.

The theory went like this; if ever the general population of humans realized that there was a supernatural world all around them and that fairy tales were true, the Veil would come tumbling down and the supernatural world would collide with the human one.

Chaos, war, death, and destruction would follow. Great fun from Silas' perspective, however, it is also believed that this will hasten the end of the world and the Vatican is not convinced humanity is prepared for the rapture.

That is where he came in. The Project summoned him to help fight against the encroaching Pale. They found a body for him to possess and a contract to bind him. The contract had straight forward rules or so he had thought. He was bound to help them by taking missions for which he was paid. That payment was a point system, when it reached a certain number he was free to let loose the shackles of the Vatican and roam the Earth as a free demon until his human form expired.

"How much is the fee on this one?" Silas asked.

"Ten thousand."

"Ten grand? What the fuck? That's chump change, not even worth dragging my ass out here." Silas slammed his fist down again on the table, this time leaving a dent in the wire mesh. This drew more stares to their table, Silas ignored them.

"Well it is just a fairy," Mort said.

"Fuck," Silas moaned and leaned back in his chair.

"Hey Silas, it adds up."

Silas stood and dropped his cigar into the fresh coffee the waiter had just set down for Mort. It hissed, Silas liked the sound.

"You taking the mission Silas?" Mort asked.

"You know the answer to that Mort."

"I already took care of the surveillance. This time keep it quick and quiet."

"Sure, no problem."

"And absolutely do not harm civilians," Mort said and tried to look Silas in the eyes. Not an easy task to do to a demon. Mort failed.

Silas smiled and turned toward the apartment building. He walked across the street and stopped outside to look up at the building. The old brownstone fallen into disrepair, as were most buildings on this street. He supposed Mort would say he should come up with a plan. He stared at the building a moment longer.

"Fuck it," he said, he never was much of a planner.

He headed up the steps to the front door. Silas looked over the tenant list on the wall beside the door and noted that the Willamet apartment was on the fourth floor. The front door was locked with a simple deadbolt that looked almost as old as he was, or his current mortal form at any rate. He scanned the edges of the door and ran his hand along the seam. No security, but that didn't surprise him. A slumlord couldn't be troubled to protect the tenants. Any cameras inside would have been disabled by Mort, but based on the lack of security on the front door Silas didn't think it had been any test of skill for Mort to do so.

He pushed and the lock ripped out of the door as the door opened inward. He caught it before it slammed against the wall. Contrary to what Mort said, Silas could be subtle when he needed to be. To someone on the street it would have looked as if he had just unlocked the door. Of course, if someone entered the building they would see the lock on the floor and assume a break in. He better make it quick.

The foyer and stairs were in the same state of disrepair as the door; workable, but barely. When it was first built, the woodwork would have been beautiful. Much of it had been replaced with cold lifeless pieces of particle board and faux wood paneling. Silas shook his head. As much as humans loved to charge into the future, they ignored the past and the beauty there.

Silas skipped the elevator. He didn't trust them and if there was a fairy in this building and it saw him coming the elevator would have been the perfect place to work its mischief. Of course that meant eight flights and that wasn't much fun either.

Before he reached the fourth floor Silas could smell it. It was the meaty rotten stench of death, of carrion. As much as that reminded him of home, it was out of place here. The scent was faint and only his demonically enhanced olfactory sense allowed him to detect it.

At the top of the stairs he looked both ways, the hall was empty and quiet. Not even the sound of a TV. To his demonic ears, the only sound was coming from the street outside. According to the mailbox list at the door most of the fourth floor was deserted, at least most of the apartments didn't have a name on them, but he hadn't expected the whole building to be empty.

The apartment at the end was Willamet's, but Silas went to the door across the hall from the stairs first. The door was unlocked and he pushed it open, ready to lunge forward if someone was inside and he had to shut them up quick. The apartment was empty.

Something was not right. He could feel it in his demon bones, magic lay thick about this place. He walked through the abandoned apartment.

It wasn't completely empty; odds and ends lay strewn about. Some clothes and boxes were in the back rooms. Some boxes contained junk, but he thought humans would have felt they were important. He found pictures in one, old baby toys and clothes in another. Whoever had moved out had been in a hurry.

On impulse Silas reached into his jacket pocket and brought out a little vial. In it was a plant. He opened it and pulled out a little leaf. From his other pocket he pulled out a packet and shook out a small measure of blue powder. It was dried bluebell. He put both the leaf and dried flower in his mouth and chewed. If something supernatural had occurred here then the herbs he just chewed would interact with his human-demon physiology and he might catch a glimpse of what had happened.

It would also make him high as a kite.

He knew his target was in the other apartment and he should be there, the broken lock would go unnoticed for only so long. Maybe not though, there weren't many tenants left to stumble upon it. He began to feel the slight tingling that meant the narcotic was going to work. It had a similar effect to dropping acid only instead of just hallucinations he would actually see the residue of supernatural events.

He walked around the apartment, stumbling occasionally. He was enjoying the euphoric effect of the leaf that activated the bluebell. Bluebell was common and by itself did nothing, but when combined with the leaf of the larthean plant, only found on the Plains of Tartarus or in a quaint little apothecary on the Upper East Side, it opened the mind to the mystical.

If he had come here to do battle with anything other than a relatively harmless fairy he wouldn't have taken a chance on the intoxicating effect, but even high he should be able to deal with a fairy infestation.

He pictured himself in an Orkin man uniform wielding a spray can full of iron dust. He burst out laughing and it took him a moment to catch his breath. Oh yeah, the drug was working.

The visions began with tracers similar to LSD, but that is where the similarities stopped. They began to coalesce into faint shapes. He saw a little man running through the living room. The little man was chasing a mortal, an old guy, but the image was too faint to make out exactly how old. He appeared to be poking the old man with a little stick. The image faded as Silas stumbled to the bedroom door.

In the bedroom an image appeared of the same little creature, a brownie Silas realized, pushing books and paper off the bookshelf to rain down on the old man's head. The old man took a swing at the brownie with his cane, but the fairy danced away.

Before he lost the effect of the leaf, Silas went out into the hallway and opened the door on the next apartment. Not yet approaching the one Mrs. Willamet lived in. As Silas had suspected this one was empty also, only there was more junk in it. The previous tenant hadn't even bothered to pack half their stuff.

In this apartment he saw a flying creature, a pixie, he thought, swooping like an angry bird and pulling at the hair of an old lady who ran around the room, mouth open in a silent scream.

Silas staggered out into the hallway. The effects of the leaf were coursing through him and he thought he might have used too much.

"Nahhh," he said and chuckled.

He pulled out his phone and speed dialed Mort.

"Yeah?" Mort asked when he picked up.

"See if you can pull a list on any submitted plans or notice of public use that involve this block or this building," Silas said.

"You sound funny, you Okay?" Mort asked.

"Yep, just fine, never been better."

"Jesus Christ Silas! Are you high? You haven't been out of my sight for more than ten minutes. Couldn't you have waited until you got home?"

"Sorry doctor's orders," Silas said and hung up on Mort's outraged squawk.

He focused on Willamet's door. It wavered a few times, then stood still. He stood leaning against the stair railing letting the drug burn itself off. It was fading. He should wait awhile, let the larthean leaf work its way out of his system.

"Hah, it's only a fairy. Don't need more than a fly swatter or a rolled up newspaper," he slurred.

He walked to the door and knocked, maybe a little too loudly. He waited a moment and heard a shuffling on the other side. A moment later the door opened and a large woman looked around the door. She had to be more than three hundred pounds, wearing a stained housedress and a dark red bandana held her hair back.

"Yes?" she asked, her voice rough and wavering as though unused for a long time.

"Plumber," Silas said.

"But I don't need a…"

Silas didn't wait for her to finish. He pushed open the door, using more strength than he intended. That was a lot of meat to push aside. The woman uttered a little screech as she fell back into the room. Inside the apartment the layout was the same as the others except nothing was packed. Apparently, the lady was not bothered by the pests. The apartment, however, was a mess. Clutter littered the tables and furniture, cigarette butts and old beer cans lay on the floor. The smell of rot was stronger here.

"You can't just barge in like that. What kind of plumber are you?" The woman said.

Silas looked at the woman. He could see a blue aura faintly around the woman. She had some strong magic on her. Unfortunately the hallucinations remained, her red bandana was shinny as though wet. Even as he watched it appeared to melt and drip onto her forehead.

This was a bad trip.

"I'm not really a plumber, I am more of an Orkin man," Silas said. "Where is your bathroom?"

"Orkin man?" she said, confused.

Silas sighed, she wasn't of much use, it was as if she wasn't all there. He was beginning to think he was going to have to kick down every door in the place.

"Second door on the right," she said pointing off down the hall.

Silas turned to the hallway and bright blue light swam before his eyes. Briefly the whole apartment lit up like a blue flame. This was definitely the source of the infestation.

"Put the seat down," the woman called from behind him as he approached the bathroom door.

The smell of rot grew stronger the closer he got, he opened the bathroom door and looked in. Nothing. The bathroom was empty. Silas stepped inside and looked around. Everything looked normal and shimmered with a faint blue aura, so faint that it was almost undetectable. The drug was wearing off. With his foot he flicked up the toilet seat. Still nothing.

Was it hiding from him? Did it know who he was? No, how could it? He shook his head trying to shake off the last of the fog. Based on the condition of the last apartments he thought the fairy should be in a full rampage trying to drive out the last tenant. It should have seen him as just another victim.

He looked under the sink and in the medicine cabinet. It occurred to him that not only were there no fairies, but he had not discovered the source of the smell. He went back into the hall and saw the woman not more than ten feet away, eyes wide as she looked at him. He turned his back on her and approached the door nearest the bathroom.

Here the smell got stronger and was mixed with the smell of feces and urine. It made Silas think of approaching an animal's den. He kicked open the door this time, in case there was some creature in there waiting for him. The door ripped partially from its hinges and slammed up against the wall with a loud crack.

It was a slaughter house inside. Three bodies dangled from a makeshift rack secured to the ceiling. All three were naked with long cuts running the length of their bodies. Below each were bowls full of blood gathered from the victims, two young men and an old woman. There was movement from the bed behind the hanging corpses.

A large older woman lay naked on the bed, arms tied to the bed posts. Martha Willamet, Silas guessed, grimacing. Although he couldn't be sure since the woman had been tied to the bed for a long time, she was covered with filth and sores. Her eyes rolled in her head and Silas was sure she had not been fed nor had anything to drink in a while.

So the large woman, now right behind him, had not been Martha. He looked to the bowls again and thought of the red bandana on the woman's head and how it shined almost like it was moist. He now realized that the red drips on her forehead had not been a hallucination, it had been fresh blood.

"Red Cap," Silas muttered, now he was sure he would kill Mort if he survived this.

Silas turned. The creature was now inches away from him. So close Silas could smell its foul breath. It had dropped all pretense of the disguise. The creature's face had melted away, revealing the stretched grin and elongated nose common to the Red Cap species of Fey. Sharp teeth, slick with saliva and rotten meat sprouted from that grin. It was large, stretching the woman frame to its limit like some gigantic blob of silly putty. The bloody red cap for which it was famous sat on its head, fresh blood soaked its dirt matted hair wiggling with maggots. It had fed well and had grown powerful.

"Hi," Silas said.

Before he could move or react, the creature grabbed him by his jacket lapels. In one smooth, powerful move Silas was thrown across the room. He grabbed the wooden frame of the window as the rest of his body slammed through, shattering glass, parts of the window frame, and the bricks surrounding it. The rubble plunged to the street below, but Silas held the remaining part of the window dangling forty five feet above the sidewalk.

Yeah, it was powerful.

He heard screams from below and looked over his shoulder. Mortimer was standing up from the table across the street and looked as if he didn't know what to do. Which he probably didn't

"You said fairies," Silas yelled at him. "Not Fey."

"Is there a difference?" Mort yelled back.

"Is there a difference? You son of a bitch, when I get out of this I'm going to…"

Silas didn't finish, a large clawed hand covered his face and another grabbed his shoulder, dragging him back into the apartment. He was thrown onto the coffee table shattering it. Pain exploded across his back and the rest of his body ached from his turning the window into a door. The body he currently possessed was large and powerful, but even it would have been shattered beyond repair if not for the demonic soul that infused its flesh.

For a moment Silas' vision swam, he was still groggy from the drugs. The creature's head came into view. It grinned and pounced.

Silas thought it might be time to show the red cap who the hell it was fucking with. He brought his legs up with inhuman speed and slammed them into the red cap's chest sending it flying into the ceiling. It must have weighed five hundred pounds, but it hit the ceiling with enough power to split wood and send debris down.

The red cap fell next to Silas with a thud and a grunt as it rolled to its feet. By then Silas was also on his feet. They circled each other, the red cap now weary of what it was facing.

Silas reevaluated the situation. He dug into his ancient memories to a time when he had possessed a witch that had often interacted with fairies and Fey. They were closely related, but the Fey were vastly more powerful and much more dangerous. This particular one started off as harmless as a fairy, but infinitely more evil. Red caps sought to murder humans and soak their caps in the blood of their victims. The more victims, the more powerful the red cap.

The red cap charged. Silas was caught off guard by its speed. He dodged to the side, but he wasn't fast enough. It hooked Silas around the middle. With a heave the red cap threw him through the living room wall. Plaster shattered and wood studs splintered. He landed unceremoniously in the bathtub. The porcelain rang out with a dull thud as his head bounced off the lip of the tub.

The world spun. He knew he had to move. As his vision cleared he was jerked to his feet and thrown through the wall again, this time into the kitchen.

He fell against the sink and hung there hoping he appeared dead or at least unconscious. He had to surprise this thing, he had to buy himself some time to think this through.

He felt the thump as it pushed through the hole he had made in the wall, splintering wood and plaster. Shit, he thought, it was moving carefully. Maybe it wasn't as stupid as he had thought. No chance to change the plan now, he had to lie still hoping it would get closer before striking.

Red caps are notoriously hard to kill. The best-known way was for their caps to dry out. If they don't get a regular infusion of blood by soaking their caps in their victims, they weaken and fade into the mists of their world. That cap had been dripping with fresh blood and Silas was pretty sure he wouldn't be able to hold out long enough for the blood to dry.

He felt it behind him. Still he did not move. It sniffed Silas like a large dog. Under other circumstances he was sure they could have been friends.

It was now or never.

Silas spun, throwing his fist out in a back handed strike. He had once possessed a Japanese warlord in the early fourteenth century who had been quite accomplished at martial arts. His fist slammed into its chin.

Silas heard a snap as the red cap spun away. It stumbled into the living room as it tried to regain its balance. Silas sprang through the air and brought his right foot up stomping the creatures face as it tried to recover from the first blow. This move he didn't learn from the Japanese warlord, the stomp was pure slam dancing 101 circa 1991.

Its jaw disengaged from it skull. Silas could see it swinging loosely as the red cap fell on all fours. With a battle cry worthy of the Hun tribal leader he possessed around 400 AD, Silas leaped onto the back of the red cap. The red cap reared its misshapen head up and bellowed.

It was like riding a bucking bronco, or because of the red caps massive girth, a bucking cow. A big, pissed off cow. To keep from falling off as the creature tried to stand Silas grabbed the cap. His fingers sunk into the sticky wet mess and he remembered there was another, trickier way to kill a deranged red cap.

He gripped the cap as hard as he could and yanked. It stayed stuck firmly to the red cap's head. He pulled again putting even more of his demonic strength into it, this time he felt it give a little, like prying sticky gum off the sofa. The red cap felt it also, because it jerked up, rapping Silas's head on the ceiling, denting the popcorn texture and splitting the drywall. Consciousness wavered, but Silas held on.

With a final heave Silas yanked and twisted the cap. It stretched briefly, with stringy flesh, like cheese on a deep dish pizza connecting it to the red caps head. The cap only appears to be a cap and it can be taken off to dip in blood whenever it so desires, but the rest of the time it is connected like any other organ.

The cap came away and the sudden release from the creature's flesh caused Silas to fall off the back of the monster. He landed with a thud in the Lazy Boy.

The creature paused in its thrashing and reached its hands up to gently probe the top of its head.

Uh oh, now it is really pissed off, thought Silas.

The red cap raised its claws above its head and bellowed. It shook the walls and shattered the widows. It sounded like Godzilla stubbing his toe.

Silas shot out of the chair and lunged passed the screaming red cap, angling for the kitchen door. The red cap lashed out to catch Silas, but striking him across his already bruised and aching back instead. The force of the blow propelled him into the kitchen.

He fell prone on the linoleum floor, blood from the cap and his numerous cuts and scrapes streaked across the white surface as he slid.

The kitchen was small and the angry red cap would be on him in seconds. He rolled to his feet, ignoring the stabs of pain from almost every joint and muscle in his body and grasped the side of the sink. From the corner of his eye, Silas saw the red cap come into the kitchen preparing for a final, enraged charge.

The other way to kill a red cap when you can't wait for its hat to dry, was to soak that cap in its own blood. It would be vulnerable for a moment. Obviously, this was very hard to do and probably the reason it was not so well known.

Silas stuffed the cap quickly into the drain. The red cap cried in surprise and ran to the sink as Silas stepped back holding his bruised ribs. It shoved its bloated hand down the drain ignoring Silas as it tried to retrieve its precious cap.

Red caps tend, like many Fey, to be anachronistic and not up to speed with modern technologies.

Like, for example, a garbage disposal.

Silas reached over and hit the switch on the wall next to the sink and the blades roared to life. The red cap threw its head back and screamed. Silas seized a cleaver from the knife rack on the counter top. He swung the cleaver at the red caps throat chopping the head from its body and cutting that ear piercing scream short.

Silas looked around the corner of the sandwich shop. People that had been sitting at an outside table were standing and looking at the gaping hole in the side of the apartment. Several passerbys had stopped and were looking. In the distance he could hear sirens. Somebody had called the police, so much for that famous New York ambivalence.

He could hear the bystanders talking. One had thought it was an explosion, perhaps a gas main igniting. Another thought it was a failed suicide attempt because he had seen somebody hanging from the edge of the window, but was dragged back in by an incredibly fat and ugly woman. Of course another thought it was a terrorist related incident, some bastard cooking up a dirty bomb. That made the bystanders nervous and they began moving away.

Silas knew that most of them will have forgotten the details of what had happened by dinner time. The few who had actually seen him dangling from the window wouldn't be able to describe him accurately. They would even forget that he yelled. The details would fade to a large man hanging from the windowsill. The gas main exploding would most likely be the explanation that stuck in their heads.

That was the way it was when most mortals brushed against something from beyond the Pale. Most mortals were completely oblivious of the danger growing around them day by day. But then again, that just meant job security to Silas.

After decapitating the five hundred pound Fey, he had slipped down the back set of stairs. Although slipped might be the wrong word, perhaps stumbling, limping, half falling down the stairs would be better, he had made it to the ground floor as fast as he could. He found a back door to the alley behind the apartment and he had looped around to the sandwich shop. Moving was painful, but so would be hanging around for the cops to arrive. Every bone in his body ached and many cuts and bruises adorned his fierce face. He was definitely not his hell born fury self.

Mort sat calmly at the table, tapping away at his laptop. Silas slipped up to him and sat in the chair. He reached out and slammed the laptop shut. Mort pulled his fingers away just in time.

"It was not a fairy," Silas said quietly.

"The report said it was thought to be a fairy. Maybe if you had read it you might have picked up some detail that would have warned you."

For the second time that day he really thought he could kill Mort, maybe take his ears for a souvenir, his skull would make a snazzy candle holder.

"Why did you want me to check out the surrounding buildings?" Mort asked

Silas pulled himself from a fantasy about ripping off Mort's arms and then beating him to death with them. If he just wasn't so God damn tired.

"Did you find anything?" Silas asked.

"Yeah, it looks like the same development company bought up a few of these buildings. They're trying to renovate the area, like this sandwich shop. The owner of this building was the last holdout."

"The owner was no hold out. I think he wanted to sell as fast as he could. I think he knew somebody or knew enough himself to call up some fairies to drive off the tenants who had long term or even permanent leases."

"He was buying the co-ops in the building over the last couple of years. But I thought you said it wasn't a fairy?"

"Well I think Mrs. Willamet might have been a little in the know herself when it came to the supernatural. My guess is the fairies didn't bother her so he had to call in the big guns and made a deal with the Fey. Which is only a little bit better than a deal with the devil."

His eyes flickered over to Mort's

"Or the Vatican," he continued. "Somebody played a cruel trick on him though if they gave him a red cap."

Mort let out a little gasp, "A red cap?"

"Yep, he has been the one killing mortals out in these parts, to feed. I'm sure the landlord didn't know what he had unleashed."

Mort had opened his laptop again and was typing away. Probably updating another report, Silas thought. He pulled out another cigar from the folds of his jacket.

"So the woman is dead," Mort said, he didn't mean it as a question.

"Oh no, she is still alive," Silas said around the cigar. "She's chained to the bed and severely dehydrated and malnourished, but alive. At least she was a few minutes ago."

"The old lady is still alive and you didn't help her?" Mort asked, his voice rising.

"Hell no, I was tired. Besides the police are coming. Mortals can take care of their own."

Speaking of which, a couple of patrol cars were pulling up, sirens blaring. Time to go. Silas didn't fear the cops, but he didn't like them. They could be very annoying when he was trying to do his job. He stood and made his way to the motorcycle. He sucked up the pain and hid the limp, no use drawing attention to himself with the boys in blue nearby. Mort shut the laptop and grabbed his bag to hurry after.

"Silas, we need more time to debrief," Mort said.

"Debrief? What are we? In the CIA? You're watching way too much TV," Silas said.

He swung his leg over the bike and fired up the engine. It roared to life and instantly Silas felt a little better, a little more relaxed. He sighed in pleasure.

"Just have the funds transferred into my account, Mort," Silas said loud enough to be heard over the exhaust.

Mort opened his laptop, supporting it with the palm of one hand and ran his fingers over the keys with the other.

"Of course, after we deduct a fee for the damages I will be happy to transfer the money, if any is left, to your account."

"Fee? For damages? I almost got killed back there," Silas said. "What was I supposed to do? That thing threw me through the windows and walls."

"Nothing proper planning might have avoided. As per section 741 subsection J sub paragraph three of the Infernal Binding Contract, or IBC, we may deduct damages and expenses above and beyond..."

Silas didn't hear the rest, his demon spirit raged and he revved the engine to drown out the sound. Christ he hated priests. There was no bargaining with Mort, he followed the Vatican's rules to the letter and those old codgers could give a rats fucking ass about what Silas went through. What the fuck had he been thinking when he agreed to that summoning and signed that contract? But he knew what he was thinking, he was thinking about the world above, the world beyond hell. He was thinking about the lusts, the passions, the drinks, the air, the meaning, and the life of this world. It was the most seductive of drugs and he was an addict.

With a grunt he throttled the bike, leaving rubber on the asphalt and exhaust billowing around Mort as he tried to yell at Silas over the sound. In his rear view mirror he saw that Mort had inhaled some exhaust and was coughing.

That, at least, made him feel a little better.

2

"Doug," Father Delentante called out, sounding shriller than he intended. He couldn't help it. They were going deeper and deeper underground. First they had entered the subway and from there a small access tunnel, which Father Delentante felt wasn't strictly legal for them to use. That access tunnel had led them to old train tunnels where the homeless watched from deep in the shadows as they passed. They moved through this area rather quickly as though Doug realized there was danger in those tunnels. *At least the young man had some sense.*

Doug might have been an urban explorer, as he liked to call himself, but he was still young and reckless. If Father Delentante hadn't known him all his life, he had christened him as a baby, he would never have followed the young man down here. Although if he were honest with himself, that might not be one hundred percent true.

They shared a love of the past, Father Delentante as a historian and Doug as an anthropology student. When Doug had come to him asking Delentante to follow him under the city, telling him that he had discovered something extra ordinary, it had been the passion in his voice that had tugged at Father Delentante. He trusted Doug and whatever the boy had found must have been significant. So it had been part love for Doug and part selfish curiosity that drew him down here into such a foreign place.

But this was getting ridiculous; they had been walking a long time, deeper than even the homeless travel. He would be surprised if some of these tunnels had seen anybody for thirty years. When they passed the sewer tunnels originally built in the 1800s he had had enough.

"Doug," he called out again.

Doug paused twenty feet ahead of him and turned back. Father Delentante thought he looked distracted, but they only had the lights of their flashlights to see by. He wondered what they would do if their flashlights went out. He couldn't find his way out of here without Doug, let alone if there was no light. He tried not to think about it.

"Yeah Father Del?" he asked.

"You didn't say we would be journeying to the center of the earth to see this interesting find of yours. I am not sure we should be going much further, it is getting dangerous."

"But it is just a little further Father Del. One more tunnel I think."

"Doug, this is foolish. We could get trapped down here or even accosted. Can't you just tell me what you saw?" Father Delentante asked.

"I can't tell you, because I am not sure what it is. A little further, please Father Del. Up the tunnel a little more," Doug said and turned. He started walking again without waiting for a response.

The Father looked down at his feet. His boots were caked with mud and soaked to the bone, he was sure his clothes and face must look as grimy. All the city's refuse found its way here, they were at the bottom of the New York trash can. With a sigh Father Delentante followed him.

After another bend in the tunnel he noticed that the tunnel walls were no longer brick, but appeared more natural, hewn from rough rock. Where the hell were they?

Father Delentante's flashlight was pointed at the walls so he almost walked into Doug before he realized that Doug's flashlight had stopped moving. The young man had pointed his light at the opposite wall washing the surface in a bright yellow light.

"Here, this is what Lily and I found a few days ago," he said.

Father Delentante looked at the wall illuminated by Doug's light. Pictures were carved and dyed into the rock wall. They were old, very old. The carved edges had worn smooth and the dye had mostly faded and flaked off, it was hard to make out the original colors. He stepped closer and ran a finger gently against the carvings.

"Careful Father, this could be an important archaeological find," Doug said.

Father Delentante nodded. The pictures, the style of art, he recognized them.

"This might be the work of the Lenape nation," he said quietly.

"So it is Native American?" Doug asked.

"Yes I believe so, but old, very old. I can't be sure it is the Lenape, but it is definitely Native American art and the Lenape were in this area. They were like the grandfather tribes for the other Native American people in this part of the country."

"I knew it. How old? I knew this was a good find. Is it like pictographs?"

He smiled, Doug was excited like a child discovering a new animal or seeing a magic trick.

"It is not pictographs in the traditional sense. They didn't really have a written language, most Native American people didn't. But like any culture they used art to tell stories."

He ran his fingers over one of the pictures again. It was of some sort of large animal, perhaps a lizard. Its eyes looked as though they were closed. Men stood above it spears and clubs at the ready. The animal was surrounded by an image commonly used by the Lenape to symbolize evil.

"Is that animal's eyes closed?" Doug said.

Father Delentante almost jumped he had been so engrossed with the pictures that he hadn't noticed Doug come up behind him.

"Yes I think so, it must be dead," Father Delentante answered.

"Or sleeping," said Doug.

"Perhaps, but see these men above it? I think they are hunters and have killed something they perceived as evil," Father Delentante said and pointed to the ring of men above the beast. A line separated the two images. The ground maybe, since they were underground now.

"Or they are watching it, guarding it. See how their clubs and spears are raised as though ready," said Doug.

Father Delentante was about to ask him why he was having such dark thoughts when he heard a noise. Doug heard it too and they turned to look up the tunnel.

It was a quiet shuffling noise and it faded quickly.

"Rats?" Doug guessed.

"Kind of big to be a rat," Father Delentante said.

"Well they grow them big here under the Big Apple. Do you know what the pictures mean?"

Father Delentante looked for a moment down the hall from where the noise came, but there was nothing. Perhaps Doug was right and it was a big rat. The desire to examine this amazing discovery overcame his concern.

"Well," Father Delentante said turning back to the picture. "This is going to require a lot of study by minds far better versed in the Native American cultures that existed in this part of America, but I would guess it is either a picture celebrating the end of a great hunt or, as you pointed out, a depiction of warriors guarding against a monster or evil thing. In that case perhaps it was created as some sort of lesson?"

"Or warning?"

"Perhaps. Who knows what they were..."

The sound came again, louder. This time the shuffle was followed by what sounded like a moan. Then the light clink of metal on stone.

"That doesn't sound like a rat," Father Delentante said quietly.

"What's that?" Doug asked.

His flashlight splashed against the other side of the tunnel, the side that had been behind their backs while there were studying the carvings. Words were sprawled across the stone in bright red ink. The ink looked new. It took Father Delentante only a moment to realize that the words were written in a modern phonetic alphabet of the Lenape language.

"It looks like Lenape, at least the modern way it is written," Father Delentante said. He had forgotten the sound up the hall, he stared at the words slowly sounding them out.

More noises came from the tunnel. Grunts followed by the occasional moan and heavy footsteps echoed from the walls.

"Ummm, Father Del? I think we should get out of here," Doug said.

"Just a minute. I almost have it."

And he did almost have it; the words were on the tip of his tongue. It had to be important, being across the tunnel from the ancient writings. The old and the new juxtaposed together. The key was here.

A cry from the darkness, vaguely human, but animalistic echoed down the tunnel.

Doug grabbed his arm and pulled on him.

"Father Del, we have to go. There's something coming."

And then he had it.

"The monster wakes," Father Del whispered.

"What? Come on let's get out of..." Doug started.

A figure emerged from the dark of the tunnel. It shot forward, a massive human with clothes torn on its body exposing glistening skin with a metallic sheen. It became a blur that slammed into Doug, throwing Father Delentante against the wall. Doug screamed as he hit the ground and the man was on him.

It was more creature than man. Its massive body strained at the clothes covering it, half of its head seemed disfigured as though its cranium grew too large causing its face to enlarge and distort. From its back sprouted bony structures like the spikes of some prehistoric monster.

Doug screamed and squirmed underneath it, but its weight as it crouched on his torso held Doug in place. It wore a human shape, but it was no human. Father Delentante wanted to do something, wanted to save the boy, but he could only lay there, body akimbo shaking his head in a silent scream as the creature grabbed Doug's hair and looked at Father Delentante casually ignoring the writhing person underneath it.

The creature's eyes glowed in the near darkness. If Father Delentante thought there was any humanity left in this poor thing, it was dispelled the moment those eyes found his. They were slit like a cat's and the pupils flickered and waved as though burning on the inside. Doug's flashlight had fallen when he was struck and it now rocked back and forth strobeing its light across the monster, treating Father Delentante to fleeting glimpses of a melted face and bony facial structure. And teeth, teeth like a canine, if that canine were a hound from hell.

With a sickening tearing sound it ripped Doug's head from his body, its eyes never leaving Father Delentante's. He was vaguely aware the creature had turned, he had become its new target, but still he couldn't move. That was when he must have passed out for a moment, because the next thing he knew, there was a man standing over him.

The creature was still there, but Father Delentante was free of the eyes. He gazed up at the stranger. He was a Native American. He wore simple jeans and a button up denim shirt, but his hair was pulled back by a leather strap and feathers intertwined with his locks.

The creature still crouched over Doug's body and looked thoughtfully from Father Delentante to the man standing over him. Surely this creature could tear them from limb to limb if it so desired, but it hesitated. Then Father Delentante noticed the club in the man's hands. The thick piece of hardwood glistened as though recently oiled. The tip was banded in knotted leather and tapered to a hand grip at the other end. Intricate carvings wove around the entire shaft. An impressive weapon, but against this inhuman thing it looked like a toothpick.

The man held it aloft and the thing flinched back, like a vampire confronted with a cross. With a deep growl, the monster rose and had to hunch over to avoid hitting its head on the ceiling. For a moment Father Delentante thought it was going to charge them, but then it turned and ran off down the tunnel.

The man stood poised for a moment ready for the thing to come charging back down the tunnel. When it didn't he looked down at Father Delentante and silently offered him his hand.

"Thanks," Father Delentante said and he grasped the hand and hauled himself up. "What the hell was that..." his voice trailed off as growls and roars echoed through the tunnel. There were more of those things.

"We had better get out of here," Father Delentante said.

The club moved so fast all Father Delentante saw was a blur as it streaked towards his head then it was all gone, swallowed by sweet oblivion. The last thing he saw before the darkness took him was the stoic look on the Native American's face.

CARDINAL JULIAN LOOKED at the clock on the wall, the big hand clicked into place at one o'clock. He had been waiting here for over an hour. He glanced at the priest behind the desk, Father Moreales' secretary. For the entire hour and fifteen minutes Cardinal Julian had waited the priest had not looked up at him. He had worked studiously at his computer and phone pausing to eat a few bites of the salad that made up his lunch. Cardinal Julian did not have a salad. Cardinal Julian was starving.

The secretary had successfully ignored Cardinal Julian's glowers and frowns for over an hour. If he had not announced himself when he had entered the room and stated that he had urgent business with

Father Moreales he would have thought the priest didn't even know he was there. He sighed loudly, coughed and exaggerated the uncrossing and crossing of his legs.

Nothing. *The impudent little bastard.*

"Do you suppose you could see if he is ready for me?" Cardinal Julian finally asked.

"He is not. I let him know you were here, however, he is not done with his lunch," the priest said.

Cardinal Julian hated this and he hated Father Moreales. The bastard thinks he runs the Vatican. He thinks that just because he has the ear of the Holy Father he can insult the cardinals. Cardinal Julian had to talk to his holiness about this. He didn't know why the pope put so much trust in Father Moreales, but it was becoming unbearable. It was one thing to ask for his advice on occasion, but it's inappropriate that he looks the other way when Father Moreales was engaged in practices bordering on blasphemy. *Investigation of the Miraculous my ass.* Moreales was a step away from the "exorcists" the church appoints. As if demons really could possess people... hell as if they even existed. Sometimes Cardinal Julian wondered if the church was tied too much to the superstitions of the past.

He would not even be here if it were up to him. If it wasn't for the silly report in the folder he carried, he would right now be dining in his own office. But his Holiness had let it be known that any reports of the supernatural or miraculous had to be quickly turned over to Father Moreales for "archiving". Whatever the hell that means. Out of spite, Cardinal Julian chose to interpret 'quickly' in his own way. He had sat on this particular report for over a week.

The phone rang with a digital shrill. The thin, pinched secretary picked up the handset and listened.

"Yes, of course sir," he said and put the phone down. "You may go in now Cardinal. He is done eating."

The little prick didn't even look up. With a huff he stood, smoothed his cassock and strode through the door.

Father Moreales sat at a rather small desk in the middle of a very large and very opulent room. It had to be at least fifty feet long and almost that wide. The floor was marble interlaid with mosaics. Against the sides of the room intricate statues stood from different time periods. Paintings and prints of ancient maps were tastefully integrated with the renaissance murals covering the walls.

"Can I help you Cardinal?" Father Moreales asked without looking up from the document in his hand.

"Yes you can Father..." Cardinal Julian stumbled over his words as the secretary slipped past him. The secretary quickly began gathering the plate and silverware from Moreales' desk. Once he had them in hand he did not leave, but stood off to the side of the room.

"I have a report for you. You know, the type that we were asked to deliver personally when they showed up?" Cardinal Julian didn't bother to hide the sneer in his voice.

"Ah, very good. Thank you, please put it on my secretary's desk on your way out."

The Cardinal's mouth dropped open.

"You mean I could have just... you mean I didn't have..." he sputtered and looked at the secretary. "You didn't tell me I could just drop it off."

"I am sorry sir, but I did not know the reason you were here. As I recall your exact words were; is Moreales in? I have to speak with him immediately," the secretary said.

Cardinal Julian knew his face was red. He spun on his heels and stormed out of the room. Slamming the door behind him and throwing the file folder onto the secretaries' desk, scattering papers onto the floor.

Moreales would pay for this. That insolent asshole was done here.

Father Moreales looked up as the Cardinal stormed out of the room and slammed the door behind him. He let out a long sigh.

"You know Christopher? There is so little opportunity for humor in what I do that I thank God all the more when one occurs," Moreales said.

"Of course sir," his secretary Christopher said.

"This report that he was delivering. It is the same one you procured from his office computer last week I assume? The one related to the other reports from New York?"

"Yes sir. The one regarding the attacks and monster sightings in and below the city."

"Our original theory is a troll or some abnormally large gnome," Moreales said.

"That was the theory sir, and until we had this report, we had no concrete information on how the creature or creatures looked. All the other reports were third or fourth hand originating mostly from street people, who are unreliable at best. Other than a vague notion of a 'monster' we did not have much to go on."

"And now?"

"After running this report by the rest of the team we have concluded that it does not fit any known physical characteristics of any mythical creature."

Moreales glanced up from the report at this assistant.

"So what you are saying is we don't have a clue."

"Yes sir," Christopher said. "Also this latest report is from a well-respected priest as seen with his owns eyes and we confirmed the disappearance of the anthropology student Douglas Perkins. The involvement by the Lenape native American and their writing also lends, if not authenticity, at least curiosity that we need to take note of."

Moreales leaned back in his chair hands clasped lightly in his lap and chin lying against his chest with his eyes closed. This was his thinking position although on occasion it could also be his napping position.

"Suggestions?" Moreales asked.

"Assign an agent; he can investigate the cause of these monster sightings and disappearances. I think we have enough information now to conclude that this is a matter for the Inquisition and not some false hysteria by the homeless and poor."

"So you vote for action? I agree, something is going on over there in New York, in the bowels of that city. Notify Mortimer and Silas of this report and have them look into it."

Christopher didn't move.

"Do you have a concern Christopher?" Moreales asked.

"Yes sir. I don't think Silas is the one for this task. At least not initially. Once we know exactly what is going on and we need some brute strength to go confront the problem he would be an ideal candidate, but for now I think we need someone a little more subtle."

"So you don't think the mind of a demon is subtle or devious enough to handle this job?"

"Of course I do sir, just not the mind of this particular demon."

"Silas is a little rough around the edges, but he has proven very effective and knowledgeable for the inquisition. Your point is taken, but I would like to use Silas."

Moreales leaned back and stared at one of the murals on the wall. It depicted a female saint slaying a dragon with sword.

"Perhaps it is time Silas had a partner," Moreales said.

3

The heavy metal door creaked loudly as Silas opened it. He winced. He would have to have that fixed; it made sneaking out of his basement apartment almost impossible. It didn't matter this time anyway. Father Deluca was standing across the alley at the foot of the concrete stairs leading to the back entrance of the mission.

If there was any human Silas could say he liked it would be Father Deluca. He had spunk and grit. Father Deluca spent day and night with the lowest of mankind--the homeless, the broken, the drug addicts, and the crazies--yet through it all he did not back down. He consistently battled to help them, even those who didn't want to be helped, even the ones who wanted nothing more than violence. He was a tireless crusader. Or maybe he was just insane; the jury was still out as far as Silas was concerned. But that didn't stop him from enjoying the priest's company.

Silas was about to call out to him, but then hesitated. Father Deluca was staring off down the alley, a frown creasing his brow. He glanced at his wrist watch, then back down the alley. Then to Silas's surprise he paced back and forth a few steps. For a man who was the soul of patience pacing was out of character.

"Father Deluca?" Silas finally called out quietly, not sure why he was quiet, but feeling the tension from the priest.

Father Deluca looked up sharply. Obviously he had been too lost in thought to hear the loud door.

"Silas," Father Deluca said, a faint smile touching his lips. "What are you doing home at this late hour? It's midnight. Shouldn't you be off saving the world--or at least putting on a rock and roll show?"

It was a Saturday night; as far as Silas was concerned he should be three sheets to the wind by now down at the bar.

"Just getting a late start Father. Had to press the old leather jacket and jeans and all that," Silas said.

Silas pulled a pack of smokes from his inside pocket, shook one out and offered it to the Father. Father Deluca looked at the pack, and longing flashed in his eyes. It was his vice and they often enjoyed a smoke together in the early evening or at dawn if Silas was sober enough. The priest seemed to enjoy the conversations and Silas enjoyed the little corruption he could inspire in the priest, so it was a win, win. This time, however, Father Deluca shook his head.

"No Silas, not tonight. As much as I might want to, I am waiting for someone."

"Suit yourself Father."

Silas flipped one of the smokes into his mouth and sucked in slowly as the tip lit with a bright red glow. He then took out one cigarette from the pack and slipped it into Father Deluca's breast pocket and winked at him.

"For later Father," he said.

Father Deluca chuckled.

"Thanks Silas. I can always count on you to be the devil on my shoulder."

"You betcha. So what brings a priest out to a dark alley? What would the parishioners say if they could see you skulking around like this?"

"Actually I am waiting for one now. Well at least one of the regular patrons of the mission."

He seemed to consider for a second. Then he said:

"Silas, I know that you are not one of the regular employees of the church, and you know that the archbishop has asked me to take special care to watch over you. I know that you provide discrete services for the church, and although I admit I don't know the exact nature of the services maybe you can help me with this. You spend a lot of time on the streets right?"

"Well not really with the homeless. They smell funny," Silas said. He was curious what the priest would ask of him. Father Deluca knew about Silas' nature and his arrangement with the Vatican, but he was not privy to the details, which was probably for the best. He knew that Silas had some skills bordering on the miraculous, but the priest did not know that his smoking buddy and sometime confidant was one of the bad guys... one of the really bad guys.

"No, but you hang out at some of the most disreputable and broken establishments in the worst parts of town right?"

"Oh that. Yep, pretty shitty places."

Father Deluca looked off down the alley for a moment and then back at Silas, the frown back on his face.

"When I started working at the mission about twenty years ago it was falling apart and I took it as my personal goal to reestablish it as a presence in the community."

Silas didn't change his expression, but if this was going to be an impromptu history lesson on the parish he was going to regret offering Deluca the smoke.

"Since that time the community has grown slowly," Father Deluca continued. "And the mission with it. The people that we helped ebbed and flowed obviously, but overall the number of people we helped continued to grow."

Silas looked down the alley; his bike was at the other end. Perhaps he should start walking toward it.

"That was until recently. It seems that the people coming to the mission, the ones that need the help the most, are disappearing."

"Maybe it's just that it's working. I mean maybe all this help, you know the food and the talking, is really helping. Perhaps some of the people are pulling themselves out of this life," Silas said, hoping he sounded convincing.

Father Deluca raised an eyebrow.

"And you and I both know that is bullshit," he said.

"Then why do you do it? If you think it is all bullshit then what's the point?" Silas asked.

"I didn't say it was all bullshit. I think the church...I think we help people a little, give them a foothold maybe, to start pulling themselves up as you put it, but I don't believe that we can clean the streets and make it all better. I know the statistics and I know that for every person I help just a little, ten more fall deeper into their hell."

"Oh no Father, don't be so hard on yourself. Hell is much worse than this," Silas said and smiled reassuringly. He told Mort he could be sensitive when it was needed.

Father Deluca grunted.

"The point is Silas...this is different. This isn't the slow, natural attrition of the streets claiming their own; there have been an alarming number of our regular visitors that have disappeared. Ah, here comes my informant now."

Father Deluca nodded towards the end of the alley. Silas instantly detected movement at that end, though whoever it was was trying hard not to be seen. The small shape clung close to the brick wall, scurrying between trashcans and crates piled against the walls.

Silas tensed and instinctually stepped in front of Father Deluca. It might have been one of the Fey or even an imp, although Silas didn't think Father Deluca would have anything to do with one of those. The shape was thin and lanky enough that it could have been the homunculus of some minor sorcerer, but his demonic senses detected a heartbeat, body heat, and the smell of sweat. No. Homunculus was out of the question.

The form stepped from the shadow, and Silas saw that it was just a boy, fidgeting nervously from foot to foot.

Jesus Christ! I need a vacation, Silas thought, slowly reining in his fury and letting the tension out of his shoulders and fists.

"Michael," Father Deluca said and stepped around Silas. "I am glad you made it."

Father Deluca's hand disappeared into his breast pocket, and for a moment Silas thought he was going to offer the boy a smoke. Instead, he pulled out a small candy bar.

"I stole this from Father Tiernan; his gut's big enough. I don't think he will miss it."

Father Deluca tossed it gently to Michael, but it bounced against the boy's chest and hit the ground. Michael was staring, eyes wide, at Silas.

Uh oh. Silas recognized that look. The boy was about to make a break for it. Silas stepped back into the shadow. With his size he could not completely disappear, but the demon in him pulled the shadows closer to hide as much of his intimidating visage as possible. Normally, scaring off the neighborhood kids was the look he was going for, but in this case he wanted Father Deluca to be able to talk to the boy.

"Don't worry Michael, Silas is my friend. He won't hurt you. He just looks tough. Really he is as tame as a pussy cat."

Silas had to chuckle at that. It came out as a deep rumble and probably didn't help the situation. Apparently Father Deluca agreed because he gave Silas a sharp look.

"In fact, I asked him to be here. I have asked him to help us find out what is going on and where your friends have gone."

Michael's eyes flickered back and forth between them then he nodded slowly and seemed to come to some conclusion. He walked over to Silas and tilted his head to look him in the eye, like David confronting Goliath.

"I am not afraid of you," the boy said.

And Silas believed him.

He turned his back on Silas, dismissing him. Very few grown men could do that. Hell, very few grown demons could do that.

Silas was quickly changing his opinion of the youth in the neighborhood.

"Come, let's sit over here where there is more light."

Father Deluca guided the boy to the stairs and they sat. The boy had retrieved the fallen candy bar. He opened it and started shoving it into his mouth.

"Michael here lives with his brother, sometimes on the streets, sometimes at the mission. I have tried to get them to meet with Child Protective Services to talk about options, but he always seems to know when they are about and makes himself scarce. Right Michael?"

Father Deluca ruffled his hair, but stopped when he saw that the boy had stopped eating the candy bar and was staring at the ground. Father Deluca hadn't seen it, but Silas had seen when the boy stopped eating the candy; it was when Father Deluca had mentioned his brother.

"He's gone," the boy whispered.

"Who is?" Father Deluca asked.

"Jared. Jared is gone. They took him."

"Who took him? What do you mean gone?" Asked Father Deluca.

"He said he was going to look for the others. The ones you were asking about, his friends... my friends."

"You saw somebody take him?" Silas asked. This was getting interesting. Maybe this was something in his bailiwick.

"No. He just left me, said he would be back in an hour. Said he thought he might know something about what was going on. Why all those people were dropping out of sight. Then he took off."

The boy was lying, Silas could smell it. Demons were some of the best liars. It was an art, and just like you wouldn't show off your doodles to Picasso, you don't lie in front of one of Satan's little helpers. If the boy wasn't lying he wasn't telling the whole truth.

"Maybe he was late. He said he would be back in an hour. When was this?" Father Deluca asked.

"This morning."

"Father, you had asked these two to look into the disappearances you were talking about?" Silas asked.

Father Deluca looked away from Michael reluctantly. Worry etched his face. "Yes. I was saying too many people I was trying to help have just faded away, some that the brothers were close too. I asked them about it, but they did not know what was happening. I..um..."

Father Deluca paused, worry had turned to guilt.

"I asked Michael and Jared to look into it. See if there was some connection. I thought maybe there was some new drug or maybe even a new mission or other place helping. If I had thought for one moment that it might be dangerous I would never have asked the kids to help."

"There is no other mission Father," Michael said. "Just you and the other shelters that have been around a while. It's like some of these people we see every day on the same street corner or in the same line for food all decided to get the fuck... um...I mean, leave town."

"There was nothing common among them? Some of them, the ones you actually talked to on a regular basis, were they all doing something? Some connection? Maybe a new drug?" Silas asked.

"No, there are no new drugs, just the same ones day after day Mr. Silas." Michael scrunched up his face in the universal child body language of "I'm thinking".

"There was one thing..."

"Yes?" Father Deluca prompted. "Don't worry you can tell us. We want to help."

"But you might think I'm weird. I'm not even sure I got it right."

"Trust me, you don't know shit about weird kid," Silas said.

"Well, now that I think about it, they were depressed," Michael said.

"They live on the streets; it ain't fucking Disneyland. Of course they were depressed."

"No dumbass, I mean more depressed than usual," the kid said.

Silas grunted. Kid was ballsey as hell.

"A couple of them--Sam the old guy that worked his mouth like he always had a wad of chew in there and Lisa, the crack ho that came into your mission once in a while--talked about getting away from it all, about finding a way out. I thought they were talking about killing themselves or some shit like that," Michael said and brought his hand up shaped like a gun to pantomime blowing his head off. "Others that have disappeared said the same shit."

Father Deluca sat next to Michael and pulled him in close in a hug. Michael resisted a minute then allowed himself to be pulled against the Father. Tears were forming in his eyes.

"I shouldn't have let him go. I knew that... I tried to tell him, but he didn't listen, Father. I let him go." the boy said into Father Deluca's shirt, but Silas could hear him clearly and thought for a moment that the boy almost let slip what he was concealing.

"No Michael, it is not your fault. You couldn't have known. Jared is eighteen years old; there is no way you could have stopped him. He was much bigger than you. You did the right thing telling me." To Silas he said, "So how about it? Do you think you can help?"

"Not really much to go on here now, is there Father?" Silas asked. "I mean some street people disappearing? Maybe a suicide pact. What am I going to find, a room full of bodies and pitchers of Kool-Aid?"

The boy winced and pulled closer to the priest, Silas thought he heard a sob. Father Deluca shot him a hard look. It occurred to Silas that this might be one of those moments Mort was referring too when he called him insensitive.

"This is unusual and I know you specialize in the unusual Silas. I know this might not be as important as what the Vatican asks you to do, but I was hoping that you might be able to help me. Help us."

Silas looked down at his watch. It was late and he needed a drink.

"Okay Father, I'll look into this if I can. I can't promise anything of course, and like you said this might not be my number one priority if his holy upittyness decides I need to chase my tail on something else, but I'll do what I can."

Father Deluca nodded and stood, pulling the boy up with him.

"I'll take Michael to the shelter for now," he said quietly.

"Sure, I'll catch you later," Silas said and headed down the alley.

"Silas?" Father Deluca called to him after he had taken a few steps. He turned just in time to catch the candy bar. Father Deluca patted his breast pocket, smiling. "I guess we know each other's vices."

Father Deluca chuckled as he opened the door and entered the shelter with the boy in tow. Silas had eaten the candy bar before he reached the end of the alley.

4

_____

A man staggered out of the subway tunnel, passing from the gloomy dark into the pale florescence of the station. An unfortunately empty station.

"The people? Where are all the people?" cried the man.

He did not know what time it was. Days, minutes, and hours had no meaning in the Undercity.

"It must be late, that's all. I will find people." He just hoped it wouldn't be too late.

He looked over his shoulder, but he could hear no pursuit.

"They're coming though. Oh yes, they are after me," he said in a harsh whisper.

Carefully avoiding the third rail he ran to the platform and climbed up. A train would come soon, a train to take him away. He clutched a satchel close to his body and the clink of glass rattled through the silence of the station. The vials were safe. They had not broken in the mad dash from his home. His clothes were dirty and ill fitting. Holes were ripped throughout the cloth and raw skin covered with welts and scrapes lay exposed. He was missing one shoe. He squinted up at the light trying to find a sign that might tell him when the next train would come. When he found it, he stood dumbly trying to read it. It had been so long since he had read anything.

Perhaps he should go up the stairs; there had to be people up there. But there were other things up there as well. Like big open spaces, loud noises all around even more people... even more confusion... His heart thumped and his stomach ached just thinking about the world above. No, he was not ready for that,. Not yet, no way.

He heard a sound from the tunnel and he jumped. It might have been the rattle of bones on brick, the slither of scales on mud. His mind worked at all the possibilities. He knew he was going mad, but these sounds were real. He knew that much.

Again he considered the stairs to the world above, but even as he watched, a shadow passed across the top of the steps. A large shadow, vaguely humanoid but misshapen with what the man knew would be boney protrusions ripping through clothes and flesh alike.

Sweat broke out on the man's face and his skin went cold. He looked at the sign praying to a god he had long forgotten that the train would come now. A roar echoed down the tunnel. The man drew himself closer to the back wall of the station, trying to wedge himself as deep in an alcove as he could. He squeezed the satchel again and felt the precious round vials within. He considered for a second just throwing the satchel behind. Maybe that would stop them, maybe if they had this precious treasure they would let him go. But he knew that would not happen; he knew too much. No, Webb could not let him go now.

He could hear whatever was on the steps starting to make its way down. It grunted a bestial sound.

Another roar came from the tunnel, louder and closer, but this time as it faded it blended with the approaching sound of the train coming the other direction. The man almost gasped in relief. People, there would be people on the train. Safety in numbers. They would do nothing in front of the norms.

As if to prove it, when the man looked back at the stairs the shadow was gone. He had made it.

The train sped into the station kicking up a strong breeze and scattering a few pieces of paper trash. It kicked a little grit into the man's sensitive eyes, and his vision blurred with tears of relief. The train slid to a halt. As the doors opened, he stumbled in and fell on the floor of the train. A young man jumped up to help him, but seemed to think better of it once he got a good look at the state of this clothes; perhaps he had also caught a whiff of his unwashed body. The man did not mind though, he giggled in relief as he pulled himself onto a bench seat. A few people had gotten off at that stop, but enough remained. He was safe.

The train rocked gently as it hurtled down the tunnels that had been his home for many years. He was free now, and he knew it would take time for him to get used to the world above, but he could do it; the path was clear to him now. And after selling the vials he would not have to worry about money.

"Woe to the man who forsakes family and the love of his lord and master."

The voice echoed through the train car and the man jerked in his seat. His blood ran cold and he began to shiver all over. He knew the voice. It was the voice of his master, Mr. Webb.

The owner of the voice stood at the front of the car. There was no doubting it was him, even in the flickering light of the train. He was tall and slim, wearing an antique suit that was too small for him. As always, large aviator reflector sunglasses covered half his face and his head was topped with oil-slicked hair too long to stay in place. On anybody else such an outfit might have looked silly, but on Mr. Webb the look was menacing.

The man knew the sunglasses were only there to conceal the red rimmed eyes brimming with blood that spilled over in constant crimson tears. Mr. Webb's right hand held the blood splattered white handkerchief that he used to dab away those tears. That same hand was covered in gold and silver rings, so many that it seemed impossible for him to make a fist. But he did make a fist, squeezing the other hand tightly. He was angry.

"Why Jeremy? Why have you forsaken me?"

"No," Jeremy whispered, but he could hear the panic in his own voice. "I didn't... I couldn't. I never meant to forsake you."

Jeremy looked around wildly. There had to be some escape, it couldn't end like this, could it? But the train roared on.

"You took something precious from me, Jeremy. You took my blood--my essence--from me. If that is not a betrayal, I don't know what is."

Mr. Webb looked around at the handful of passengers, his arms spread slightly as though seeking their support. Most kept their heads down, the ingrained training of a New Yorker taking over when a drama unfolds on the subway.

"Whatever buddy, just sit down and shut up," said a large burly man seated near the front of the car.

Mr. Webb chuckled and began walking toward Jeremy. He swayed with the movement of the car, gliding easily down the aisle as though floating.

Jeremy's mind raced. He thought maybe he could run, maybe he could run out of the car door and try to keep away from Mr. Webb until the train came to a stop. Then he dismissed the idea. If he ran he might accidentally run into a deserted car and then Webb would have him exactly where he wanted. No, he had to hold it together until they arrived at a crowded station.

"You think I won't act, don't you? Because of all the other passengers?" Mr. Webb asked, as though reading his mind. "You think these ignorant slaves will save you by their presence?"

"Hey!" said the large man who had spoken earlier as he stood. "Who the hell are you calling ignorant?"

Mr. Webb ignored him. The other passengers were watching nervously as Mr. Webb made his way down the aisle.

"These people won't stay my hand. Maybe before, while I gathered strength. Now, though, it is almost time for us, the faithful, to show ourselves to the world and the weak inhabitants of the upper city. No, these witnesses will not stop me this time. I will simply have to kill all of them."

"You're a terrorist!" screamed one woman. This caused several others to scream. Jeremy could see that in a moment this car would be in pandemonium.

"Terrorist? Mr. Webb asked to no one in particular. "No. Maybe terror though..."

"Okay, enough of this shit," said the large man as he walked toward Mr. Webb. "I don't know who the hell you are, but you are going to sit down and shut the fuck..."

He was interrupted as a long arm covered with boney plates punched through the ceiling of the car like it was made of foil and a hand twice the size of any normal human hand wrapped around the man's neck and lower jaw. With a jerk the man was pulled up and through the hole in the ceiling, leaving bits of his flesh along the jagged rim.

Someone screamed. The lights went out, causing even more screaming. And soon wet tearing sounds added to the confusion. He could see nothing except as a strobe from the passing tunnel lights. Flashes of demonic visages, talon-like claws, ripping fangs. Bloodied, screaming human faces stretched in frozen moments and burned into his mind.

Jeremy felt the satchel he had carried from deep in the Undercity ripped from his hands. His treasure, lost forever.

"Poor Jeremy," Mr. Webb said.

His breath touched Jeremy's ear and his voice cut through the din of the slaughter.

"You were never truly one of the faithful. You always denied me. And for that Judas, you die."

Jeremy felt the cold blade slip between his ribs--the cold searing pain of steel, not the claws and teeth that tore at the others on the train car. As oblivion took him, Jeremy thought that maybe he should be honored. The others were of no consequence. He was Mr. Webb's kill.

The strobe flickered again and Mr. Webb was gone. The cold steel that seemed to suck his soul from his body was gone. The last thing he saw was the blood-washed train car and the fading image of one of the monsters that had slaughtered the people on the train. It was twice the size of a normal man.

SILAS GRIPPED the microphone tight enough to feel the metal creaking beneath his fingers. The bass thumped, and he belted the lyrics in a voice reminiscent of the screams of the damned--only he was in tune. A guitar dangled from a strap across his back, swinging as he swayed and coming within inches of hitting the microphone stand.

He didn't fucking care.

The music had him. Walt, on rhythm guitar, pounded out power cords that shook the bar. Kitten, the drummer, threw sweat from her brow across the stage as she pounded the skins and thumped a double bass. Carl, one of the fattest and ugliest bass players Silas had ever seen, alternated between slapping the bass strings and smoothly grooving to the rhythm.

It was always like this. When he was on stage, he ruled the world. He wasn't a demon, and his audience wasn't a bunch of mindless humans. When he was on stage, he and his audience were the same. Just a bunch of assholes that wanted to rock. In the ages he had existed, he never had felt more alive than when he had a guitar in his hands and a microphone inches from his mouth. It wasn't the fact that it was music--he had played instruments for centuries--it was rock and roll that called to him. He liked drugs as much as the next guy, but nothing beat a rock high.

Music, including rock and heavy metal, was scorned in Hell. It empowered the listener and empowering the damned was frowned upon below. So it was only when he walked the surface world that he got to indulge his passions.

The chorus had ended, and now Silas' fingers flew across the fret board of his guitar in a searing solo. For a brief period in the eighties he had possessed Eddie Van Halen, so his hands flew confidently across the guitar with all the skill of a guitar god. He had also possessed Ozzy Osbourne, but it was only a couple of hours before he couldn't take it anymore. That guy was a serious freak.

The audience was eating it up, screaming and rushing the stage. Occasionally a random bottle was thrown, once striking Silas in the head. He shrugged it off, taking it as a compliment.

Only one thing could put a damper on his high, and he was just walking into the bar. Across the mass of screaming sweat sacks pressing against the stage Silas saw Mort slip into the room. At least he didn't immediately cover his ears as he had last time.

Probably wearing ear plugs, Silas thought.

Mort took a seat in a booth, as far from the stage and PA system as he could. Silas hoped he didn't try to order milk again. For Christ's sake, he had a reputation to protect.

The song ended and Silas threw the microphone stand down as he pulled free the mic.

"Gonna take a little break, be back in a minute," he said and spit into the audience.

Walt walked over to Silas.

"What's up Si? Why cut it short? It's so fucking hot in here, I thought Carl was on his way to dropping a couple of pounds in this set alone," he said.

They looked over at Carl. He had taken this opportunity to start eating nachos from a plate on top of his amplifier. He saw Silas and Walt looking at him and shrugged before going back to his cheesy snack.

"Maybe not," Walt said.

"Got to meet with the missus," Silas said and nodded towards Mort at the back of the room.

"Hmm... you ain't going to disappear on us for a week or two like you did a couple of months ago are you?" Walt asked.

Silas hoped not, but to Walt he said, "Nah, probably wants me to beat the shit out of somebody."

Silas took off his guitar and propped it up against his amplifier, then jumped off of the stage. There was an impromptu cheer and hands slapped him on the back. Girls reached out to touch his shoulders and arms. He was no superstar, but he could get used to this local fame, even if it didn't extend further than the front door of the building. The pats and touches faded as he moved across the room. By the time he reached the booth that Mort had selected, somebody had turned on the iPod and recorded music blasted through the PA, albeit at a much lower volume than Silas' band. His fifteen minutes of fame were over for now as the bar danced to the big-selling sell outs. *Fickle bitches.* He slid into the booth.

"See. This is much better than some sort of coffee shop," said Silas.

Mort removed foam ear plugs from his ears. Silas noticed the cup of tea in front of Mort.

"Have you even tried beer? A shot maybe? I could get you one of those fruity girly drinks." he said.

"Alcohol clouds the mind. Besides, one of us needs to stay sober," Mort said.

A waitress set three shot glasses down and a pint of beer on the table.

"Brought your usual, Silas," she said and winked at him.

"Thanks babe. Can you bring me another round? My friend Mr. Sunshine here thinks he's the weather man. I get to get all cloudy."

Silas looked over at Mort before continuing, "I have a feeling tonight I'm going to need a little extra anyway."

"Sure thing," she said and disappeared into the crowd.

Silas slammed a shot back and put the glass on the table.

"It might cloud the mind Mort, but it is the gut that feels the fire."

As Silas took a generous swallow of beer Mort pulled out his laptop.

"Just don't spill any beer on this," Mort said.

Silas glowered at him, "What do you want Mort? I take it I have another job?"

"Yes, and this one is a biggie."

Now Silas was interested; he leaned forward. He pulled a cigar from his jacket pocket. It was illegal to smoke in public bars like this one; however, he thought he'd smoke where ever the hell he wanted until told to put it out. Then he would put it out in the face of the person telling him. So far no one had told him to put it out.

"What's got Moreales' panties in a bunch this week?" Silas asked.

"Attacks in the city. Someone or something is singling out victims and, well, tearing them apart."

Silas nodded, "Sounds like my kind of party."

"The initial reports came from street people, the homeless."

That caught Silas attention because of the conversation he had had with Father Deluca and that kid.

"They came as word of mouth reports up through the mission and soup kitchen system."

"Was one of these reports from Father Deluca?"

"Yes, I believe so. Why? Do you know something?" Mort said and narrowed his eyes at Silas.

Silas ignored him, "Go on, tell me the full deal."

"Well, it seems it started as a rumor of monsters stalking the backstreets and alleys of New York, also some told of sightings below the city, in the sewers and tunnels deep below. The reports were inconsistent at best and borderline incoherent at worst. You know, descriptions of hulking shapes, big teeth, violence, and boney protrusions."

"Sounds like a family photo."

"If it wasn't for the fact that there were so many, the Vatican might still be ignoring it. At least until we got this."

Mort slid a file folder out of his laptop bag and dropped it in front of Silas.

"That's a report from a well-respected priest named of Delentante. In this report the description is a little more detailed and describes an encounter between one of these things and a Native American while the priest was in a tunnel beneath the city."

"What the hell was an Injun doing in the sewers and dirty tunnels? Aren't they tree huggers, preserving the forests and all that crap?"

"We don't know what the Native American was doing down there since the priest lost consciousness, and you shouldn't call them Injuns. You sound racist."

"Mort. What a horrible thing to say. I'm hurt. I'm not racist--you know I hate all humans equally."

"Anyway, apparently the Native American knocked Father Delentante unconscious. So we don't even know what his intention was. The next thing Delentante knew he woke on a subway train a long way from his parish."

"Well what was the priest doing beneath the city? Looking for the gates of hell?"

"Actually, he was down there with a friend. The friend was an anthropology student from the university and a long time parishioner of Father Delentante. The Father had known him since he was a kid."

"What happened to the student?" Silas asked.

"He was killed by the creature."

Silas sat back and said, "Perhaps you should tell me the whole story."

"Ya think?" Mort said. "If you could refrain from interrupting me for more than a few seconds with a sarcastic remark or questions perhaps I could."

Mort told him what had happened to Father Delentante under the city. Silas feigned disinterest and even kept from interrupting him, until he got to the writing on the wall.

"What was that? What was on the wall?" Silas asked.

Mort sighed, "I really wish you would pay attention. *The monster wakes* was written in Lenape on the wall."

"It couldn't have been written in Lenape. They had no written language."

Mort raised a surprised eyebrow.

Silas waved his hand. "I possessed Meriwether Lewis for a while back in the early 1800s."

"I see. Well it wasn't technically the Lenape language; it was a phonetic spelling of the spoken words."

"So whoever wrote it knew enough about Lenape culture, but was desperate enough to bypass the normal oral tradition route to get a warning out."

"Or he couldn't tell anybody personally because he doesn't want to expose himself."

"Then why write it where it was unlikely to see the light of day? I mean, why not write it somewhere it would be easily found?"

"I don't know," Mort said.

"Let me see the words."

Mort spun the laptop so he could see.

"Huh," Silas said.

Mort waited a moment then said, "That was very profound Silas, but would you mind letting me in on the revelation?"

"No," Silas shook his head. "Look, this seems a little complicated. Don't you have something I could just kill? That's more my speed."

Mort spun the computer back and nodded. "I agree and so does the head office. Straight from the Vatican itself. You're getting a partner."

"A partner? You mean besides you?"

"Well Silas, I am flattered that you have raised me to the level of partner, it is so much better than my previous status of lowlife human piece of shit, but yes someone besides me."

Silas was stunned. In all his years of service he had never had a partner. It had never even been suggested. Other agents worked in pairs, he had heard, but not him. He would get a partner killed. Hell, Silas would probably kill them himself. He worked alone.

"No way Mort. You can tell the Vatican to shove it up his Holiness' anointed fat ass."

"This came directly from Morales himself."

Silas slammed his fist down on the table. A crack formed down the middle and the shot glasses bounced. Just then the waitress reappeared with a new round of drinks. She frowned at the table and overturned glasses.

"Don't worry honey, I didn't spill a drop. All the booze was gone," Silas said, glaring at Mort.

"Silas what the hell, why'd you go and break the table?" the waitress asked.

"I just got some shit news."

"What like your mom dying or something?"

"Yeah, or something."

His eyes never left Mort's. Was that sympathy he saw in the human's eyes? If so, was it for him or this new 'partner'.

"Just give me the booze and go away. I'll pay for any damages."

She set the drinks on the table quickly.

"Screw you Silas. Mark's gonna be pissed. I bet he fires you."

As Silas turned his attention to her he did not have to call for the demonic fury inside. She stared into his eyes and words caught in her throat. He let a little of what he was poke through his human facade. Then he spoke in a deep rumble.

"I said go away."

She dropped the serving tray and the glasses it held. They crashed to the floor with a loud bang. She brought her hands up to her throat as the blood drained from her face. He broke eye contact so she could leave. When he turned those fiery eyes from her, she ran. Not back to the bar, not to the back rooms; she ran to the door and out into the night. Silas was pretty sure she would never be back.

"Silas, that wasn't necessary. She was just an innocent girl. You didn't have to traumatize her."

"So who is this partner? Let me guess, an ex-Navy Seal or Green Beret yahoo who thinks he's the biggest baddest mother fucker in the..."

"She," Mort said and Silas could have sworn he was holding back a smile.

"Come again?"

"She, Silas. Your new partner is a she."

Now Silas was sure Mort was fighting a smile. *Smug bastard was enjoying this.*

"You can't be serious? They want me to babysit some chick? Oh wait, am I supposed to use her as bait or something?"

"No you can't use her as bait Silas."

"Then what good will a woman be? I already have to deal with you. She'll just get in the way, and I am sure as hell not going to protect her. At least an ex-seal or special forces might tell some good dirty jokes before he gets killed."

"She's not just anybody, Silas. She's a Saint."

Now that was a surprise. Silas sat back in his chair and swallowed the contents of a shot glass. A Saint. He had never worked with one before. He had heard of them, of course, and knew of their nature, but they were rare. Most agents of the Inquisition are mortal, albeit with special knowledge and skills. Only a few were supernatural like him. These Saints were another. They weren't the traditional saints of the Catholic faith, the ones painted on walls and carved into figures. The term Saint was just a name for these beings.

A Saint was once a human, normally a kind and just person--your basic goody two shoes-- who died. What happens next is a little like guess work. That person passes on to heaven, but stays around the fringe of the great kingdom until a gateway is opened by rituals known only to the Inquisition. It is a one-way gate through which only the Saint can pass. But they must want to, that is the key. To come back as a Saint you had to have unfinished business, such as vengeance or a desire to protect someone. So while a Saint will help the Inquisition out of goodness and nobility, they also have their own agenda. This can make them a little tricky.

"Which one?" he asked, but thought he already knew the answer.

"Saint Abigail," Mort said and looked quickly down.

"Oh shit, Mort. What the Hell is Morales thinking?"

"Yes, the former Miss Abigail Lee."

"He knows her record I assume? Christ, Mort. I killed her back in... back in..."

"1863, but it was by accident, at least that is what her record says. I assume the report is not wrong?"

"Well no, it's not, but that doesn't change the fact that I killed her and her whole family."

"She was never told that of course. Saints are never told about their past in the living world. If they were busy righting perceived wrongs from when they were living..."

"Like vengeance on the guy who killed her and her family?" Silas interrupted.

"...they would virtually be of no use to the Inquisition," Mort finished, ignoring Silas. "And their memories from the time before are hazy at best."

"When does this partner get here?"

"She is already here," Mort said.

Silas sat up and looked around.

"Not here in the bar Silas, I meant in the city. She is already in the city."

"Oh, well yeah," Silas said trying to looked relaxed. "When am I supposed to meet this slut?"

"Saint."

"Saint, that's what I meant. When do we meet?"

Now it was Mort's turn to look a little nervous.

"I am not really sure," he said. "Saints kind of make their own schedule. Then again Silas, you should know a lot about that. It's not like you are known to play by the rules."

"Maybe, but there's only room for one rebel in this organization. They want me to have a partner, so they give me one who might want to kill me and say she will show up in her own good time."

"Yep, that's about right."

"Business as usual for the Vatican. So we'll move ahead and her royal highness can show up when she is ready to grace us with her presence."

"I assume you are going to go talk to the priest who was attacked? His address is 359 west—"

"Not now Mort," Silas said and stood. "I have a set to finish, and rock 'n roll is one mean bitch when you deny her."

Silas ran and jumped up on stage, grabbing the microphone just as the drummer hit the first beat. The rhythm of the guitar burned through his head. Yeah, it was good to be him.

5

Silas hated the sun. He stared up at it through his darkly tinted sunglass. In his experience, which was significant, nothing fun ever happened during the daylight hours. Case in point, here he sat on his motorcycle outside the Dominican Friars monastery.

The building was out of place, a Gothic throwback wedged between two typical New York buildings. It was five stories tall and topped with soaring steeples. The facade gleamed a decaying green color in the bright sun.

This is where the priest that had been attacked was recovering. Silas assumed Mort had meant spiritually, although this place had a reputation as a poor man's hospital. Rest and recuperation--basically a priest's Club Med.

He lowered the kickstand of his bike and swung off it. The large wooden doors atop a set of brick steps towered over him and gave him a moment of nostalgia as he remembered the time he had possessed a Crusades-era knight during the breaking of a siege. Surging past that broken gate as they had torn into a city ripe for pillaging had been a good time, even in sunlight.

He rang the bell. Moments later a young monk opened the door.

"Yes?" asked the monk, thick glasses dominating his face. A vow of chastity was no stretch for this one.

"I need to speak with one of your guests."

"Is this an emergency?"

"Not yet," Silas said.

"Can you please return in a few hours? It is currently quiet time here and we don't want to disturb the peace. If you could come back in about three hours I could take you to Brother Talbot and see if we…"

"Quiet time huh?" Silas interrupted him. "That's a shame, because I'm pretty loud."

He pushed open the heavy door and stepped past the stunned monk.

The young monk sputtered. "Look sir you can't just barge in here, we are monks, but we can call the police like anybody else. I don't know what you think…"

Silas put his arm around the monk and pulled him close, steering him down a hallway. "Look kid, I ain't here to play games and I don't want to hurt anybody, but I will if that's what it takes. Now I need you to take me to Father Delentante."

The young monk paused. "You're Silas, aren't you?"

"Why yes. It seems my fame precedes me."

"Brother Talbot said you would be coming."

"And who is this Brother Talbot?"

"Secretary to the Abbot," he said as though that should impress Silas.

Mort must have contacted Brother Talbot about him.

"Good. Now that you know who I am and we are all buddy buddy, take me to Father Delentante," Silas said.

"I can't. But I can take you to Brother Talbot."

Silas thought for a moment then nodded. The quicker he saw this brother, the quicker he could see Delentante.

"Lead on oh, bespectacled one," he said. "What's your name?"

"Harold. I'm Brother Harold,"

"Oh, your parents must have hated you," Silas said.

Brother Harold shrugged off his arm and led him down a hallway. The interior of the monastery was a mixture of old and new. Well-maintained woodwork resided next to chipping plaster. They passed several side hallways. As they passed the last, Silas caught a flash of movement. When he turned to look down the dark hallway there was nothing.

He had seen something, however. He hooked Brother Harold's arm to stop him and turned him toward the hall. At the same time he enhanced his human senses and the dark hallway opened up to him. Nothing.

"What's down this hall?" Silas asked. The young monk tried to pull away from the painful grip, but Silas would not loosen.

"Nothing, just storage," he answered.

"I saw movement," Silas growled.

"I suppose a brother could be down there, but it is unlikely. This place is old and dark; I am sure it's just your mind playing tricks on you."

Silas looked at Brother Harold and let a little of his demonic fury through. "My mind does not play tricks on me. Take me to this Brother Talbot." He released Brother Harold.

The young monk stumbled back against the wall, his face draining of color. He crossed himself and then hurried off down the hall. Silas allowed himself a smile before following him.

They arrived at a non-descript door and after a quick knock the young monk ducked in.

The room beyond was strikingly different from the hallway outside, well maintained, almost luxurious. The office furniture looked impressive. A large desk dominated the room and behind it sat a large man. This must be Brother Talbot.

He was older, but broad shouldered and barrel-chested. He looked as if he could hold his own in a barroom brawl. Silas liked him already. The young monk was talking to him.

"This is Silas; he has come to see Father Delentante," the priest mumbled.

Brother Talbot's eyes darted to Silas. Silas had the distinct impression he was being sized up like livestock.

"So this is the great Silas Robb. The Inquisition's special agent." Brother Talbot stood; he was almost as tall as Silas.

Brother Harold stepped back against the wall as though he was trying to disappear. His face still pale.

"Why Silas, whatever did you do to the boy?" The words, spoken in a heavy southern accent came from behind him.

Silas turned to see a woman against the back wall; the door had hidden her when he came in. She was tall also, more than six feet and slim. Blond hair fell past her shoulders. She wore jeans and a tight fitting vest. Curves in all the right places. She was stunning and glowed with an inner strength. She annoyed him already.

"Abigail," Silas said quietly.

"Yes. Silas Robb meet Saint Abigail," Brother Talbot said.

Two stilettos crossed at her belt--long, slender and deadly. Just like the Saint herself. Her lips were red, as if she had been drinking blood. She stepped forward, coming into the full light of the room.

"Just call me Abigail."

"Whatever you say, Toots," said Silas and turned back to Brother Talbot. "Now if you could take me to Father Delentante..."

He was interrupted by a scream, followed by the quick rapport of gunfire.

"God damn it!" yelled Brother Talbot. He reached under the desk with his right hand and the cabinet along the wall near Brother Harold popped open, revealing several large assault rifles as well as a handful of smaller fire arms. "Don't they know it's quiet time?"

Brother Talbot grabbed a rifle and threw one to Silas, who caught it out of reflex. Brother Harold quickly chose one himself. St. Abigail had her stilettos in her hands.

"Templars?" Silas asked, although he already knew the answer. Brother Talbot nodded.

The Templars were the special military unit of the Inquisition

Project, taking their name from the famous order of knights. They were the Green Berets of the Vatican; however, they worked exclusively for the Inquisition reporting to Father Morales.

"Why didn't anybody tell me there was a Templar unit in the city?" Silas asked

"It should have been in the city dossier they gave you when you were assigned here." Brother Harold said as he threw a belt containing ammo cartridges over his shoulder.

"Another report? Can't anybody just tell me these things?" Silas asked.

Another crack of gun fire rang out, followed by a loud crash.

"It sounds as though it's coming from east wing," Brother Harold said.

"Let me guess, that's where Father Delentante is," Silas said.

They looked at him eyes wide.

"Dammit," Brother Talbot said again. A burst of static came from under his robe and he pulled out a small radio.

Silas didn't wait for him. He dropped the rifle--it wasn't his style-- and ran out into the hall. St. Abigail slipped up behind him.

"Do you think they are after the Father?" She said, her southern belle accent out of place with the evil looking stilettos in her hands.

"Don't know, don't care except that I need to get to Father Delentante before they do."

Behind him he could hear Brother Talbot speaking into the radio.

"Central, this is Talbot. What is going on?"

"Sir, this is Central. Sir we don't know exactly. We detected intruders and spotted them on surveillance, then almost immediately our systems went down."

"So you didn't see how they got in?"

"Sir, they were already in when we spotted them. And sir, they're not human."

"How many are there?"

"We don't know. Two were spotted before the system went down. Alpha and Epsilon unit have both ceased communication. We believe they are on the second floor of the east wing and they appear unarmed. Except for natural weapons."

"Natural weapons?"

"Yes sir, claws and big teeth. They are more monster than man."

That was all Silas needed to hear.

"Talbot, which way to Father Delentante's room?"

"That way," Brother Talbot nodded down a large hall.

Silas took the lead running down the passage. A door to his right burst open and a creature sprang at him. All teeth and claws, it was man-shaped, but green, plate-like scales covered half its face and shoulder. Oddly out-of-place sunglasses sat awkwardly on its face. The glasses were twisted and stretched to fit over its huge head. It was almost as tall as Silas and heavily muscled. Claws flashed toward his face. Silas dodged to the side, grasped its extended arm and heaved against its chest letting its momentum add to his as he slammed it against the far wall. Bits of plaster and chunks of the ceiling fell as it hit.

Shots rang out from the Templar's rifles, but the thing was already moving with preternatural speed. The bullets scored the wall where the creature had been moments before. The monster was fast, but so was Silas. He had his hands up just as the creature was on him again. He managed to get his hands under the creature's jaw and around its neck to hold back its snapping jaws, but its arms were long and he could feel its claws sinking into his shoulders.

Suddenly, St. Abigail was on it from behind. Her stilettos darted in several times with quick punches, slicing between the scales that covered most of its back. Its grip loosened on Silas' shoulders. It tried to turn to address this new threat, but this time Silas held on, refusing to let it turn to St. Abigail. She got in three more strikes before it went limp in his hands. He let it fall to the floor.

It was a man, or had been a man, he thought. Scales gleamed through torn holes in old baggy clothes, next to flashes of pale human skin. It looked like half man half lizard. It even had a tail, jerking like it had a mind of its own.

"What the hell is it?" Brother Harold asked.

"An over-sized gecko," Silas offered.

More shots came from ahead.

"Up the stairs," Brother Talbot said.

More monks were streaming down the hall, armed to the teeth. But Silas didn't wait for them; he took the stairs two at a time. He did note that St. Abigail was right behind him. He heard the radio crackle.

"Sir, all teams report that the other wings are clear. It seems the intruders are only in the east wing."

Of course they are, thought Silas, *they're after the same thing I am.*

Silas crested the top of the stairs and found his way blocked by five of the creatures. Dead monks lay strewn about the floor and the smell of discharged weapons drifted through the air. As the newcomers arrived at the top of the stairs, the creatures leaped forward. Gunfire erupted around him as Brother Talbot and the other monks opened fire. The creatures moved at inhuman speeds, but even so, they could not dodge the hail of gunfire. Two were hit, but it only slowed them. One sprung effortlessly to the ceiling, using its claws to find purchase in the plaster. It swung from its arms straight at Silas, who grabbed its swinging legs and pulled down. Its claws ripped free of the ceiling and the creature came crashing down.

Silas didn't hesitate; he slammed his fist into the back of its head. The back of its neck felt like it was armor plated. If Silas had been human his hand would be broken, but it was just incredibly painful. The creature fell forward at the blow, but lashed out with its left arm at Silas. He caught the appendage and with both hands yanked the forearm back, slamming his knee against the creature's elbow. It howled in pain as the bone splintered, leaving the arm at an impossible angle. St. Abigail slit the creature's throat as it stretched its head back in a roar of pain.

She turned back to the fighting, if you could call it that. The monsters had waded into the monks like a farmer harvesting wheat. The guns were of limited use in the confined space and any shot had just as much a chance of hitting one of their own as one of the creatures. Even St. Abigail was cut in a few places from claws. But she was more than a match for these things. As she fought she moved more like a dancer attempting a complex, but beautiful choreography.

He looked at the creature she had killed; it had dark goggles on its eyes also. In fact, all the creatures fighting them did.

A sixth creature stood down the hall, but this one was different. Larger than the others, maybe close to seven feet tall, it was somehow less bestial. It too wore goggles around its head. Most of its body was covered in scales, but they shone silver as if they had been polished, whereas the others' scales were a dirty, mossy color.

This, Silas thought, is the leader. As he watched, the creature opened the door next to it and stepped inside. Silas guessed that was the door to Father Delentante's room. He stepped forward to pursue then looked back at the slaughter happening behind him. He should leave them and get to Delentante before that thing, but at the same time these creatures would soon kill all the monks and then his back would be unprotected. One of the creatures looked at him, a large grin forming beneath those dark glasses.

Dark glasses!

Silas reached out with his demonic fury and created a small ball of fire in his hand, about the size of a lighter flame. Recalling words he had learned while possessing a sixteenth century sorcerer who specialized in sympathetic magic, he murmured quickly as the monster crouched to pounce on him. Silas felt the power of the words gathering like a thunderstorm and could feel the pull and push building in the air around him. He directed the pull toward the flame in his hand and the push at the lights along the wall. It was good they were incandescent, as this little trick wouldn't work with florescent bulbs.

The creature sprung at him and he released the power. Instantly the flame went out in his hand and the lights flared to life, making the hallway ten times brighter. The creature flew past him clutching at its eyes. The other monsters fell back and covered their eyes, screeching in pain. While bright for the creatures, in truth the hall wasn't much brighter than a sunny day, so the surviving monks quickly took up positions around the stunned creatures.

The monks had more of an even chance now, although Silas suspected the bright light wouldn't keep their adversaries at bay for long. But he had other problems to deal with now. He ran to the door that the big one had gone through. St. Abigail was right behind him, apparently she assumed the monks could handle it also.

"I saw one go into here," she said.

Silas didn't answer, he kicked the door down, tearing it off its hinges. Inside the leader stood over Father Delentante. The Father's throat was a bloody mess and blood flowed freely from the wound. The creature's right hand dripped with blood and flesh. It looked up as they barged in, and Silas thought he detected surprise on the thing's face. Surprise turned to a smile and then the creature leaped through the window.

Silas ran to the window and looked out as the thing landed on the ground and started to run down the alley at incredible speed. Silas glanced at the Father. The gouge in his throat was weakly pumping blood now, but the priest already had a glassy look in his eyes. It was too late.

"Go after it. I will take care of the priest."

Silas needed no further encouragement, the priest wouldn't live to tell them a thing. He jumped through the window and landed thirty feet below on the pavement. The large creature stopped at the mouth of the alley and swung back to look at him.

This one seemed unaffected by the sunlight, although it wore glasses. It looked from the window above, then back down to Silas.

"What are you?" it asked, its voice deep and rumbling, but human sounding.

"Just a rock 'n roll singer," Silas answered.

With a roar the creature charged at Silas.

Hmmm... must be a country fan.

Silas dodged to the side, but the creature was too fast. Its hand lashed out, hooked him around the midsection and spun him against a large metal dumpster. Silas kicked out with his right foot and caught it in the face. The power of the kick knocked it back a few feet. It shook its head. Obviously it had not expected resistance like this.

"Why did you kill Delentante?" Silas asked, as the creature carefully squared off against him.

It struck at his face and Silas realized this was probably not the time for an interrogation. Silas brought his hand up to block, then slammed his fist into the creature's stomach. It grunted, but otherwise seemed unfazed. The creature returned the blow to Silas's nose using its scale-plated forehead. Pain exploded across his face and tears blinded him. He fell back against the dumpster, blood gushing from his nose.

This is one tough lizard thing, Silas thought through the red haze of pain. He struggled with consciousness, awaiting the next blow. It didn't come.

Bullets rained down from above. The creature was hit three times, the first two rounds glancing harmlessly off the silver scales covering parts of its back and chest. The third round, however, cut through the remnants of clothing the thing wore and found soft flesh. It roared and looked back up at the window to Delentante's room.

The pain had receded and Silas had stayed conscious. Up in the window he could see Brother Talbot and another monk, each with rifles in their hands, firing at the monster in front of him. Two more bullets bounced off the creature's scales and with a final roar it ran off down the alley, moving with that same supernatural speed. When it reached the street beyond, it sprang into the road and onto the top of a car, crushing the top. The car slammed on its breaks and slid into the one in front of it. The creature sprang from that car to another and then out of sight into another alley.

Silas couldn't follow it. It moved too fast and his body was too bruised and battered. He walked to the service entrance of the monastery and kicked it open before ducking back inside.

WHEN SILAS RETURNED to the room, he was nursing aching ribs and had one son-of-a-bitch headache. Monks had been clearing the wounded and the dead from the hall; it looked as though the battle was over. The bodies of the creatures had disappeared.

"What happened to the ones we killed?" Silas asked a monk helping with the injured.

"They retreated shortly after the lights flared, but they took the time to grab their dead before leaving," the monk answered in a thin voice, his face pale. He was still in shock from the combat.

"Which way did they retreat?"

"We saw them head down to the first floor, but none of us followed. We were in no condition to chase after them. If they hadn't retreated..."

The monk left the rest hanging. He didn't have to finish. That any monks had survived was a miracle. Silas nodded and went into Delentante's room.

St. Abigail sat on the bed leaning over the body of the priest. Brother Talbot was speaking with another monk in the corner. Two monks with medical bags were packing them up next to the body of Father Delentante. Brother Harold and another monk looked out the window, rifles at the ready. A priest stood over the father's bed speaking the final words of the last rites.

Silas knocked the bottle of oil from the priest's hand and shoved him back against the wall. The surprised priest fell splayed against the wall. St. Abigail jumped up from the bed, shock on her face. Brother Talbot turned from the monk he was speaking with.

"What the hell is wrong with you Silas?" he asked.

Silas looked at the monk to whom Talbot was speaking. "Get me three candles and brazier, or something else I can start a small fire in."

To Talbot he said, "I need something important to him, something sentimental, the older the better." Silas started to take off his jacket.

"Look Silas, I have no idea what you think you're doing, but you can't just start shoving people around making crazy requests. I just lost ten men and a lot more are injured."

"And do you want answers as to why those men died? Back in the early eighteen hundreds I poss—knew a guy who was a necromancer. I can try to get the answers we need. If he had completed the final prayers of the last rites it would have made it harder."

Brother Talbot looked stunned. "Are you saying you want to use Delentante in some sort of ritual to talk to the dead? I can't allow that blasphemy and desecration of his body, not for some superstitious mumbo jumbo"

"Why not? This is all for God's work right? We are all on the same side here, at least in principle. It's not as if I'll be keeping him from moving on in the afterlife. It's just a delay. You know, like a layover."

"Let him do it," St. Abigail said. "He's right Brother Talbot, we need information. You have read his file and know what unusual talents he has."

"But St. Abigail, talking with the dead? All of us in the Inquisition have had our experiences with the supernatural, but this is just unnatural."

It's not really, just a different definition of natural. Brother Talbot, the report we received from the father was good, but it was incomplete, told while he was in and out of unconsciousness. We needed to speak to him about the details after he was moved here to recover. We have to make sure we didn't miss anything."

Talbot looked back and forth between them. "But you won't actually harm the body right? No cutting or mutilation?"

"Of course not, I'll just need a chalice for drinking his blood."

Talbot's eyes widened.

"Just kidding, no funny business with the body. Just get me those things I asked for. It might already be too late."

Brother Talbot nodded to the monk who immediately left the room in search of the items.

"And some booze if you got it. The stronger the better," Silas called after him and began to take off his shirt.

In the distance Silas could hear sirens. Police responding to the gun shots.

"Don't worry, we will keep them away. We will tell them there has been some gang activity in the area or something like that. We are, after all, just harmless monks. You know how it is dealing with those who have not seen beyond the Pale. They will believe almost anything that sounds rational. You won't be disturbed," Talbot said.

FIFTEEN MINUTES later the room had been cleared of everybody but Brother Talbot and St. Abigail. Silas sat on the ground by the bed, three candles burning in a triangle around him. Father Delentante's rosary was on the floor in front of him. They had closed the curtains at Silas' instructions.

Necromancy, or specifically the calling up of dead spirits, was tricky. Everything had to be perfect and there was not a lot of time between the moment of death and the soul's passage beyond the afterlife. Too much time, and it was impossible to contact. The more troubled the soul, the longer it would linger close to this world. Father Delentante was probably strong in his faith and therefore had a direct line to heaven. There would be very little time to connect with him, and in fact might already be too late. Silas just hoped the method of his death was enough to keep the spirit here for at least a few more minutes.

A monk came in with a bottle, handed it to Brother Talbot, whispered something to him and left the room.

"We couldn't find anything stronger than wine, but this is one of our oldest vintages and very potent. It's priceless." He handed it to Silas.

Silas looked at it disapprovingly for a moment then said, "This will do." He brought the bottle to his lips and took a long drink from the bottle. It was delicious and potent. Not usually a wine drinker, he was beginning to see the allure.

"Thanks, necromancy is thirsty work," Silas said.

Brother Talbot's jaw dropped.

"Are you sure this will work Silas?" St. Abigail asked.

"No, but it's worth a try. Necromancy is a complex and rare style of magic. It's dangerous to the practitioner because it can open a gate for all sorts of supernatural entities to come through. So we are going to wing it."

"Wing it?"

"Yep, for example we are going to shorten the ritual and cut right to the chase by using the essence of both heaven and hell. Which means I am going to need a little blood, oh hallowed saint."

"You need my blood?"

"Yep and a little of mine. That should be enough to open a gateway."

"I'm not sure this is a good idea," St. Abigail said.

"Look it's either we short cut the rituals with our blood or we need to spend hours, if not days trying to gather everything we would need for a more complicated ritual. By that time Delentante's soul will be long gone."

She nodded reluctantly.

He pulled the brazier closer to him and lit the paper inside on fire. The he nodded to St. Abigail. "Let's begin."

St. Abigail pulled one of her daggers out and sliced into her thumb, Silas offered his and she did the same, maybe cutting a little deeper than necessary. Then he pressed his thumb against hers letting their mingled blood drip into the fire beneath their clasped hands. He felt power where their blood touched, far more than he had expected. And there was something more, something just as powerful passed between them. He was shocked for a moment, then it subsided, but he saw in her eyes she had noticed it also. He began speaking the words of the ritual.

They started as just words, but soon developed a weight of their own. He droned the words in a monotone voice, letting his own words hypnotize him just as he had learned long ago. It was while possessing the necromancer that he discovered a way to circumvent necessary rituals of mortals and reach into the spirit world. There are many worlds beyond, in what many would call the afterlife, but the two polarizing elements were heaven and hell, or good and evil, or whatever words were used in religions.

While he could navigate and travel these realms, it was not as easy when he was confined to a human form. Then he was more beholden to the rules of mortals, but he could bend them when needed.

The room darkened even more than it already was. The air became thick and heavy. The objects in the room, especially those on the periphery of Silas' vision, started to blur and turn a dull gray as though the life was being drained out of the world.

Next to him St. Abigail gasped. She would have traveled through this realm on her way to heaven and again when she was pulled back, but she would not remember the desolation. Besides, they were not fully into the afterlife; they had merely created a small space that allowed the mortal world to overlap with the land beyond for a short period of time.

St. Abigail could see the change because she was part of the ritual, but Brother Talbot stood leaning against the wall staring at them, oblivious to the change around them. Silas looked for the shade of Father Delentante, hoping they weren't too late.

"There," said St. Abigail pointing to a spot just beyond the bed in the gray and lifeless room.

Silas saw it. The blurred spot came into focus as he stared at it and willed it to form. Soon he could see Father Delentante standing by the bed. The shade looked up at him and immediately it began to dissolve. Silas quickly picked up the rosary and held it up so the shade could see it.

"Wait," Silas said.

Father Delentante's eyes were drawn to the old rosary and his imaged re-formed.

"That was my grandfather's rosary," Delentante said. His voice faint and hollow sounding as though from far away. He looked sadly at Silas. "When I pass, when I go, will I have these memories?"

"Not sure. I've never died before and probably never will," Silas answered. "I need to know what happened to you underground."

The shade's look turned from melancholy to confusion. Then that too faded and the shade looked at his body on the bed. They were losing him.

"You will remember," St. Abigail said next to him.

She stepped forward seeking the shade's attention.

"You will keep some memories, but they will be different. But that isn't what matters. What matters is what those experiences and memories have made you now. That is what you take with you into these new worlds."

Silas wondered how many memories she carried with her now after passing through. He was beginning to wonder if he could trust Mort's assurances that she had no memory of the time on earth before her death.

Delentante nodded slowly as though understanding and then came around the front of the bed. "The two of you don't belong here. But I don't think you belong back there either." He nodded toward the gray and blurred figure of Brother Talbot standing against the wall.

"Father," St. Abigail tried again. "We need to know what happened under the city. What happened when that creature attacked you?"

"Yes the monster, the writing. The writing on the wall. Old drawing, well carving actually. Old even before the Europeans arrived in the country. And next to it writing, modern phonetic. Lenape maybe?"

"What were the drawings? What did the writing say?" Silas asked, he was getting impatient. The reports had mentioned writing and drawings, but no details. They were taking too long; they would not be able to hold his shade much longer. Already the image was beginning to dissolve again.

"Doug can take you to it. He remembers," Father Delentante said. His voice was definitely getting weaker.

"Doug's dead Father. He ain't going to be of any help to anyone," Silas said. He was holding back his anger.

St. Abigail gave Silas a harsh look and stepped closer to Father Delentante regaining his attention. "Please father, is there anything you can tell us?"

"Lily, she can lead you there. She was working with Doug."

"Lily who?" St. Abigail asked.

Delentante shrugged. "The Native American will help, I think. He had a headdress and a club."

He was fading fast, Silas held up the rosary again, but Father Delentante ignored it. He was losing his grip.

"What did the writing say Father, what were the words and the pictures?"

Delentante was almost transparent by now.

"Tell Doug I think he was right. They were guardians not hunters, they had not killed it."

"Silas," St. Abigail whispered. "Something is coming."

Silas could feel it too. Something was coming.

"What do you mean guardians? What are they guarding?"

Again Delentante just shrugged.

"Silas!" St. Abigail cried.

Silas saw it. In the corner of the room a black swirling mass had appeared. "What did the words say?"

Father Delentante spoke his last words before fading away. "The monster wakes."

"Silas, we need to go," St. Abigail said.

The blob of darkness in the corner had grown and shifted into a churning mass of forms. Some human, some not, shifting and sliding through each other. Mouths and other orifices opened and closed in silent screams as the mass flowed into the room.

St. Abigail was right. Silas was not sure what this thing was, but it was a creature of this in-between realm and was probably dangerous. He had had enough fighting for one day. He leaned down and blew out the candles.

Instantly the room returned to normal and the black tide of spirits was gone. Colors flowed back into the world, the necromantic door was shut. Talbot stood up straight, surprised at their sudden return.

"Did it work? I saw you sort of fade, but not completely disappear."

"We got something, but I don't know how useful it will be," Silas said.

Silas pulled out his cell phone as St. Abigail continued to fill in Brother Talbot. He called Mort.

"Mort. I need you to look up the name Lily at NYU. I don't know her last name, but she would be doing post graduate work in the archeology or anthropology department."

"Did you go see the priest? What more did you learn? He was in and out of consciousness when he made his report."

"Well he gave us the name. Apparently she was working with this Doug," Silas said.

"I will look her up for you. Did he say anything else?"

"Just something about an Indian with a club, guardians, and a monster waking up. Got to go."

"A monster waking up? Guardians? What the..."

Silas hung up on him. Monks were coming in and out of the room now talking with Brother Talbot and then rushing off to carry out his orders.

"Sir, I know how they got passed our perimeter security. They never went through it," Brother Harold was saying.

"Come again?" Talbot asked.

"They came from within the building."

"Let me guess. The storage rooms have access to the basement," Silas said.

Brother Harold nodded. "There are stairs to the cellars."

"And I bet we could find some old, unused tunnels that connect or at least come close to the sewer system or utility access tunnel," Silas said.

Again Brother Harold nodded. "I have already begun assembling a team to learn where they came from."

"Be careful, they might still be lingering below. I want everybody working in teams of no less than five," Brother Talbot said.

"Do you have any idea what those things were Silas?" St. Abigail asked

Again, Silas noticed how out of place the southern belle accent was on such a dangerous individual. And the fact that she touched upon the one question bothering him did not make him feel any better about her. He didn't know what they were, but he should have; he knew something about every type of supernatural beastie out there.

"I have no idea," he growled.

"I read your file, you are the most experienced agent of the Inquisition and you don't at least have an idea?"

"No," he said.

He turned to leave, but she grabbed his arm. Demonic fury leaped into his eyes as he looked down at her.

"It won't work with me Silas. You don't intimidate me, I'm a Saint remember? I have been beyond and your fury does not threaten me." She noticed she was still holding his arm and pulled her hand away. "Look, Moreales wants us to be partners in this and I am no happier about it than you, but we have to find some way to work together."

"I work alone," Silas said.

"I know, and so do I usually. But this isn't your usual burst into the room all guns blazing type of mission. You will need a little subtlety, some investigative skills." She crossed her arms and looked up at him with a little smile on her lips. "That's why I am here."

"Look lady, Moreales made you my partner because he thinks I need a babysitter. I can't do my job if I have to turn around every other step and protect you. You'll just slow me down."

"Well the Vatican was wrong about one thing; you aren't stupid," she said, righteous fury blooming in her face which, Silas noticed, made her southern accent all the more pronounced. "You're right Moreales did see me as a babysitter of sorts. He seemed to think you might have a problem staying out of trouble with this one. So don't get all pissy with me, he's the one who thinks you need help. If you've got a problem, give him a call. As for slowing you down, I think I did alright back there. In fact, I think it was me who got one of those creatures off you."

That accent was pretty attractive, especially when she gets mad, Silas thought. He remembered the first time he ever saw her. She was dressed in a high-necked blouse and long skirt standing out front of the general store in Tattle, Oklahoma. And she could handle herself in a fight... *what are you thinking? No Silas, you work alone.*

"You can do whatever you like just stay out of my way and don't expect me to slow for you or take care of you."

"Why Silas you do say the sweetest things. I think I'm growing on you," she said.

Her smile was sickeningly sweet. Probably the same smile a black widow gives her mate just before she kills him. He grunted and moved past her into the hall.

"So I guess this means we are heading underground."

She was keeping stride with him as he walked down the hall.

"Good luck with that, let me know how it turns out," he said.

"What are you going to do?"

"I am going to visit an old friend and maybe have a few drinks."

He smiled at the confused look on her face.

6

M r. Webb stood at the edge of the roof, leaning over the street below. It was not a tall building, but there was a strong breeze and the cool wind felt good on his face. The wind was sweet, carrying the stink of the city and the noise of its cars and people. He could hear the sirens and voices of millions, so loud compared to the voices of his people below.

It was late and the shadowed rooftop was dark enough to hide him and this meeting, but still it was a risk. Worth it though, so he could see and feel the upper city again. He needed this inspiration to help him prepare to lead his people to the surface again. He would live in this world once again.

Coth stepped out of the shadows behind him, three other of Webb's personal guard stood off to the side. They gave him solitude when he needed it, but they would be there in an instant to fanatically protect him. That was the way with all his children, they loved him. Then he remembered Jeremy. Perhaps not all.

"I miss this Coth," Mr. Webb said, absently dabbing at the blood leaking from his eye. "I've been underground too long."

"I don't. I don't remember much from before my rebirth, but I think it was a horrible place. I remember suffering up here. Down there I found my family," Coth said.

Mr. Webb smiled. "I remember you Coth, before you came into the fold. You were suffering; it was a hard life that this world forced upon you. And it was not of your choosing. I am glad I could save you, give you a sense of purpose and of..." He let the words trail off, knowing Coth would finish them.

"Of family," Coth finished. "All the others feel the same."

"Even the flawed? Even the ones whose souls were not pure enough and did not survive the rebirth with their minds intact?"

"As you say, their souls were impure; that was not your fault. And we clean up after them as always, as I am doing now."

"And you come to the point as always. I can count on you and that is why you are my favorite." Mr. Webb said and turned away from the edge of the roof. "Then report, is the priest dead?"

"He is dead. However, the monks were much better prepared than we had thought."

"What do you mean?"

"I mean they were surprised, but they actually had heavy weapons and reacted more like a military installation than a monastery. We came in through the tunnels as planned and bypassed much of their security. Stupidly they focused on threats from beyond their walls not from within."

"Yes, few know the extent of the Undercity. Most think it merely uninhabitable sewers."

Coth nodded. "But soon after we were discovered, we ambushed what appeared to be a sentry group, heavily armed. We had knocked out some of their security systems, but they were back online very quickly, indicating that their security was much more sophisticated than we had thought."

Interesting. He would have to file that information for later.

"But you were able to complete the mission?" Mr. Webb asked.

"Yes, the trespasser is dead; however, there is one other problem. Just after we reached the priest's room more Monks showed up, and with them were a man and woman who were not part of the monastery."

"Oh?"

"Yes. They did not appear to be mortals either. I left them to fight against my team and my brothers should have been enough to deal with humans. But soon after I killed the priest the man and woman entered. I escaped by jumping out of the window. The man followed by jumping a distance no mortal could survive. We fought briefly, and while he did not overpower me, he possessed great strength and stamina."

Mr. Webb thought for a second. Something with the strength and power equal to Coth? Their enemies had just become more danger-ous. Who were they and where did they come from? Were they working with that Indian?

"What did the man look like? And this woman too?"

"He was large for a human. Looked like he was a biker--leather jacket, old jeans, t-shirt with some sort of band logo on it. He moved fast and I definitely got the feeling that there was something powerful inside him. The woman was tall, blond hair and athletic. I did not confront her, but I saw her fighting some of my brothers and winning."

Mr. Webb looked sharply at Coth. "Winning? Were there casual-ties on our side?"

"Yes, but we took the dead with us. No evidence was left behind."

This was almost unheard of. The brethren had lost one of their own? That did not happen. Only that Indian had ever killed one of his children.

"This is disturbing. We have managed to keep our existence hidden from others, even the other denizens that live in the Under-city, and that is no small task. There will come a time when we will be forced to reveal ourselves, but not yet. It is too early."

Mr. Webb dabbed again at the blood tears forming in his eyes and dripping past his glasses. He came to a decision.

"We must accelerate our time table; that is the only answer. That should not be a problem I think the flock is ready." He turned to Coth and put a hand gently on the large creature's arm. "And you must take care of this man and woman. Discover who they work for if you can, but the most important thing is that you find and destroy them. They will not ruin my plans. If we move quickly enough it will be too late for our enemies to do anything to stop us."

Coth fell in beside him as he walked back to the roof access door. He towered over Mr. Webb.

"Recruiting is up. The services to the forlorn and downtrodden are going well," Mr. Webb said.

"Yes sir. You are the father to a very loving flock," Coth said, adoration in his voice.

"Have you found anything about that Indian?" Mr. Webb asked.

"Not yet. I have searched a large section of the Undercity, which is not easy when you want to stay away from prying eyes. It's as if he just disappeared after saving the priest, which didn't do any good in the end anyway."

"Didn't do any good? We just had to stage a major assault on a monastery in the upper city, exposing ourselves to two new enemies. I think whatever the Indian's intention it definitely put us in a more dangerous position. That might have been his intention all along."

Coth nodded, properly chastised.

"I am returning to the Undercity; there will be a mass service tonight and I am curious to see how large my flock has grown. When we meet again I expect to see blood on your hands. Or at least some information."

Mr. Webb opened the roof access door and headed down the stairs wondering who these new players were and what part they would ultimately play in his plans

SILAS HAD JUST GRABBED a beer from the fridge when the computer beeped, indicating he had a call. The entire basement of the church

had been remodeled into a living space for him—a large area for working out, one wall containing racks of weapons, mostly melee type, but with the occasional firearm; his bike sat on a lift at one end; the other contained most of his musical equipment and an isolation room for his guitar amplifiers so the holy rollers upstairs didn't flip out every time he got the urge to pick up an axe and tear out a nasty riff.

By far, however, two features dominated the large warehouse space (well, three if he counted the sixty inch flat screen; working for the Vatican did have its perks). One was the large technical center that Mort had insisted on installing. Multiple computer monitors, large and small, hanging from brackets in the wall. Silas thought it was a waste of space-- computers were pretty much good for Google and porn and that was about it. Not that porn wasn't important; he just didn't see the need for all the extra fire power.

The second feature was a block of racks that stored all the equipment a small army would need. Or perhaps an intelligence organization. Everything from night-vision goggles to tracking devices lined the shelves. Microscopic cameras, systems for wiring people for recording, other high tech weapons that he wasn't even sure how to use. He hardly ever used any of this equipment; he just liked it because it made him feel like Batman. Only Silas had real super powers and wasn't really one of the good guys in the strictest sense of the word.

His real pride and joy, however, lay behind a small, unassuming door in the corner. He had made a deal, or rather won a bar bet, with a Djinn and had him carve out a room from the space between worlds, effectively making his own little universe. It contained all his mystical possessions; his books, his apothecary storage, and some choice artifacts that he had managed to get a hold of.

The computer beeped again before Silas reached the keyboard. As he switched on the monitor and web cam, Mort's face swam into view.

"Took you long enough Silas—oh! Jesus Christ, Silas, couldn't you put some clothes on?" Mort looked away from the screen as though it hurt his eyes.

Silas looked down at his naked body, he looked good. He shrugged and pulled on a pair of jeans from the floor. Humans can be so sensitive.

"It's okay Mort, I've covered the naughty bits."

Mort peeked as though unsure; once he saw Silas wasn't lying he turned back to the camera.

"Silas, you can't just go around doing that. You gotta warn a guy..."

"Stimulating conversation Mort, but when you're done glaring at me can you tell me why you called?"

"I found the student you asked about, Lillian James."

As he spoke a second monitor came to life, displaying Lily's face and location information.

"Lillian James, is currently at NYU working on a graduate degree in anthropology. Well specifically she was in the Institute for the Study of the Ancient World. She seems fairly accomplished with several publications to her credit."

"What? Like Playboy's Girls of NYU?"

Mort just glared at him again. Silas smiled back.

"I sent the location of her apartment and the office she works out of on campus to your cell phones."

"Cell Phones? Why the plural?" Silas asked, but realized the answer right away.

"Well, you and St. Abigail of course."

"Oh, so now you are working for her is that it?" Silas was not sure why this made him angry, but it did.

"I don't work for her and I don't work for you. I work for Moreales and the Inquisition. Moreales says she's your partner in this, so I share my intel with both of you."

"Intel huh? That's a pretty fancy word for Google."

"Well maybe this was pretty basic research, but I got the info." A smile crept across Mort's face. "Oh yeah, I also told her where you live."

"Great, now I got to get out of here before she shows up," Silas said and hit a key on the keyboard to end the call. He threw on a shirt and pulled on his boots. After grabbing his keys and wallet, he hopped on his bike and hit the button for the lift.

He started the bike and relished the throaty roar of the exhaust. Already he was feeling better. As the lift stopped in the upper garage he opened the garage door. Outside, blocking the exit sat St. Abigail on a sleek racing bike. She was dressed in tight, all-black racing armor. Damn, she looked sexy.

Silas killed his engine, swung off the bike and walked over to her.

"Crotch rocket huh?"

She looked him in the eye. "Faster than yours."

Silas grunted. "Yeah, but mine is cooler and bigger."

"Well, you know what they say about a man with a big bike. He's compensating for other shortcomings."

Silas stepped closer to her. The smile never left her face and she didn't back down. He could have said it was the supernatural in her now, but he had met her when she was a human and thought even then she would not have backed down.

"Aren't there rules against Saints wearing outfits like that? Shouldn't you be wearing an ankle length dress or maybe a heavy robe? Lead us not into temptation and all that?"

"Why Silas you say the sweetest things, I don't know why some woman hasn't snatched you up yet."

There was movement from the alley. Silas turned, ready for an attack. St. Abigail pulled a stiletto from somewhere, but with an outfit that tight Silas had no idea where she had concealed it. A shadow flickered across the alley.

Silas sniffed the air. He recognized the scent. He reached out a hand and gently pushed St. Abigail's deadly knife down.

"Come on out, Michael."

The shadows shifted, but the boy did not emerge. Silas turned to St. Abigail.

"Michael's brother has disappeared along with a few other patrons of the mission. Father Deluca asked me to look into it."

"Have you looked into it?"

"Not really," Silas shrugged. "Been busy with this other stuff about monsters roaming the streets of New York."

"I knew it!" The boy sprang from the alley. "I knew you didn't care."

"Look kid..." Silas started.

"You're just like the rest, you don't give a shit about us," the boy cried. "He was right, nobody cares; everybody just wants us to disappear."

St. Abigail moved past Silas, stepping a little closer to the kid. Silas instantly felt the shift in her demeanor. Just as he could radiate malice and danger, from her he felt calm, peace, and love. Yuck! His demonic nature flared briefly, but he tried to rein it in. It was too late; he instantly saw the change in the boy. One moment he was enthralled by the approaching saint then as Silas' own power flared, it canceled out whatever energy Abigail was projecting. The boy went back to the balls of his feet, ready to run in an instant.

"It's okay Michael, nobody here wants to harm you," St. Abigail said.

"I know, nobody cares," he said tears shown in his eyes.

"I care. Silas cares, even though it doesn't seem like it."

For a moment Silas believed her; just as it was his nature to inspire fear and hate, she emanated trust and peace. He knew it was working on him, because he could feel that maybe he wanted to help the kid. The streets may not have been like his Hell, but they couldn't be good for a kid. Especially one who had lost his only family.

What was he thinking? He shook his head as if to clear a bad dream. He had to watch it; her power could get to him.

"He said we're all on our own and he was right. We need to stick together," Michael said.

"Who said that Michael? Who said you were on your own?" St. Abigail had taken a few steps closer to the kid.

"The preacher guy."

"Father Deluca?" Silas asked.

Michael glared at him, "No, the street preacher."

"Michael, can you start from the beginning?"

He shot an evil look one last time at Silas and then slumped against the wall, giving up.

"He was just a street preacher, maybe not as crazy as some others that roam the area. He didn't scream about God's vengeance or how everybody was a sinner. In fact, he doesn't mention God that much at all."

He shuffled his feet a little and gave St. Abigail a little smile. "I guess that doesn't make him a very good preacher."

"If he doesn't talk about God what makes you call him a preacher?"

"I don't know, I guess prophet is a better word. He calls the people who listen to him his flock. And he says things like, we have been baptized by fire since we live on the street. Mostly he just sounds like one of those preacher guys you see on TV."

Silas stepped forward and leaned to her ear. "We don't have time for this. We need to go fight the bad guys, the real bad guys."

She ignored him. "Were you and your brother part of this flock?"

"Not really. We listened to him a few times, sometimes he made sense. He talked about how most people don't understand us and think us homeless people are all drug addicts and scum. He tried to tell us how we did not need this society. I'm not sure what he meant by that, but he spoke about you people, the people that don't have to live on the streets, with contempt and hatred. He tried to tell us there was a path to a better life, but my brother and I didn't believe it. The streets are our only life."

"But maybe your brother started to think there was something to what this guy was saying?" St. Abigail asked.

Michael's eyes got wide and he shook his head. "No, Jared wasn't buying it, but..." he looked at Silas, a little sheepishly. "I didn't tell you the whole truth the other night with Father Deluca."

"No shit? A street punk lying? Get the fucking action five news team, we got a scoop," Silas said.

St. Abigail held up her hand to silence Silas.

"Now might be a good time to tell us everything Michael. We can only help if you let us," St. Abigail said.

Michael nodded. "When Father Deluca asked us to look into the disappearances we noticed that a lot of the missing we had seen listening to this preacher guy and his buddies--acolytes he called them--so we followed him around awhile. We could never find where he slept at night or where he went when he wasn't speaking to people on the street. I think my brother found out where they might be having a meeting though; I think that was where he was going when he disappeared."

"Why didn't you tell any of this to Father Deluca and Silas when you saw them?"

"'Cuz I was scared," he stood a little straighter on the wall. "This preacher guy and his buddies are creepy, nobody fucks with them. Besides this was all my brother's theory, about the preacher being connected to the disappearances. I didn't know what was going on. Now because I was scared, I might never see Jared again."

He started crying and Abigail reached out to him, pulling him into a hug.

"It takes a brave man to admit he is scared," Abigail said quietly. Michael cried all the louder into her shoulder and squeezed her tight.

Silas thought for a moment while they did the mushy stuff. The boy had said nobody fucks with this street preacher. Strong choice of words and it didn't jive with his image of a wasted-looking guy spouting gibberish on the street corner and wearing a sign that says John 3:16. They were the type of guys you definitely did fuck with. This was getting more interesting. Maybe he should follow up on this when he had some time.

"Look, I'm glad we had this breakthrough, but I ain't Doctor Phil and this ain't the Oprah show. Abigail, we got some pressing problems at the moment. Can we get a move on?"

The boy pushed away from Abigail and screwed up his face, mixing anger and tears only the way a kid could. "Fuck you Silas. I know you don't care about shit. So go fuck yourself. I don't need your help," Michael screamed. He turned and ran off down the alley sobbing and kicking empty boxes and trash out of his way.

St. Abigail watched Michael run off down the alley. She didn't try to stop him. She turned back to Silas.

"You are a dick," she said and walked back to her bike.

Silas looked back to where the kid had run. St. Abigail's aura was still working because he could almost feel a pang of guilt... almost.

"Come on Silas, let's go see your friend. If he is your friend, I am sure he will be a real charmer. Probably likes to drown puppies in his spare time. I'll follow you."

Gone was the almost flirtatious air that they had just enjoyed. Now she hated him again. It was probably for the best.

7

They pulled up in front of the bar and looked at the sign above the outdoor table area. "Faust" was written on it. Silas grunted at the irony. Mephisto always loved that story, though it was completely made up. Ever since it was popularized by Christopher Marlowe he was always flaunting it in other demon's faces. kind of like Hell's equivalent of a reality show celebrity. Now he had named his bar after it and boy, did it look snooty.

Maybe bar was the wrong word. It was more like a fancy restaurant, a bistro they were called. Silas was definitely underdressed, but this wouldn't be the first time.

"Silas, when you said you were going to have a few drinks with a friend I pictured something a little different. Something a little less sophisticated, maybe something more beer soaked and smelly."

"I may have exaggerated when I said he was a friend; he's more like a lifelong enemy who would just a soon stab me in the back with anything handy than help me. If he were really my friend he would be beer soaked and smelly, so don't be too hard on yourself."

"But if you had told me where we were going I would have dressed differently, something more appropriate."

He eyed her up and down.

"You look very appropriate to me," Silas said, hoping to recapture the mood from before. It didn't work.

"Who is this friend we are seeing anyway?" Abigail asked.

"Mephisto."

"You mean Mephistopheles? One of the grand dukes of hell?"

"Yeah, I'm surprised he settles for this dump as well. Could do better."

"I wasn't referring to his bar."

She stepped in front of Silas, blocking his way into the building. A valet stood off to the side, apparently unsure of what to do about the motorcycles blocking the curb.

"He is one of the most powerful demons in Hell. Do you think he is just going to let us walk in there, ask for his help—I am not even sure why we are here anyway—and then let us leave?"

"He's like family. I'm sure he'll be civil, besides he won't want to damage his nice establishment. One thing though--don't mention that you're a Saint because he will kill you... again."

"Then who am I supposed to be?"

"You could pretend to be my girlfriend," Silas said.

St. Abigail just raised an eyebrow.

"Yeah, you're right. You don't look slutty enough to be my girl-friend. Just tell him you're working with the Vatican on special assign-ment. He'll just assume you're mortal. He knows all about my um... predicament."

She did not look convinced, but it would have to do. He stepped past her and into the swanky restaurant. The inside was just as nice as the faux stone and dark wood exterior suggested. The restaurant was crowded and the bar area packed with a little spill over onto the restaurant tables nearest it. His eyes passed over the patrons gathered at tables dressed in their look-at-me designer evening wear. Rich men with cheap plastic faces stared at cheap silicone women, not listening to each other, just being seen. Yeah this was Mephisto's place alright.

And it only took him a moment to see the proprietor. He sat in the back of the restaurant, in a private room. He could see him through the open door, but it was draped in shadow and if he had been mortal his eyes would have slid right passed it. As it was he saw Mephisto himself sitting in front of a large pile of pasta and stuffing his face. For a moment Silas almost did wish he was mortal and his eyes would slide past the sight in front of him. Mephisto was large. No, that was too kind. He was morbidly obese. His bulging frame was draped by an impeccable Italian suite like a tarp covers a van. His second and third chin lay jiggling like Jell-O as he stuffed his face with meatballs and pasta. Jowls that would have impressed a bull dog dangled below deep-set eyes.

"Is that him? That's one of the grand dukes of hell?" Abigail asked, disbelief in her voice.

Silas had been so engrossed in observing his fellow demon that he had not even heard her enter behind him.

"Yeah, he kind of let himself go. I guess he let the fame go to his head," Silas said.

"Should we wait until he is done? We might get accidentally eaten."

Silas chuckled. "I wish we could, but I have a feeling it might be a while. He doesn't look like one to skip dessert if you know what I mean."

Now it was her turn to laugh. Two men, definitely not obese, but built like tanks stood against the wall near his table. Silas had heard Mephisto was playing at the Mafioso roll lately, He had always been a ham for clichés. Time to get this over with.

Silas navigated his way through the drunks and diners to Mephisto's table. The two thugs noticed his approach and detached themselves from the wall to intercept him.

"Those are Screamers--low level entities, but definitely a threat to our mortal forms," Silas whispered quickly to St. Abigail. He slipped his hand into his pockets and found his earplugs. He had them for gigs, but rarely used them.

One of the thugs held up his hand to block their approach.

"Is Mr. Duncan expecting you?" The Screamer asked, his voice high-pitched and out of place coming from such a large figure.

"Mr. Mephistopheles will want to see us," Silas said.

The Screamer looked back to the table. Silas could see Mephisto look up from his feeding. He glanced at them, eyes widening a little in surprise, then with his fork he made a small gesture for them to come forward.

"Are you armed?" Asked the other Screamer. His voice was impossible low.

"Only with charm and wit."

"Silas, where have you been hiding? Come over, come over," Mephisto called.

Silas shoved passed the Screamers and sat in the chair Mephisto gestured to. As St. Abigail sat next to him, Mephisto gave her an appraising look and raised an eyebrow to Silas.

"And who is the young lady?" Mephisto asked.

"She's my assistant. I know she isn't much to look at, but good help is hard to find nowadays," Silas said. St. Abigail put her hand on his knee under the table, but not in the good sort of way, more like the nails biting into flesh and bruising sort of way.

"An assistant? For you Silas? You've always worked alone."

"Not really my idea. My employers sort of forced this one on me; I guess Mort just couldn't keep up."

"Your employers?" Mephisto laughed. "You mean your masters? Yes, masters, and it serves you right gallivanting around looking for any chance to be summoned and bound to human flesh. No wonder your binding name became known to the Enemy."

"I have tasted more of human life than any of my brothers."

"Brothers," Mephisto laughed. He pointed the fork at Silas flicking a piece of pasta onto his jacket. "You are and always will be an outcast, not even a gnat in the hierarchy of the damned. You are not of our world."

"But I savor this one. I know this one, perhaps better than any of you. You know I am an asset for the Final Accounting, when souls are divvied up between heaven and hell."

Mephisto stared at him for a moment, his puffy face seeming to deliberate between anger and disgust. Then he laughed loudly.

"I suppose so. Are you hungry? We have great Italian food here," Mephisto said.

"You do realize Faust is German, not Italian?" St. Abigail asked and Silas almost winced.

Mephisto gave her that same puzzled look as though trying to decide how he should kill her when he suddenly laughed again.

"Oh, I like her. She's got a tongue that one," he said between barks of wheezing laughter. "And brave too."

He stopped laughing after that last sentence, but the smile remained on his face.

"Well, if you are not here for my food, why are you at my table?"

"Information," Silas said.

"Information, huh? That can be expensive stuff. What kind of information?"

"Have you heard of a new breed of supernatural creatures appearing in the city? Maybe coming from underground?"

"Underground? You mean the sewers and subway tunnels?"

"Yeah, or maybe even deeper."

"And a new breed you say? One you haven't encountered before? That's saying a lot, because you've been around my boy."

"My guess is not natural, probably man-made or some artificial creation."

"Ah! Possible transmogrification? That is why you have come to me," Mephisto said and sat back a little in his chair, which creaked under the weight. "You think I made these little beasties and set them loose on the city?"

"No, these creatures have been attacking civilians, including a priest and in at least one case tried to assault a fully armed branch of the Templars. I don't think you would risk the anger of *your* masters by upsetting the balance directly."

Mephisto's smile was gone, replaced by a cold stare and slight twitch in the eye. Silas guessed he didn't like having the word master turned back on him, but they both knew that was the appropriate word. Silas may not have been in the hierarchy of hell, but that was exactly the way he liked it. Mephisto, on the other hand, was a card-carrying member reaping all the pros and a large pile of cons.

"Then why are you here?"

"It's your area of expertise. I know you've trained many sorcerers over the years in that specific skill," Silas said. "I thought you may have known someone in the area who would be capable of this."

"Nope, no one," Mephisto said and went back to his meal.

Silas blinked at the abrupt ending. "Well then, I guess..."

"Wait," Mephisto said, once more holding up his fork and spitting another piece of pasta onto Silas' jacket. "I might know somebody. How many of these creatures are there?"

"Not sure, I saw about seven at one time, but there are probably more."

"Nope, nope," Mephisto said shaking his head. "Couldn't be this guy. He wasn't that powerful. Holding a transmogrification that long on that many humans would require more power than most mortals possess. Unless..." Mephisto said and gestured with the fork again, but this time Silas was ready for it and leaned away from the pasta projectile. "Unless he had help."

"What kind of help?" St. Abigail asked.

"Well like another sorcerer or supernatural being. Or perhaps a catalyst."

"A catalyst?"

"Yes a catalyst--some sort of alchemical substance that enhances the transmogrification. That is why some sort of potion is used for effecting a long-term or potent transformation. It's in all the stories."

"Could this person be using some sort of catalyst?" St. Abigail asked.

Silas was getting tired of all the questions. If Mephisto would just give them a name, they could go find out for themselves. "Can we get a move on here? Just get a name maybe?"

Mephisto and St. Abigail ignored him.

"Well, maybe, but it would have to have been one hell of a cata-lyst, and I am sure this guy wouldn't have been able to create one alone. He was your run-of-the-mill sorcerer and dabbled in alchemy, but he was strictly amateur."

"But if someone helped him, maybe gave him a little guidance? You think this guy could do something like this?" St. Abigail asked.

"You mean morally?" Mephisto laughed. "This guy was a nutso. He had ideas about taking the human race to a new level. Very racist individual, thought he could perfect mankind. Almost religiously fanatical about it. Anyway, he came to me a few times for some help-- wanted all sorts of exotic arcane lore. I thought he was going nowhere, so I taught him just enough for him to get into trouble. Then blew him off. But yeah, he could do something like this if he had help or was given a catalyst."

"Okay, great, who is this guy?" Silas asked.

"Come now, Silas. You didn't think it would be that easy did you?" Mephisto said, a smile sliding across his face. "Information is not free. Why should I help you?"

"This guy is breaking the rules, rules even your masters play by," Silas said and leaned on his elbows close to Mephisto. "These things are brushing against mortals, and I don't mean just the ones that know of the Pale. I'm talking about civilians. And keep in mind these things could look like demons to your average mortal."

Mephisto shrugged, but Silas could see a little concern in his eyes.

"What do I care if there is a little chaos? We welcome that, you know that just as much as I," Mephisto said.

"Sure. What's a little chaos and fear among friends? Sounds good to me, I'm all for it. But what happens when this nutso, as you described him, decides to really change the whole human race. He won't be able to of course, but he will sure as hell cause an imbalance. And if he grows his little menagerie and directly confronts the mortals, do you think there will be any balance? What happens when mortals begin to understand what's really amongst them? What happens when mortals realize the monsters are real, the fairy tales are real and the very fabric of reality is to be questioned? What happens then?"

"A little dramatic aren't we Silas? I know what *could* happen. Theoretically we are talking Armageddon, but that seems like a large jump. I mean we don't even know if this guy is the nutso in question."

"But what if it does happen? If this grows and the imbalance is created and the Final Accounting comes early, do you think the infernal host would like that? Are we that certain things are tipped in our favor?" Silas said, and dramatic or not, he was right. Exposing the Pale to humans too early would bring about Judgment Day prematurely and the remnants of humanity would be divvied up between heaven and hell. This is the primary reason the Inquisition project was created--to protect humanity until they were ready. They may have different definitions of ready, but for now their goals were the same.

"Look at it this way Mephisto," St. Abigail said. "We are helping you clean up a possible liability. You yourself said he was a nobody, that you blew him off. What does it matter if you let us check him out? He might be the guy or he might not. Either way it seems like we are really just helping you. Working for you as it were."

Silas looked over at St. Abigail. He was impressed. She was working him over good by playing to his vanity and making it look as though they were really doing what he wanted. And it was working; she had him wrapped around her finger.

"Well I suppose you could clean up this loose end for me Silas, I certainly can't be bothered with anything so petty. The name's Webb, Nicholas Webb. He had an apartment in Jersey, on Kensington Avenue."

"Great. Well then we will just be going, get out of your hair..."

"I said *you* could clean this up for me Silas. The Saint is mine, that is my payment and of course it is not negotiable," Mephisto was smiling big now, smug he had pulled one over on them.

Silas heard the door close behind them and the two Screamers stepped a little closer, expecting trouble. Mephisto leaned back, out of the way of the violence. He could take care of himself, but probably preferred to have his minions deal with them. Abigail tensed. If she made a move those Screamers would start and it would be over real quick. He had to do something. Mephisto was right, there was no negotiation. If he had figured out she was a Saint he would have to destroy her, his demon blood would not let such an enemy walk free out of his domain.

"Fine," Silas said.

They both looked at him like he was crazy. Apparently they had both expected a fight.

"I mean she is sexy as hell, but damn does she talk on and on, drives me crazy. Come on Mephisto, do you really think I like having a goody-two-shoes look over my shoulder. I mean when the Vatican saddled me with this one, they really made my life a living hell, no pun intended. If you could take her off my hands, that would be cool."

He looked over St. Abigail and smiled at the fury reddening her face. He couldn't kill her easily, but if Mephisto got his hands on her, she could end up trapped in hell for all eternity. "I could just file some report or something saying she was disposed of in the line of duty. Doing me a favor really."

Mephisto was scowling, probably trying to figure out Silas's game. But then he seemed to accept it. "Didn't think it would go down that easy, but okay,"

"One thing though, she is a fucking banshee in bed. Can I just give her a kiss goodbye so I can keep a taste of that?"

"Silas you old dog," the smile was back on Mephisto's face. "You had a piece of that? Sure go ahead."

Silas knew St. Abigail was going to do something any moment, so he had to be fast. He slipped the earplugs from his pocket, then moving as fast as he could, he grabbed the sides of her head and kissed her as her lips opened in shocked protest. Knowing that any moment those stilettos could plunge into his gut, he slipped the plugs into her ears. Her eyes widened even as she tried to push him away. He didn't know if she understood what he was doing, but the stilettos never came, and he took that as a good sign.

He pulled away from her and felt a stinging slap across his cheek. It would leave a mark, but it was a lot better than a knife in the gut. Looking her in the eyes he pointed at his throat, she wouldn't hear him so he hoped she got it.

"Now," he said and turned to the Screamer nearest him.

He covered his ears with his hands and kicked it in the groin. The Screamer screamed. It leaned forward, its large jaw swinging loose and distending much lower than any mortal mouth could. To Silas it looked like a snake unhinging its jaw to eat a rat. Then, as its face swelled like a fleshy mega horn, the sound came. Like the long distance whine of a train whistle, the sound ripped out of its mouth. Silas' hands were useless now--he had to keep them up to protect his ears.

It only took a moment for the second Screamer to figure out what was going on. It too distended its mouth in preparation for a scream. St. Abigail's blade streaked through the air and impaled the screamer in the throat even as the whine began.

The one that Silas had kicked was quickly reaching its full volume. His hands would only delay the inevitable; a screamer at full volume will kill. He kicked it in the gut. The Screamer paused in its wail long enough to cover its midsection.

The second screamer had given up trying to remove Abigail's stiletto from its neck and lunged at her. St. Abigail jumped onto a chair, then onto a table, then, using her momentum, she leaped and spun in a somersault over the Screamer and its chomping mouth. As she passed over, her blade struck out, slicing across the demon's eyes. She landed in a crouch facing the creature's back.

If Silas had a score card with a ten on it he would have held it up. The creature covered its eyes, blood oozing from between its fingers.

Mephisto had stepped back from the table and ripped open his jacket and shirt revealing rolls of fat and flab. He grabbed a hunk of his own flesh in both hands and tore it off in globs then tossed each of the flesh lumps onto the ground where they instantly began to grow. Silas wondered why his brethren had to be so gross.

Silas kicked at the Screamer, aiming for its throat, but this time it was ready and blocked his kick. Its scream was loud enough that he could feel it piercing into his brain.

He swung his fist at the creature and it brought its arm up to block, but at the last moment Silas changed his target and grabbed the Screamer's outstretched arm instead. It was not expecting this and he caught it off balance.

He looked at St. Abigail and yelled.

"Now!"

He knew she wouldn't hear, but he hoped she would know what to do. Her eyes flashed and then she was leaping, slamming into the back of the blind screamer with her legs. The creature was knocked forward, off balance by the unexpected blow. In a moment Silas was going to be the meat in a Screamer sandwich. As the three collided he shoved the arm of his Screamer into the chomping maw of the blind one.

The scream turned into a roar and lost some of its piercing quality, for which Silas was grateful. Silas ducked and rolled, coming up on a few feet from Mephisto. The two lumps of flesh that he had thrown to the ground were growing. Whatever they were becoming Silas was sure they would not be healthy for him and St. Abigail.

Within moments he and St. Abigail were forgotten by the screamers as they tore at each other in rage. The low level demons were always predictably stupid.

"Silas!" St. Abigail cried and pointed.

He could barely hear her through the ringing in his ears, but he looked at where she pointed. The blob of flesh was finishing its transformation into a giant Rottweiler. But this was no man's best friend.

"Hell hounds," Silas said.

It snarled at Silas and drew its mouth back, revealing four inch teeth. It took a small step forward as its form solidified. They had only seconds before these creatures pounced.

"Time to go," Silas said.

Mephisto had already removed two other pieces of flesh. They could not fight that many hell hounds. He grabbed the edge of the nearest table and heaved, swinging it like a flat, giant baseball bat. He slammed it into the newly formed hell hound just as it crouched for a strike.

The force of his blow knocked it back into its brother and they landed in a tangle on the ground. Silas continued the arc of his swing and using its momentum, he threw the table through the tinted glass windows, shattering them into a thousand pieces and knocking a pedestrian down.

"Come on!" Silas yelled to St. Abigail and jumped through the window.

The two hell hounds were already on their feet and the other two were almost fully formed. Silas wasn't sure Abigail had heard him, but from the corner of his eye he saw her follow him through the window.

Humans scattered out of the way as they ran from the restaurant. Tomorrow all they would remember is that a pack of dogs chased two people out of a restaurant. Mephisto might get a visit from the health department, but that would be about it.

He and Abigail climbed aboard their bikes just as the hounds exploded from the restaurant window. They roared out onto the street, sending two cars sliding into oncoming lanes as they swerved to avoid two bikers and a pack of wild dogs the size of horses.

Abigail had already shot ahead of him--maybe he should look into one of those crotch rockets after all—and there was no question that their bikes could out run the hounds, but New York traffic was another devil entirely. They were slowed immediately as they wove in and out of cars. The hounds took advantage and leaped from car to car, snarling and chomping. They left huge dents in the hoods and roofs they pounced on, claws tearing huge gouges in taxi cabs and SUVs.

The lead hound came close to Silas and lunged at him. He stood on his foot pegs and leaned to counter balance, then he brought his fist down like a hammer on top of the beast's head. It fell off the taxi it stood on and hit the street. Silas couldn't take the time to see if it was going to get back up, a second was coming up to take its place.

Ahead of them the cars were at a stop. A red light. He gunned the throttle to catch up to Abigail and to avoid a large claw swiping at him. He felt the claw wisp through his hair and then heard a bark of frustration, although it was barely audible to his numb ears.

Abigail hit the throttle at the intersection and went up on one wheel as she raced through, squeezing between two cars. *Yep*, thought Silas, *she is growing on me.*

Silas entered the intersection where a semi-truck came bearing down on him. He throttled and felt the wind of the passing truck across his back just as he cleared the lane. The hell hound closest behind him was not as lucky. In his mirror Silas saw the hound plaster the grill, crushing part of the hood and radiator. The truck driver slammed on his breaks, sending the trailer sliding sideways. Silas hoped it would slow the others down.

A hound appeared on top of the trailer and bounded over it, but Silas didn't see where it landed because the road ahead needed his attention. A wooden barrier was blocking off the lane for road construction. This explained the bad traffic so late at night. Silas couldn't see what the construction was, but Abigail burst through the barrier, probably to take advantage of the briefly open stretch of road. Silas followed.

Abigail blew past a man in an orange and yellow safety vest, a cup of coffee forgotten in his hand. Two more workers jumped out of Abigail's way, but she didn't slow. Then she was up in the air like the bike had just become a bucking bronco. She was airborne after hitting a large pile of dirt and asphalt. Silas wondered what the hell they were jumping even as he hit the make shift ramp and gunned the throttle. Whatever it was, he hoped it wasn't too large.

As he left the ground, Abigail landed. His bike was much heavier than hers and not really designed for this kind of riding. Fortunately, he had had the forethought to put a supercharger on the engine, which might have been what saved him this time.

Beneath him was a hole in the ground and a serpentine mess of pipes and cables a good ten feet below the surface. His back wheel scraped the helmet of a worker at the top of the access ladder.

Then he was slamming to the ground. The suspension barely held and his ass slammed into the seat with enough force to knock his teeth together. He heard something scrape underneath the bike, but it didn't slow.

"Come on baby, hold together," he whispered to it.

In his mirror he saw the two remaining hounds leap over the hole. The second slammed into the back of the first and fell into the open pit. Gas jetted out and sparks flew as the creature flailed in the mess of utility conduits. The first had cleared the opening and seemed to not notice the fate of its brother.

As far as Silas could tell they were down to only one hell hound, but while the odds were better, even one hell hound was too much. They were back in traffic, but now that they were past the construction it was picking up.

Only one more block, was that too much to ask? Apparently it was. The hound lunged at Silas and slammed into the side of the bike, sending him off balance. He stayed on, but only by wrenching the handle bars and riding onto the sidewalk. The beast slammed into him again with its shoulder, Silas could have sworn it had grown to the size of a large pony, knocking him off the sidewalk and straight at the plate glass windows of an elegant, if a little ostentatious, shopping mall.

Silas hunched his shoulders, thought for a moment that helmet laws might not be a bad idea, and slammed into the window. The bike shattered through the glass in a hail of sparkling shards and slid sideways on the slick floors and glass. He felt small slices across his unprotected face and scalp. He stayed on the bike until it stopped against the far wall of the mall.

Late night shoppers scattered away from the bike and broken window, screaming. Directly across from him, elevator doors opened to reveal oblivious shoppers, their mouths dropping open in shock.

The hell hound plowed through the window next to the one Silas came through. Its claws clicked on the smooth floor as it tried desperately to stop itself before slamming into the marble wall and creating a cloud of plaster. Silas didn't wait for it to recover.

He gunned the bike and headed straight for the open elevator. The shoppers inside tried to run. At last moment he spun the bike backward and slid into the elevator. A family was pressed up against the wall of the car, looking as if they were trying their hardest to disappear into the side.

In front of him, the hound was getting to its feet and shook its head a couple of times. Its eyes found Silas in the elevator.

"Sky bridge please," Silas said to the man standing by the elevator buttons. The man didn't move, he just looked at Silas like he was the hell hound. Silas pointed to the buttons.

"Sky bridge level and you better be quick if you don't want to be puppy chow," Silas said.

The man looked out of the elevator and saw the recovering hound. He screamed and started hitting all the buttons, including the sky bridge level. The hound, sensing its prey trying to escape, started running at them. The man screamed harder and started slamming his fists into the buttons.

Silas willed the doors to close. He didn't like being in the enclosed space. Having him, this family and an enraged hell hound in the tiny elevator would be like hanging out in a giant food processor. They weren't going to make it, the hound would reach them before the doors closed. Silas grimaced, there was only one thing he could do.

He twisted the throttle and leaped off the bike as it bucked underneath him and shot forward into the chest of the hound. It yelped as seven hundred pounds of steel slammed into it knocking it back. Silas joined the man on pushing the buttons. The doors shut before the hound stood up.

The entire family cringed in the corner as the elevator rose, except for the boy, who pulled away from his sister and stared up at Silas.

"Cool bike," he said.

Silas heard him through the ringing in his ears.

"Yep, it was," Silas said promising himself that he and Mephisto would settle up some day.

"Who are you?"

"David, you leave the nice man alone," the boy's mother said and pulled him close to her. "He doesn't mean to bother you..."

"Listen kid, I'm what happens when you skip school, stop listening to your parents, listen to rock and roll, and do drugs."

It was the closest Silas had come to a public service announcement. The boy's eyes grew wide.

"Cool!"

Silas smiled, "Yeah it is."

Ding.

The doors slid open. Silas poked his head out; the family appeared to have no intention of leaving the elevator. About a hundred feet away was the sky bridge. He looked both ways, no hound. People were gathered by the windows looking down at the mess he had made below. In the distance sirens were approaching.

He was about halfway to the bridge when a door behind him burst open and the slavering dog came through.

"Shit."

Silas ran. The hell hound had grown to the size of a large horse. Silas's running caught its attention and it charged after him. He ran down the sky bridge as shoppers dove out of his way, screaming.

Some fell in front of him and he had to hurdle them. He wouldn't be able to out run the hound on foot.

Through the lower window of the sky bridge he saw a familiar motorcycle rolling up the street. He went through the large double doors on the other side to the parking garage, plowing through a woman. Designer clothes boxes went flying as the woman screamed. Silas ran down the aisle of parked cars as the hound crashed through the glass behind him. He could feel the beast's breath on his back. He veered toward the parking garage railing and without looking he jumped, hoping he had timed it right. *I mean, if cowboys could do it?*

He missed. He jumped the three stories and landed on a moving car just to the right of the motorcycle. He slid across the roof of the car and fell to the asphalt a few feet in front of St. Abigail.

St. Abigail slammed on her brakes and came to a stop inches from Silas.

"You do know how to make an entrance," St. Abigail said.

Silas got up with a moan and limped to the back of the bike. He could hear her even with her helmet on; his ears must be getting better.

"How did you know where I was?" Silas asked.

"Mortimer. He traced your cell phone GPS."

"Son of a Bitch."

Silas thought of the phone in his pocket and wondered how often Mort followed him. He did not have long to think about it. Above him the hell hound peered over the railing and looked straight at them. Silas hopped on the back of the bike and hoped nobody he knew would see him.

"Hold onto my waist," St. Abigail said.

Silas did as he was told and put his arms around her, *maybe this wouldn't be so bad.*

"Silas, those aren't my waist."

Or maybe not. Silas sighed and lowered his hands.

With a roar the beast sprung from the parking garage with a lot more grace than Silas had.

"Now would be a good time," Silas mumbled.

St. Abigail twisted the throttle and the motorcycle surged ahead. To Silas the bike felt like a toy between his legs, but he had to admit it was fast. They zipped ahead as the monster crashed to the ground. St. Abigail slid the bike out onto the main arterial street through a red light. Traffic was much lighter and in seconds they accelerated to over sixty miles an hour. Any cops in the area were probably congregating on the other side of the shopping center. Silas looked behind them.

The hound loped after them, but it was drifting further and further behind. After a few turns and side streets they could no longer see it. Abigail finally pulled up to the curb by the river. She pulled off her helmet as Silas got off. He kept an eye behind them; hell hounds were not always easy to lose.

"So those were hell hounds? Nasty pets your kind keeps."

"Well they're good for hunting. I don't think they were really hell hounds though. I suspect they were something else transmogrified by Mephisto. He is an expert at that."

"They seemed pretty real to me. Why do you think they were fake?"

"It was too easy to escape them."

"Too easy? You look like someone took a baseball bat covered in razor blades to you and you called that easy? I would hate to see what you consider hard."

Silas shrugged. Sometimes it just paid to be mysterious. She got a serious look on her face.

"Look Silas, I want to thank you for what you did back there. I know that you could have just left me. You had what you needed, but you saved me."

"I would never have heard the end of it from Morales if I have lost you. Besides, you are proving more useful than I had thought."

St. Abigail smiled.

"Okay Silas, we'll play it your way. Either way, I owe you one."

"You could sleep with me," Silas suggested.

"Do you actually practice saying the absolute worst thing you can think of at exactly the wrong moment?"

"No it's just a natural gift."

St Abigail sighed and put her helmet back on.

"I'll meet you back at that rat hole you play at," she said.

"What about me? Aren't you going to give me a ride?" Silas asked, then smiled when he realized what he had just said.

"Take a cab," Abigail said and pulled away from the curb.

"What? What'd I say?" Silas asked loudly.

St. Abigail didn't answer as she roared off down the street.

8

S t. Abigail was waiting for him on the curb as Silas pulled up. He moaned; she looked bright and chipper while he was hung over. Whose idea had it been anyway to meet at ten in the morning? Who in their right mind gets up this early? Last night after the meeting with Mephisto was a little blurry. They had met back at the bar with Mort to go through what they had learned. He had started ordering shots and it had kind of gone downhill from there. He remembered the discussion of going to Webb's apartment and St. Abigail had said going during the day might be safer especially after what had just happened. But had he really agreed to ten in the morning? The driver of the black Cadillac limousine got out of the car and opened the back passenger door, allowing Silas to stumble out.

"A limo? Really?" St. Abigail asked.

"Hey, I lost my bike in the line of duty. I'm expensing this until I get it back or they find me a replacement."

St. Abigail shook her head in exasperation. "You look like shit, Silas."

"It was your idea to meet at ten in the morning," Silas said.

"It's almost noon."

"Whatever. Can we get on with this?"

"What about him?" Abigail nodded toward the driver. "Isn't he a civilian?"

"Right, good point. I'll take care of it," Silas said and walked over to the driver.

"Is this the correct destination, sir?" the driver, who couldn't have been more than twenty five, asked.

"Um yeah. Listen, just wait out here for me to get back. I might be a while. Oh, and if you hear gunfire, screaming or explosions just sit tight; that kind of stuff happens all the time around me."

"Sir?" the driver's face dropped into a worried look.

Silas patted him on the shoulder and glanced at his name tag. "You'll do fine, Sam."

"Steve," the driver corrected him.

"Your company does provide medical insurance right?"

"Well, uh..." Steve started.

"Forget it. Doesn't really matter. See you in a few."

Silas left the stunned man standing by the car.

"You really think he will wait?" Abigail asked when they were out of earshot of the driver.

"I think so. You're really good at spotting the goodness, compassion, love and all that crap in a person, right?"

"I suppose that is a benefit of being what I am."

"Well, just think of it as me being good at spotting the bad-ass in people."

Silas turned away from St. Abigail and took a good look at this apartment building. It was big and obviously abandoned. Paint was peeling, windows were cracked, and part of the roof even looked like it was sinking in.

"Uh oh... this place is off the grid," he said.

"What do you mean?"

"It's an abandoned apartment complex in the middle of New York, but there is no one around, no city signs condemning it, no signs showing that a developer snatched it up."

"I can feel it too, as though the Pale covers it."

"To most humans this place doesn't even exist. It's slippery for the eyes. Anything could be in that building and it has had free rein for years. I don't think even the Inquisition has this place on its radar."

The Inquisition had one of the largest databases on supernatural locations. If they didn't know about it chances are nobody else did.

"What floor was this Webb supposed to be on?" Silas asked.

"Mort said room 502."

"Great. Top floor. Think there's any chance the elevator is working?"

"About as much chance as there is for you to get in my pants," St. Abigail laughed. "Have a plan?"

"Naw, let's just go knock."

COTH WATCHED them enter the apartment building from the shadows of the alley across the street. Somehow they had found it. He didn't know how, but somehow they had discovered this sacred place. His master would want to know. He pulled out his cell phone and held it awkwardly to his misshapen head.

"Hello," said Mister Webb on the other end. The connection was faint and cutting in and out. His master must have been in the Undercity.

"I have found them. It looks as if they have discovered your old home, before you had the revelations."

"Ah, they are moving quickly. Have you discovered who they are?"

"The man is called Silas Robb, but that's about all we have on him. The woman we can't find any information on; it's as if she doesn't exist. Actually finding data on either of them is difficult."

"I expected no less. These two are not your average investigators."

"What do you want me to do? They are defiling your birthplace."

"Don't worry Coth, there is nothing there for them. Our work is much greater than an apartment. They will only find the lesser children, the ones I told you about. The ones that weren't strong enough to join me in the Undercity. All that is left for them are the broken and weak. They will learn nothing."

"Watch them for now. Who knows? It has been a while since I resided there, there might be some interesting surprises for them. However, I would not be opposed if you see an opportunity to take care of them quickly."

"I understand."

"I knew you would, Coth. You have always been my favorite."

Coth hung up and looked back at the building. The two strangers had entered. He was trying to think of what to do next when his eyes found the limo and an idea started to form. A grin spread across his reptilian features.

THE INSIDE of the apartment building was as run down as the outside. The building, however, was hidden by the Pale, so there was no graffiti, no empty beer cans or drug paraphernalia except what might have been left over from the tenants. Unlike a normal abandoned building, this one had not been taken over as a crack house or squatters' home.

They stood in the darkened entrance breathing the stale air. Dust motes danced through the shafts of light coming from the window in the door. The walls were stained brown with mold and in a few places the plaster had flaked off, exposing wood underneath.

"You feel that?" Abigail asked.

"Yeah, there's something here, and if it's in this kind of place it's nothing we want to meet."

"Normally I'm kind of in tune with life--comes with being a Saint--but this place feels..."

"Dead?" Silas interrupted.

"No, not dead; just lacking life," she said.

"Does being wacko come with being a Saint too? How can lacking life not be the same as dead? Unless you're talking about vampires ,or maybe zombies."

"No, not vampires, just a feeling that's hard to explain. Let's just head up."

Silas caught her arm as she stepped on the first stair.

"I was just thinking his apartment might have been 502, but he owned this whole building. And by owned I don't mean he bought and paid for it. I mean he controlled it. Even if he was the strongest supernatural in the building there was no way he could have pulled this whole thing beyond the pale unless he was virtually in control of the other tenants."

"What are you saying?"

"I am saying that despite what Mephisto might have told us about his abilities, or lack thereof, he must have had some sort of strength. And that strength flowed through the entire structure, so we might have a bigger area to worry about than just his room."

Silas took the lead on the stairs. They were half way up when the thumping started.

Whump! The stairs shook beneath their feet.

"What the hell was that?" Abigail asked.

"Whatever it is, it's pretty active for lacking life."

Silas was rewarded with an annoyed scowl. He kept walking up the stairs, hoping maybe it was nothing.

Whump!

This time plaster broke loose from the walls and rained down on them.

"Keep going. Whatever it is, I am sure we will be seeing it soon enough," Abigail said.

Silas nodded and kept climbing the stairs. Scratching sounded from overhead, like a thousand rats running around on the floor above them.

"I hate rats," Silas mumbled.

Mixed with the scratching sound was the larger sound of heavy foot falls. Thumping and running sounds were coming from all around them, and every few seconds the loud, ground-shaking whump would rain plaster down on their heads.

"This can't be good," Silas said.

They started to run. An arm burst through the wall next to them, and a groping hand clawed onto Silas's shirt. The hand was dirty and misshapen, but it grabbed him tight. He grabbed the thing's wrist and snapped it. There was an ear-piercing scream and the hand immediately let go.

Silas looked at St. Abigail and shrugged. "That wasn't so bad."

Suddenly, hands and arms began bursting through the wall up and down the stairs. Hands, some ending in claws, grabbed at them and caught hold of cloth and flesh. Arms shot up from the stairs, wrapping around their ankles. The arms varied in size and shape as though creatures both large and small were trying to get a piece of them. Silas pulled away from a hand only to have three more grab him one step further up the stairs. He was stronger than these clawing creatures, but it was like walking through molasses. His skin was tearing in dozens of different parts of his body as dirty razor fingernails gouged his flesh. St. Abigail wasn't fairing much better. Hands grabbed at her hair and tried to pull her against the wall. So far all that was coming through the wall were appendages, but what would happen when a face, perhaps with a mouth full of teeth, decided to push through?

Silas grabbed another piece of Abigail's hair and pulled her away from the wall in the other direction. She screamed at the indignity of this tug of war. Her blades slashed out and sliced into the pale flesh of the arms entangled in her hair. More screams from beyond the wall as a severed hand fell to the ground. Silas broke two more wrists and Abigail sliced at a dozen. There were more screams and some arms retreated.

"Now looks like as good a time as any to get to the fifth floor," St. Abigail said.

Silas jerked his foot free from a grasping hand and nodded. They ran up the rest of the stairs. Clawed hands still burst through the walls and steps, but they were a little more hesitant after all the damage they had taken. Silas suspected they were cowards and that is why they hid behind the walls. When they were almost at the fifth floor he had the sudden desire to see what one of the things looked like.

"Time to turn the tables," he said and punched through the wall near one of the arms.

He grabbed the nearest body part he could find and yanked the owner through the wall and onto the stairs. The thing screeched as it fell on the stairs at Silas' feet. Instantly the other arms retreated, only holes in the walls remained to mark that they had been there at all. But Silas hardly noticed, he was more interested in the thing at his feet.

"Oh my God," Abigail said.

There was no doubt the thing at their feet had once been human, though its abdomen and appendages were rail thin. Silas had once possessed an officer at an extermination camp in Poland and this man was as thin as those prisoners on their death beds. His back, shoulders, and head, however, were thick with growth that looked like crustaceans, as though barnacles had grown over the upper part of his body. His eyes were a mixture of fear and madness, but they were definitely human. They were the only part left of him that looked normal. And he was crying.

Silas stepped back as St. Abigail stepped forward. Comforting pitiful wretches was her job.

"Shh...it's okay. We won't harm you," she said quietly.

Silas almost laughed. He had definitely done some harm to these things and would do so again if they tried clawing at him again. The creature's eyes flicked back and forth. He was not convinced.

"What happened to you?" She asked.

"Transmogrification gone bad looks like," Silas said. "Yep. This is probably the handiwork of our friend."

St. Abigail looked at the wall covered with broken holes. He knew what she was thinking.

"Yes Abigail, all of them. He used them as practice for his experiments. It takes a lot of practice to get transmogrification magic to work right."

"All of them are like this?" She spoke it as a question but Silas knew she expected no answer.

"No," the misshapen man said in a raspy voice unused to talking. "Some are different, some strong, some stupid."

"But all flawed?" St Abigail asked. "Who are you?"

"Lived here," the man said, but slowly as though confused about his past. "This was home."

"A tenant? You were a tenant of this building?"

The man's eyes narrowed at her, but he nodded.

"Why? Why was this done to you?" She asked.

The hatred and lunacy flared to life in his face.

"To purify us,. To give us a better life," the man said, then spit a large green glob onto the floor and laughed hysterically. Lungs, long unused for laughter, produced wracking coughs between laughs.

The man jumped to his feet and ran up the stairs to the fifth floor. Silas tried to catch him and would have, but Abigail caught his arm and he stopped.

"Let him go."

"What if he goes and gets his buddies?" Silas asked.

"Does it matter? It's not like they don't know where we are."

Silas shrugged.

"Then let's follow him," Silas said and waved his arm at the last flight of stairs. "Ladies first."

They reached the fifth floor and turned down the corridor. A man stood in the middle of the hall, but it was not the poor wretch they had captured on the stairs. He was hunched over, a large bony lump protruding from his shoulder. The lumped shifted, and Silas realized it wasn't a lump, but a third arm and it was heavily muscled. It looked out of place next to his other appendages, which were as thin as the man's on the stairs had been. These creatures looked as if they hadn't eaten in years. At the end of one of his thin arms he held a cane.

"Why have you come to this place?" The man asked, his voice firm and strong even as his body shook from weakness.

"Look buddy, we're just looking for Mr. Webb," Silas said.

The man scowled and turned.

"He is no longer here," he said as he walked down the hall.

"Yep, we kind of figured that one out. What can you tell us about him?" Silas asked, catching up to him.

The man stopped at a door and went through. Silas and St. Abigail followed.

The room beyond was not a normal apartment; it looked as though walls between apartments had been torn down, transforming the whole floor into a makeshift warehouse space. Taking up most of the floor space were chairs and tables holding test tubes, beakers, and other alchemical equipment.

"It looks like a garage sale at a mad scientist's lair," St. Abigail said.

"Or a large meth lab," Silas said.

And it did look more like a drug lab than a sophisticated research set up, like someone had built it strictly from what they could scrounge up. Dust was thick on the equipment. Bunsen burners, test tubes, hoses, and books littered many work surfaces.

"We have touched nothing since he left," said a voice from the wall behind them.

Silas and Abigail turned to see the man they had followed standing there. He was leaning against the wall for support.

"Were you a tenant of the building?" Abigail asked.

The deformed man nodded. "Most of us were; others were pulled off the street and from the depths of the Undercity. He called us his flock, as if he was some great protector."

The man limped to a table and with a violent motion smashed his cane across the table, scattering glass and metal onto the floor. Glass shattered and metal clanged.

"It wasn't by choice," the man continued, the calm in his voice belying the violence in his action. "He trapped us here, one by one, and performed his experiments. His baptism rites, he called them. Then he left."

"How long ago did he leave?" Silas asked, trying to cut to the chase.

"Years. Months. Days. I don't know. A long time I think," he said and walked to another table, smashing the contents as he had the other. "He said he had found others below the city and on the streets more worthy, stronger in their faith in him." The man finished with a laughed.

"So he left you behind?" St. Abigail asked.

"At first we were glad to be rid of him; we never saw him as the prophet he saw himself. But he sealed us in with some dark magic. Now we live this way, mutilated and unable to go out into the city."

"Times are tough all around. Listen did this Webb tell you where he was going?" Silas asked him, ignoring the glare from Abigail.

The guy laughed a little. "Underground, to the depths of the Undercity to create his army for a new dawn."

"New Dawn?"

The man looked him in the eye, his own cold, gray eyes hardening. "The dawn of a new, pure race to replace the humans. People like us," he laughed. "Only I expect they will be a little more refined."

"So you don't know exactly where in the Undercity?" Silas asked.

As they talked, Silas noticed more of the half-men emerging from other rooms--first one or two, then a dozen, then two dozen. They were all twisted specimens of humanity and all different sizes and shapes, some with extra arms, some with misshapen growths of barnacles or hardened leathery skin. It was a horrible example of the handiwork from a mad man with access to sorcery.

"No, he is gone and we can go no more than a block from this building before we are pulled back. It makes finding food very hard. People rarely get past the veil that cloaks this place. It is hard to come by fresh meat."

Silas noticed that the creatures had closed in, cutting them off from the door. He had a bad feeling about this.

"I guess we'll just be going now," he said.

"You don't understand. Fresh meat is so very hard to come by," the man said and the group drew closer.

Whump! Whump!

The loud thumping sound started again like something was trying to break out from below. The old man slammed his cane down twice, then spoke loudly.

"Yes, don't worry we will save you a leg,"

"Don't do this. We can help you," Abigail said, pulling her blades out.

Silas could tell by the drool they weren't listening. He couldn't imagine what they subsisted on, only being able to move in a one block radius. Most likely they fed on rats, garbage, and each other. Coming into this building was like ringing the dinner bell for these things.

Silas turned to one of the tables laden with glass and metal and kicked it into a group of the twisted creatures. With a loud crash the glass flew at the monsters, tiny shards flying like shrapnel. Not stopping to see what effect it had on the others, he grabbed one of the gas pipes descending from the ceiling and ripped it open, bending it toward the group behind him. Natural gas jetted out. He batted aside one of the weaker ones and napped his fingers in front of the gas. He called "fire" and the gas ignited, sending a jet of flame at the surging mass of deformed flesh.

St Abigail had run behind the pipe as he bent it like a flame thrower, washing it across the creatures. A new wave of screeches and the smell of burned flesh filled the air. The majority fell back as the wall of flame smashed into them, but others moved around the tables looking for a way to get behind them.

"This won't hold them all back," Silas yelled over the screams and roaring flames.

By now the flaming jet had ignited parts of the wall; the creatures had given up on them and were trying to escape the rabidly disintegrating room.

"Point it at the door, clear a path," St. Abigail said with a grimace.

"Now that's the spirit," Silas laughed and did as she asked.

The flames did the trick and all the creatures scurried away from his fatal hose. Just in time, too, because at that moment the pipe decided it had enough stress and ripped loose from the ceiling, ending Silas' flame thrower. But now they had a bigger problem. Gas was leaking from the line in the ceiling. In moments the flames in the room around them would ignite the gas build up and explode.

"Time to leave," St. Abigail said and ran at the burning door.

Silas followed. A flaming member of Webb's flock leaped at him from the corner as he neared the door. Greasy, half-charred hands grabbed his jacket and tried to pull him down. He punched the man in the face and he dropped away. Two more leaped at him, staggering him as he reached the door. Two blades flicked out and the flame-covered creatures fell to the ground, dead.

Whump!

Outside the flaming room they heard the massive thumping again.

"Hurry!" Silas said and pushed Abigail toward the stairs. "We don't have much time before this building is going to blow."

They ran down the stairs, stumbling every time the thumping came. Silas hoped they would never see what could be making such a massive noise. At the bottom of the stairs the floor burst with one final, ground-shaking thump.

A creature at least fifteen feet tall burst through the floor. Thick with muscles, it carried an oversized sledge hammer like it was a tack hammer. With a bellow it celebrated its freedom and then glared down at Silas and Abigail.

"Troll. Or at least that's what it looks like Webb was going for," Silas said.

"Look out!" Abigail cried.

The large beast swung his hammer at Silas. He ducked, but was not quite quick enough; the corner of the hammer caught his shoulder, flipping him through the air and slamming him against the wall.

Silas had heard a loud crunch as the hammer hit and knew something had broken. He lay in a heap at the base of the wall, pain throbbing through his shoulder. Even as his demonic essence begin knitting the bones back together, he knew that arm would be useless for a while. He cursed his fragile mortal form.

The troll bellowed again, this time in triumph, and took a swing at St. Abigail. But she was quicker, her preternatural speed making her a blur. She ducked under the blow and her blades flashed out, slashing at the troll's arm. The stiletto skidded down the tough hide of the monster. She jumped back out of the reach of its returning blow.

Silas slid up the wall holding his left shoulder and wondering how the hell he was supposed to fight this thing with only one arm. He looked up and saw flames licking at the railing at the top of the stairs. The gas would ignite any second, only luck had kept it from happening so far.

The troll's back was to him as it was distracted by Abigail. She was moving quickly, dodging in and out of its strikes. Its attention was focused on her, probably dismissing Silas as dead.

Big mistake.

With three long strides he jumped onto the creature's back, slipping his good arm under the its neck. In the eighties he had possessed a pro wrestler and had performed a similar move against Andre the Giant. Sure, it was all fake, but when it came to technique, using brute force pro wrestling could not be beat. Besides, it had worked on Andre even though Silas had gone "off script" since he was scheduled to lose that match. Silas was never keen on losing.

The Troll roared in surprise and Silas cinched up his arm, closing off the beast's throat and cutting the roar short. A large meaty hand slapped at Silas' back, but at this angle the troll didn't have much leverage. After a moment it gave up trying to hit him off its back and instead worked directly on the arm wrapped around its neck. Silas pulled even tighter as it tried to pry off his arm. The beast spun about and Silas was almost thrown from its back, but the troll was slowing now and Silas thought his choke hold might be working.

WHUMP!

A blast of heat and embers fell on him from above. The upstairs had exploded. The ceiling collapsed in places and a large piece of wood slammed hard enough against Silas that he was knocked from the troll's back. Flames and twisted metal fell around him. The entire building was in flames. Now he was in his element. Heat and fire might cause some damage to his mortal form, but it gave his demonic fury pure joy.

St. Abigail would not be as lucky. He quickly climbed to his feet and looked through the rubble and walls of flame trying to locate her. He caught a splash of black against one of the few walls still standing. It was Abigail. She appeared unconscious; a burning log lay across her back.

He started crawling over the debris toward her. He had never possessed a firefighter, but for a couple of days in the seventies he had possessed an arsonist, so he knew a thing or two about moving through a burning building. He kept low as he moved through the wreckage.

The fire was just getting going and he could feel its hunger growing. This room would be at furnace temperature in moments. He was less than ten feet from her unconscious body--at least, he hoped she was just unconscious--when a flaming sledge hammer hit the ground inches from his feet.

Silas turned to see the troll pulling itself out from under a pile of rubble. The beast was horribly burned, and its face looked like it had both melted and charred black at the same time. This may not be a true troll, Silas speculated, just some helpless homeless guy that Webb had experimented on. But he had to give the guy credit; this creature was as tough as any real troll Silas had met. Of course with only one arm, an unconscious partner and a building about to collapse on top of them, it would have been more convenient if the troll had been a pussy.

Another explosion shook the building. Silas thought much of the north side of the building might have just collapsed. The troll ignored the shaking and lifted its giant hammer high over its head, preparing a deadly swing.

There was not much Silas could do. One arm was no good and he was surrounded by flaming debris. He would have to go on the defensive and try to dodge around it. The hammer started its deadly arc and Silas tensed, then it stopped. They both looked up. The head of the hammer had become embedded in a part of the ceiling that had fallen a few feet. The troll grunted and tried to wrench it free. Silas didn't wait.

Ignoring the pain in his shoulder, Silas charged forward and slammed his good shoulder into the abdomen of the troll. He managed to knock the troll back about twenty feet, but it let out a loud woof and doubled over its stomach. Before he could follow up with a punch to its face the ceiling above it collapsed, raining several stories of burning apartments down on its head. The troll was buried instantly.

Silas took only a moment to make sure the troll was down for good before running over to St. Abigail. Pieces of the ceiling were falling around him. He grabbed the beam pining her down and heaved it away, knocking down more of the wall. He caught her jacket collar and lifted her up and over his good shoulder. His arm was still useless, so he handled her like a bag of flour. He was glad she was unconscious; otherwise, he would never hear the end of it.

A mound of rubble had fallen between him and the door, but it was still the quickest way out. He made his way to the door, kicking the smaller pieces out of the way. A handful of large boards had fallen across the door, and he wouldn't be able to move it without leverage. With his bad arm, that would mean putting Abigail down and wasting valuable time.

He was looking for a safe place to put her when the door shoved inward, dislodging the burning wood. The door moved again and the wood fell away completely. The chauffeur's head popped out from behind the open door. He saw them and smiled.

"Need some help?" he cried over the noise of the fire and collapsing building.

Silas jumped over the flames on the floor in front of the door; the chauffeur stepped back making room for them.

"You weren't kidding, what you said about explosions and screaming," Steve said.

In the distance he heard sirens and people were flooding the street to see what was going on. The building no longer hid behind the Pale; it was just another building fire drawing curious onlookers.

When he reached the car Silas laid Abigail down on the ground. She was still breathing, but the breaths were shallow. If her mortal formed died, she would make her way back to the afterlife. He thought mouth to mouth might be in order. He lifted her gently and put his lips to hers.

His demonic fury rose up against her compassion and love and it was like mixing night with day. He could feel the energy flow through both of them. He could feel her heart speed up and he could feel warmth spreading across his face, calming his racing heart. For a moment the exchange was almost painful. Then it just seemed right.

It was different from the fake kiss last night at the restaurant. Different, but Silas was not sure why. It ended the same, however; a stinging slap across his face.

"Oww! What did you do that for? I was saving you," Silas said.

"From what exactly? My virtue?" Abigail said.

"No that," Silas said and nodded back at the blazing apartment building.

She looked over her shoulder and the inferno. "Oh," she said and reached up to wipe a smudge off his cheek.

"Ah, cops and firemen are at the end of the street, guys. Do you want to get going?" Steve asked.

Silas smiled at Abigail. "Told you he had some balls."

He helped her to her feet and they got in the back seat. When they were in, Steve ran to the driver's side. His door hadn't even shut before the tires started squealing on pavement.

"Holy shit, guys! What the hell happened back there?" Steve asked. "One minute everything was quiet, the next, bam! The place exploded. What the hell was in there? Was that some sort of monster you were fighting? I could see a little in there and he was one big dude. I mean, you're big Mr. Silas, but that thing was huge."

Silas and Abigail looked at each other from where they lay exhausted and battered on the back seat. Silas reached over and hit the button for the glass privacy screen. Steve was cut off in mid speech.

"Thank you," Abigail said.

"No problem."

"Looks like we got a new convert," Abigail said.

"What do you mean? Steve?" Silas asked.

"He saw past the Pale and his conscious mind is not going to be able to cover up for it. He has seen too much."

"We can let Mort know to watch him," Silas said.

"We can send a recruiter to him; see if he can handle it. Maybe get him involved," Abigail said.

Silas shrugged, "Maybe, but for now he is my driver."

St. Abigail pulled herself more upright in the seat. "What about my bike?"

"Just text Mort and he'll send someone around to collect it. You didn't use yours to smack a hell hound, so it should be easy to get back."

She pulled out her phone and started doing just that. Silas looked out the window at the city moving by. Silas liked New York. Dirty and grimy, filled with dregs of society, but still a bastion of that spark that gives humanity its edge. The lowest of the low and the highest of potential all together in one large city.

What the hell was he thinking? Why was he waxing poetic? He looked over at Abigail and glared. It's because of the aura she has about her. It made him sick to think it had that power over him.

"Did you hear what that old man said in there?" St. Abigail asked when she was done with the text.

"You mean the geriatric cannibal?"

"Yes. He said that Webb wanted to purify them, wanted to give them a better life. He called them his flock. Who does that sound like?"

"Any given evangelist?" Silas offered.

"He said he was gathering them from the streets. Silas, this sounds very similar to what Michael was telling us about his brother and the street preacher."

Silas nodded. There were connections.

"Perhaps we should go find Michael and listen to him this time. I mean really listen," St. Abigail said.

Silas nodded again and then winced at the pain in his shoulder. Abigail seemed to notice that he was not moving his shoulder for the first time.

"How's your shoulder?"

"Won't be doing any jumping jacks anytime soon, that's for sure."

"Let me see it," Abigail said.

"Why? So you can poke and prod it and make it hurt even more?"

"Silas don't be a big baby, let me see it. And take off your jacket."

"I don't think I need..." Silas started.

Before he could finish St. Abigail reach over and yanked his jacket part way down his shoulder. She was not gentle; if he had been a mortal the pain would have been bad enough that he would have screamed, as it was he just grunted.

"We can do this the hard way or the easy way. What's it going to be Silas?"

"I like a woman who can take charge," Silas said and took off his jacket carefully.

Abigail's stiletto whipped out and sliced his t-shirt.

"Hey!" Silas said and was ignored.

"Quiet. I have a feeling this isn't the first time a woman had a knife on you."

Abigail touched his shoulder, not as gently as Silas would have wanted, and closed her eyes. "It's healing fast, but maybe I can speed it up a little."

Silas felt warmth like he had felt when his lips were on hers. He closed his eyes and tried to enjoy it. Moments later her hand fell away and the spell was broken. Silas moved his arm and tested it.

"And?" Abigail asked.

"Little stiff, but I'll be busting heads again in no time," Silas said.

"I guess that's as close as I will get to a thank you?"

Silas was about to respond when the privacy window slid down.

"Where to, boss?" Steve asked.

"The Dark Horse, off thirty Eighth Street," Silas said.

St. Abigail frowned. "What about Michael? Shouldn't we be trying to find him?"

"In the last twenty four hours I have been chased by hell hounds through a mall, attacked by a pack of mutant cannibals, and fought a troll in a burning building. To put it mildly, I need a drink."

"Cool," said Steve from the front.

"Besides, I got band practice in a few."

"We almost got killed several times, there is a religious lunatic creating monsters in the city, and all you can think about is getting a drink and band practice?"

Silas patted her on the knee and said, "Yep, and it only gets weirder from here. Sit back and enjoy the ride."

He then proceeded to follow his own advice.

COTH WATCHED the limo pull away from the blazing apartment building. That had not gone as he expected. Fire light reflected off the scales covering half his hulking body and in his eyes, wet with tears.

That Silas is a walking demolition team. Webb may not have returned here anymore, but he would be upset that this man destroyed the birthplace of his work. This was in many ways a holy site and now it was burning like any other piece of trash in this city.

Coth ducked further into the alley as fire trucks and police vehicles pulled up next to the fire. He had to leave; this place would soon be crawling with government humans. He slipped down the alley, darting through the next street. He didn't stop until he was two blocks away. Then he pulled out his cell phone.

It had been so easy to slip up to the limo. Coth was usually too big to go unnoticed, but with the distraction of the fire he could have been a giant pink elephant and still no one would have noticed him approach the limo cloaked in a heavy over coat and hooded sweatshirt. The driver had not even turned around when Coth had banged his head on the car door placing the tracking device under the frame, but by then the explosions had started and all hell was breaking loose.

Now he brought up the tracking app. Instantly, a map of New York appeared and a blip marked the location of the limo. Amazing what you could pick up at your local consumer spy store.

He glanced around to make sure no one was looking, then lifted a manhole cover and dropped down. He checked the phone again, and then he was off running through the sewers. His feet found their way through the tunnels without thought. He held up the phone and followed the red blip knowing that wherever it led him, vengeance would be waiting for him to claim.

9

"Silas, you're drunk," Abigail said.

And he was, happily so. Well maybe just buzzed, but it was hard to drink enough alcohol to get really drunk when you were a demon. He looked down at the twelve shot glasses stacked in a pyramid. It was a monument to his inebriation.

"Yes rock and roll is always a little better when you are less in control of yourself," Silas said and winked at her.

St. Abigail turned to Mort for help. "We should be heading out to find this street preacher or even heading to the Undercity. Not sitting here at a night club."

"Whoa, whoa, whoa! This ain't a night club. You see some sort of DJ in the corner spinning? Do you see bright lights blinking on and off in time with the music, anybody with glow sticks around here?" Silas asked.

"I see a drunk at the bar struggling not to puke, and a fifty year old hooker eying him like he's a catch."

"Right! This is a bar," Silas said. "Nobody here is going to show up in fancy clothes or feather boas trying to be seen. No feathers allowed."

"You might want to tell that to him," Abigail said and nodded over Silas' shoulder.

Silas turned and saw a man in jeans with a button up work shirt tucked in sitting at the bar. His hair was long and black, shot through with gray. Woven through his hair were strips of leather holding a few feathers. He was definitely an Indian. He sat facing the bar and Silas couldn't get a good look at his face.

Silas turned to Mort with a raised eyebrow. "Any chance that is the Indian that Father Delentante talked about?"

"Could be. But there are lots of Native Americans in the city; not all are dressing the part."

"I suppose I should go over and just ask," Silas said and stumbled to his feet.

"Si!" Walt called from near the stage, waving to get his attention.

Time for their first set. Silas looked around. The bar was half full and it was still early, might be a good night. He decided the Indian could wait. It was time to get the party started. He walked to the stage and jumped up, grabbing the microphone.

"This first song is dedicated to someone special," Silas said. "She's sitting in the back. She's perfect like... well like a saint. The song's called Fuck Me."

He looked over at Kitten, who looked at him as if he was crazy before beating out the four count and launching into the song. Fat Carl thumped the bass and the song was on.

The music flowed and he rode in like a wave. He let the lyrics fly from his tongue. Yeah, this was what he was meant for.

He was so involved with the music, it took him a moment to notice the strange man in the back of the bar by the door. He was a slim man wearing an old suit too small for him. His hair was slicked back, large sunglasses perched on his nose dominating his face. A speck of something red dripped down his cheek from beneath those glasses. From the stage Silas could smell it was blood.

The Indian was staring at the slim man with a stoic look on his face, but Silas could see the hatred inside him. Hate was a hard thing to hide from a demon. Slim didn't seem to notice the Indian staring at him. This was trouble, Silas could feel it.

He looked around the room as he sang searching for others who might be out of place this night, and he saw them--several large individuals concealing their bulk beneath long coats and large hats. He could see the glint of scales on some, and if it had been any brighter in the bar somebody would have noticed the creatures moving through the crowd. A group of three sat at one table and another handful scattered throughout the crowd. They were slowly making their way closer to the stage. Silas could see that they wouldn't get to the encore tonight.

He glanced at St. Abigail and could see she had spotted them also. Her stilettos were in hand, but held low to remain unnoticed. Normally Silas would not have expected such an attack out in the open; most people don't want to risk breaking the Pale so obviously, but these guys did not seem too worried about that. Perhaps that was even part of Webb's plan. He was remaking the world, what did it matter if he helped instigate Armageddon?

He looked back at the band. Walt was looking at him oddly, probably wondering why he was more distracted than usual. Silas nodded toward the audience, and after a moment of scanning the crowd Walt nodded back. Good, he had seen the creatures approaching.

They were almost at the stage. Silas looked back at the slim man. This must be Mr. Webb. Mr. Webb, the Indian, the monsters--with all the players in one room this could be over really quickly.

A group of the lizard creatures had made it to the stage. They jumped for the front. Most were going for Silas, but a couple leaped at his band mates. They were probably thinking they could take care of the humans quickly and then join the others on Silas. Boy, were they in for a surprise.

As a handful of the creatures leaped on the stage in front of him, Silas stepped forward onto the pyrotechnics stomp box. The sparkle fountains, usually reserved for a big Saturday night show, exploded up at the lizard creatures. The dazzling light display played across their glasses, like the ones at the monastery these also wore tinted goggles, and stinging sparks engulfed them.

With a combination of roars and screeches they fell back onto the dance floor, scattering people in all directions. One of the beasts leaped at Carl, who calmly slipped the bass guitar off his shoulder and swung it like a battle axe. The hardened hide that all ogres had, usually concealed by the bulky coat he wore, tore through his clothing as he put power behind that swing. It connected with the lizard creature's head and sent it spinning into the dark of the bar.

Another lunged at Kitten, who dodged aside at blinding speed, then spun and drove her custom carbon-fiber drum sticks vertically down through the collar bone and into the heart of the creature. It hit the ground dead, spilling over the drum set with a crash of cymbals and metal. Kitten's canine teeth had already lengthened. She was eager for the fight and, most likely, the blood afterward. She held the other carbon fiber stick ready--no self-respecting vampire would use a wooden stick, even if she was the drummer in a rock and roll band.

The one who had attacked Walt was faring no better. As the lizard creature, leaped it must have noticed Walt changing, growing bigger, hairier, more wolf-like. Now it found itself snapping at the neck of a werewolf. With a snarl Walt completed his transformation into an eight-foot werewolf and wrenched the lizard creature off his fury chest. With a screech of surprise, it fell back into the crowd.

Silas looked back at the slim man standing by the door, beyond the people running in all directions and screaming in confusion at the sudden violence.

"Oh yeah," Silas said into the microphone looking at Slim. "This is rock and roll bitches. We don't fuck around."

The creatures were regrouping, now more leery of this rock and roll band. Of the nine original lizard men, seven remained. They circled the stage cautiously. In the back Silas saw Slim flicker, and then there were three of him. Abigail had been moving toward him. Now she paused, unsure of which was real.

The creatures split, doubling up on his band mates, but leaving only a single one for him to deal with. Apparently these creatures thought his band more dangerous than him. Once again, big mistake.

As they rushed the stage, Silas stepped on another pedal. This one lit up the sign behind him. The band's name--Burning Soul--burst to life behind him, bathing the room in bright light. The lizard creatures pulled away, shielding their eyes. His band mates, always up for a good ass-kicking, didn't hesitate; with various battle cries they jumped into the confused group.

Silas slammed his fist into the face of the creature closest to him. It felt like hitting leather-covered metal and made his knuckles sting. What the hell were these things made of? The creature came at him, all claws and teeth. Around him his band mates were holding their own and looked as if they might be winning. Over the creature's shoulder he spotted St. Abigail as she whipped her blade through Slim. It passed through, and the image only flickered. She jumped at the second image, and passing through it, continued her momentum to confront the last image.

By now Slim had seen her coming and had time to prepare; he raised his hand in a flicking motion. Abigail immediately fell back as though bouncing off a wall.

A fist covered in scales slammed into Silas' stomach and he doubled over. He couldn't let Abigail distract him like that. He came up hammering a double fist into the creature's distended jaw. Its head slammed up from the force and Silas had the satisfaction of hearing its jaw bone snap.

Suddenly, he was surrounded by fog. Coming out of nowhere a thick, pale green cloud rolled in, instantly reducing his visibility to zero, and from the surprised cries of his band mates he knew they were having the same problem. A claw came out of the fog and before he had time to react, it had sliced a gouge in his left arm. He spun in the direction of the attack, but the creature was gone.

Pain exploded up his back as he was struck again, this time the claw sliced his jacket and flesh like butter. He spun again, but his attacker was gone. A scaled hand clamped around his boot and pulled. Silas fell onto the ground.

Apparently their attackers were not as inconvenienced by the green fog. It had to be sorcery. He racked his memories from his past. Acting more on instinct than any sensory perception, he rolled to the right. An extra-large boot with razor-sharp claws ripping through the toes slammed down where his face had been moments before.

He heard Walt bellow in a roar of pain and Kitten scream as though touched by sunlight. This wasn't good. If he didn't act quickly he might lose his band, and it is very hard to put a good band together.

He reached into his jacket pocket and pulled out a cigar. He hesitated a moment--after all it was a good Cuban--before crushing it in his fist, being careful not to spill the tobacco. The spell was supposed to be done with ashes, but this was all he had. He brought his closed fist to his mouth, but before he could do anything, a creature was on him.

It slammed into his back, sprawling him onto his stomach. Cold, leathery hands closed around his throat and squeezed. Pointed knees dug into his back, forcing him to arch his head up. It felt like the creature was trying to rip his head off. With his hand clamped around the loose tobacco he was at a disadvantage.

Abigail stumbled backward and fell into the creature on his back. Both tumbled into the pale green fog.

Silas coughed and heaved as he sucked in breath. He rolled up against the stage. He inhaled a few more times to steady his breath, then brought the tobacco to his mouth. He spoke a few words from an ancient spell and let the tobacco fall from his hand as he blew on it.

A breeze came from behind his shoulder, pushing the fog away from him. For a moment, he could see around him in a small radius. His band mates were locked in battle with the lizards, but the momentary clearing was quickly turned the tide. Even Abigail, now that she could see her attackers, was dancing around her opponent, her daggers a blur.

Silas could see Slim by the door; their eyes met. Slim grinned and then raised his hands. Instantly the fog returned, filling in the void.

Damn, he needed something stronger. He was trying to think when a clawed foot caught him in the chin, sending him backward onto the stage. Stunned, he crashed into something made of metal-- his stage fan.

Silas grabbed another cigar from his pocket. Since this was sympathetic magic, increasing one of the elements, in this case wind, should increase the force of the spell. Silas switched on the fan and crushed the cigar in his hands, letting it fall as he spoke the words of the spell again. The dried tobacco was pulled from his hands and blown out into the room.

This time it wasn't a breeze that appeared, but a strong wind. It tore through the room and shredded the green fog as it toppled chairs and tables. With their sight restored, his band mates quickly turned the tide of their own battles. Now it was the creatures' turn to hiss in frustration.

In the back Slim was raising his arms again, preparing another spell Silas guessed, when he stopped and turned. The Indian was standing near with a raised wooden stick, and he was speaking, but Silas could not make the words out.

Pain exploded in his back and he was thrown from stage once more. He landed in the middle of the floor. On stage stood the same large creature Silas had fought outside the monastery. Although similar in build, he dwarfed the other lizard creatures; his chest and arms were wrapped in scaled-covered muscles. Fire burned in his eyes and his elongated mouth parted in a tooth-lined smile. The creature's hatred was palpable.

Must still be embarrassed by that little dance in the alley, thought Silas, ready for the beast to pounce.

"Coth! Retreat!" said a voice from the back of the room. Silas guessed it came from Slim.

Coth's eyes flickered from Silas to the back of the room. The creature hesitated and stared at Silas with hunger.

"Coth! I said retreat!"

Coth growled, then reached down to pick up the body of a fallen comrade with one hand. The other creatures disengaged, grabbing their dead and injured as they ran for the front and back doors, causing screams as they ran through the kitchen. They moved with inhuman speed and agility, and Silas and his band mates were too busy recovering from their wounds to try to chase them.

The slim man at the back of the room was gone. The old Indian was putting his club through a loop in his belt. Abigail limped to Silas with a smile on her lips and claw marks on her arms and across her stomach. None of the cuts looked deep. Silas thought she never looked hotter.

"One hell of a mosh pit, huh?" Abigail asked.

"You should go to an Anthrax concert; makes this look like a night at the opera."

Mark stood up from behind the bar. Mouth open, he surveyed the destruction before his eyes stopped on Silas.

"Everybody's a critic," Silas said and shrugged.

Mark nodded his head and picked up a broom.

"I hate fucking gangs," Mark mumbled, clearly in shock. He would need much more than a broom to take care of this place.

The other staff was coming out from hiding as the last of the customers made their way out the front door. Luckily no civilians had been hurt; Silas and his friends had been the only targets. Hurt patrons would have meant cops and that was one headache Silas didn't want to deal with.

Silas and Abigail made their way to the table. Mort was still there with his laptop clicking away as though there hadn't just been a battle royal ten feet from where he sat.

"Mort open that fat Vatican purse of yours and help Tom with the repairs," Silas said as he eased himself into a seat. Every muscle ached and he was pretty sure he had cracked a few ribs. Maybe if he told Abigail, she would do the healing thing again. He would heal fast on his own, but he was pretty sure he could get into her pants if she tried something like that again.

"Sorry Silas. I can't let the Vatican pay for this. It would look really bad to have his Holiness linked to a cesspool like this. How would they explain a donation to a seedy bar?"

"Fine, give them something out of my personal account to get the place up and running again."

Mort nodded.

"It looks like our friend disappeared," Mort said and nodded past Silas.

The old Indian was gone. Then the door swung open and Steve the driver walked in looking around.

"Damn, another fight. Did you fight another troll Mr. Robb?"

Mort raised an eyebrow at Silas.

"He kind of saw what happened back at the apartment. He might be one of us now,"

"Well I can have a recruiter talk to him, maybe bring him in."

"For now he's my driver and it stays that way; at least until I get my bike back."

"He's had no training, and his limo isn't even Vatican property. He works for Fast Eddie's Limo Service for Christ's sake."

"Yeah, Eddie is my brother," Steve said.

Mort just sighed and shook his head. "Here," Mort reached into his bag and handed Steve a device that looked like an iPod.

"I want you to use this device to check out every inch of that limo of yours," Mort said.

Steve looked at it dubiously. "How does it work?"

"Just hold it within a foot or so of the car. Run it over the body; if it lights up come tell us," Mort said.

Steve nodded and headed for the door.

"And don't forget to run it underneath!" Mort yelled at him as he walked out the door.

"What was that all about?" Silas asked.

"Well, they found you , didn't they? Even if they had spotted you at the apartment, those things didn't follow you on foot. Most likely they tracked you somehow. I bet there is something on the limo."

"Come on Mort. Isn't that a little too James Bond? I mean we are talking about monsters from the sewers here."

"You can find good tracking devices at your neighborhood spy outlet; even a sewer monster could get a hold of one easily," Mort said.

"So what's our next move?" St. Abigail interrupted.

"We find Michael. Make him take us to this street preacher. Got to be connected," Silas said.

"Do you think he is going to want to talk to you after the last time?" Abigail asked.

"He's just a kid. He'll tell us what we want," Silas said.

"You don't hang around kids much do you Silas?" Abigail asked. "Besides, after the last time, he'll run the moment he sees you coming. Do you even know how to contact him?"

"Father Deluca can probably arrange a meeting."

"And whatever we use to persuade him, it will only be with words. I'm not going to stand by and watch you interrogate a kid like the Gestapo."

"Abigail, I'm offended that you would think such a thing of me," Silas said although he had assumed he would do exactly that.

Steve came bursting back into the bar holding a small piece of metal in his hand and a smile on his face.

"Got it!"

He held up the quarter size tracking device like a trophy. Silas snatched it from his hand and crushed it between his fingers. The iPod-like device in Steve's other hand stopped chirping. Silas turned to Abigail.

"These guys are more sophisticated than I had thought," he said.

St. Abigail grimaced. "I'm beginning to worry about what we're going to find in the Undercity."

10

F ather Deluca slipped out the front door of the church and came down the steps to Silas and Abigail. This time of night the church was deserted.

"He is in there. What happened between the two of you Silas?" Father Deluca asked.

Silas shrugged.

"Silas was his usual charming self when they last met," Abigail said.

"Well he sure hates you now. It was only because you said you might know something about what happened to his brother that he even agreed to meet with you. You sure you can't tell me what this is all about?"

"We will father, once we figure it out ourselves. For now it's best you don't know," Abigail said.

Father Deluca nodded his acceptance. "Remember these are my parishioners, this is my neighborhood. Please be careful."

"Of course, Father. I know how much this neighborhood means to you," St. Abigail said.

With one last stern look at Silas he walked down the steps and turned into the alley. *Smoke break,* thought Silas. He and Abigail entered the church.

The church was a large, built originally in 1877. Empty pews filled the majority of the open room, which was dominated by the ornate altar and lectern. The lights were on, but they couldn't penetrate the shadows along the outer edge of the pews.

"Never was a big fan of these places," Silas mumbled.

"Well don't do anything blasphemous," Abigail said.

At first they couldn't see Michael; then Silas spotted the small head popping up from the front pew. The kid must have heard them, but his head was down. In the quiet of the church Silas could hear a quiet sobbing.

Oh great, more water works.

St. Abigail was already moving down the aisle, quietly so as not to disturb the kid. Silas followed, not being anywhere near as quiet. They sat on the pew next to the boy.

"Father Deluca said you needed to talk to me? Something about my brother?" The boy asked. He looked up at them hopefully, but when his eyes focused on Silas he frowned and looked away.

"Well, we are not sure yet, Michael. We might have found a connection in our investigation," Abigail said.

"Investigation? What are you, detectives?"

"Something like that. We work for the Church."

He looked over at Silas and snorted. "Yeah, right."

"We need to know more about this street preacher you mentioned."

"Why? Because it's important to your investigation now? Silas didn't care about my problems before."

Silas sighed. He could see the kid had been crying. His brother was the only thing he had left in the world and now that was gone. The boy was lost, for lack of a better word. He couldn't believe he was going to do this, but he could feel St. Abigail's aura working on him. Perhaps he should just go with it for now. It might get them the answer they need faster.

"Look kid," Silas said. "I'm sorry I treated you like shit the other day. I was caught up in my job and getting impatient. I know how it can be, feeling alone in the world--no family or friends. The truth is there is some shit going on in this town and it's bigger than your brother, bigger than any one person. If we don't find out what's going on and stop it quickly, a lot of people might die."

St. Abigail was looking at him with an unreadable expression. It made him uncomfortable and he looked away.

"This thing that's going to happen, you think my brother is somehow involved?"

"Well we don't know for sure, but this street preacher might be involved in some of the disappearances, and if he's the reason your brother vanished, we might be able to discover what happened to him," Abigail said.

"So what do you need from me?"

"This preacher, could you lead us to him? Is there some area he hangs out at?" Silas asked.

"He walks the street a lot, usually stops in areas away from the public with some space for his gatherings. There's an abandon warehouse that I think he uses for large meetings. That was where my brother was going that night."

"Where is this building?"

"Oh no! It's not going down like that. I tell you where it is then I go hide up somewhere, then I never see you again and never find out what happened to my brother. If you're going, I'm going with you."

"Look kid, this is going to be dangerous, life and death kind of dangerous,"

"No shit, Silas. You think I don't know danger?"

No, Silas didn't think he knew this kind of danger. Street thugs and drugs were one thing, but the creatures that really roamed this city were a whole new level of fucked. But he also knew there was no way to convince this kid he might be out of his league.

"Fine. Can you lead us to this building?"

"Sure, but you'll never get in. He has a couple of people always on the lookout," Michael said and looked them up and down. "And you guys would kind of stand out."

"He's right, Silas. We don't really look like the poor and downtrodden. Any ideas?" Abigail asked.

"Yeah, I don't do poor and destitute very well. We can use his work against him. I might be able to come up with some sort of transmogrification."

"Transmogrification? Like magic?" Michael asked.

"How do you know what transmogrification means?" Silas asked.

"I'm not stupid. I can read and there's this place where they dump a lot of old books in the trash. Mostly fantasy books."

"Well then I guess..." Silas started.

St. Abigail grabbed his shoulder.

"Silas can I have a word with you, alone?" She asked.

Silas nodded and they made their way to the side of the church.

"Silas, do you know what you are doing here? Were you going to tell him the truth?"

"If the kid is going to help us, he'll find out anyway," Silas said.

"Yeah, but this isn't some adult with a job that can take care of himself, this isn't some monster or creature that wants to kill us. This is a kid who lives on the street. If you lift the Pale from his eyes and show him the true world, there is no going back for him. Who will take care of him in this new world?"

"Father Deluca..."

"Doesn't even know the truth himself. How can he take care of a kid that knows what's really going on. You know how this works. Once you step through the veil there is no going back. He has no stability, no grounding to fall back on. He's just a kid for Christ's sake."

"The Inquisition Project?"

"You would turn him over to the likes of Moreales and the Vatican? I support what we do and respect the church, but even I know it's no place for a kid."

Silas looked back at the boy. Abigail was right; it would be tough on him. He would be set adrift in a world he no longer understood. But he also saw that they might not have a choice.

"Look Abigail, look at him. I think it's too late."

She too stared at Michael and he could see she saw the same thing. The kid was smart and already had some idea that something abnormal was going on.

"He's gonna figure it out, maybe not today, but soon. And you're right, then he will be fucked."

St. Abigail just nodded, but when Silas went to sit beside the boy again she held him back.

"Silas you promise me you won't abandon him when this is done. There is no one for him except you."

"And you," Silas said.

"Well sure, but I need to know you are committed to watching after him once we do this."

"Yeah, yeah. Sure," Silas said waving her off.

And why not? He could always find a babysitter for the kid after this was all over. Besides, he was pretty sure Abigail would take care of him, feminine instinct and all that.

"Michael my boy, prepare to have your mind blown," Silas said with a grin.

Damn, St. Abigail was ugly!

Silas had to turn away with a grimace. The transmogrification was almost too good. Her beautiful skin had been transformed into a leathery, wrinkled shell of what it had been. Lines deep with age covered her face and long, stringy hair, most of which had fallen out, leaving pink splotches on her scalp. Most of her teeth were gone too, the few remaining stained almost black. She looked like a hag, and having quite a few of them in Hell, Silas knew what a true hag looked like.

"Well you don't look like you'll be doing the cover of GQ anytime soon, you know," St. Abigail said.

Silas flipped down the mirror in the back of the limo and checked himself out. He was still big, he would have had a hard time getting the magic to hide that fact, but a huge scar ran up part of his face, cutting through his hair line. The scar looked like it had not healed clean and most of his hair had fallen out around the wound. His nose looked broken--worse than normal-- and open sores covered most of his lip. His skin too was wrinkled with age and sun. He smiled, revealing several missing teeth. Frankly, he thought he looked good. He just shrugged at Abigail.

"How long will this spell last?" She asked.

"Not much more than a couple of hours. Transmogrification isn't one of my specialties. I picked it up from a vampire I possessed in the thirteenth century. Did you know most young vampires can't change their shape without help? This one had learned the spells from a sorcerer he had lured to his castle."

"Is sorcerer's blood tastier?"

"What? No, no nothing like that. The vampire was gay and thought the sorcerer was cute. Of course, the vampire's wife was a wraith, and trust me that is one love triangle you don't want to get in the middle of," Silas said and then paused, caught up in the memory.

"Sorry to interrupt your porn fantasy, but don't you think we should get out of the limo with some distance from the building? I think it might blow our cover to have two poor, homeless vagabonds arrive in a Cadillac."

"I think we're about four blocks away from his rally," Michael said. He looked like himself, fitting the part without magic. Of course he couldn't keep his eyes off the Silas and Abigail, seeing real magic for the first time.

Silas had Steve pull over and they got out. The street was deserted. Silas leaned over the driver's side window.

"Stay in the area, but keep moving; this isn't really a limo type neighborhood. I'll call you when we need a pick up."

"Sure, Mr. Silas. Maybe I should pick up some prostitutes? You know to look inconspicuous," Steve said.

Abigail grunted. "You picked him Silas."

"No Steve, just tool around a little; this isn't the time to cruise for a piece of ass."

"Right. Gotcha. No ass."

Silas did wonder if it had been a mistake to bring Steve into the fold. Although he wasn't the sharpest tool in the shed, there was something about him that made Silas think he would be useful.

They headed off down the street, keeping in the shadows until the limo was gone.

"Silas, you're strutting like the king of the fucking ghetto. Try to walk a little meeker, maybe shamble a little."

Silas tried, but it wasn't in his blood to be meek. Thankfully he had drunk most of a bottle of Bourbon in the limo so it was easy to manage a little stagger here and there. He also smelled the part, thanks to a bump in the road Steve had taken too fast. But the sooner they get what they needed from the preacher, the sooner Silas could grab the other bottle he had stashed under the seat.

As they approached the area they spotted more people heading the same general direction and avoiding eye contact. They all walked, staggered or stumbled down the street like a zombie parade. They were subdued like a congregation gathering for church. A few cried out here and there like the crackpots they were.

Must be something *going on tonight,* thought Silas.

They eventually merged with a small crowd outside an abandoned warehouse. Two large men wrapped in baggy clothes and hoodies stood outside the doors watching the crowd of destitutes wander through the door. Silas caught a glint of silver from under the hood of one. He leaned down to whisper to Abigail.

"I think we're in the right place, I just caught a glimpse of scales. These two aren't as far along as the others we've encountered."

"That's probably why they are on recruiter duty. They look the most human," Abigail said.

As they approached, shining eyes glared at them from beneath the hoods. Silas heard the man in front of him offer a greeting to the thugs at the door.

"Brother," the man said and nodded a greeting to the two.

"Welcome, brother," the man said, his voice gravelly, and Silas could imagine that soon it would be the same hiss he heard from the creatures they had fought. Why did he feel as if they were entering the hornets' nest? As he stepped to the door, Silas spoke.

"Hi brother, how's it hanging?"

The thug's eyes slid over him.

"I don't recognize you brother. Are you new?"

"Yep, first time. Will there be a raffle?"

The bouncer returned his question with a cold stare. Abigail kicked him in the ankle and pulled him away.

"Watch it Silas, they take this thing seriously," she whispered in his ear.

They walked by the other bouncers, but only received stoic glares. Silas tensed waiting for an attack. It wouldn't be the first time his mouth had fucked things up. But they were allowed into the building without incident.

Inside was a great mob of the unwashed. The scent hit Silas, but it was nothing compared to the great rotting pits of Hell. Still the presence of so many homeless--there must have been a hundred gathered in the decrepit building--brought out a certain stench to the air. Silas saw St. Abigail wrinkle her nose.

"Makes you wonder how Mother Theresa could do it," Silas whispered to Abigail.

The inside of the warehouse was as plain as the outside. It consisted of one large open room with small piles of trash scattered about and what looked like a makeshift stage of stacked lumber and wood pallets. Beyond the stage was a large garage door, presumably to a loading dock. Along the other wall three garage doors sat closed. The large room was lighted by old halogen lights, half of which were burned out while most of the others flickered.

The congregation--if that was the best word to describe this group of homeless misfits--gathered close to the stage. It appeared most of them had been here before, so it was an ongoing recruiting effort. Silas could identify a few newcomers looking uncomfortable as the other tried to explain the beauty of what they were about to experience.

The low din of voices talking filled the room, some more passionately than others. Silas identified these as the shills. Several televangelists had made it to Hell--actually all of them that had died so far-- and had explained that this was how it worked. You primed the crowd with a couple of people who will pump them up and lead the way.

There were also coffee and donuts. Silas made his was over to the table and picked a powdered one. Michael grinned and grabbed a large chocolate one. They both noticed Abigail giving them a disapproving look. Silas shrugged and then gave Michael a wink as he bit into the donut. The kid grinned a little wider and took a bite.

Maybe the kid wasn't so bad.

The crowd grew quiet. One of the garage doors began to open, beyond was the open back of a shipping container on a semi-truck. Standing inside was a man wrapped in an oversized trench coat, two other large men also hidden in large coats standing behind. Beyond them the lights didn't penetrate; the rest of the container was covered in shadows.

Even with the baggy coat covering the preacher's form Silas could tell it was not Webb, if Webb had been the slim man at the back of the bar casting spells, and Silas was sure he was. This guy was not as thin, and most of his face was obscured by a long beard and scraggly hair that hung in dirty dreads down his face. He stopped for a moment after noticing how large the group was, and one of the large men behind him stepped forward and spoke in his ear, gripping the preacher's arm tightly.

"Handlers maybe?" Abigail whispered in his ear.

"Maybe," Silas said. Abigail was probably right, the preacher looked a little confused, but the men behind him seemed to know exactly what to do. So that meant he was probably just a tool, the real brains were probably far from this place. Like in the Undercity.

The preacher climbed up on the makeshift stage and seemed to undergo a metamorphosis. His eyes came alive as he stared out at the crowed and a large, friendly grin spread across his face. The confusion was gone. He opened his arms as though he wanted to embrace everyone in the congregation.

"Friends. It is good to see so many of you have come. It gladdens my heart that so many have come to hear my words, which aren't really my words at all. They are the words of a man much greater than I, much greater than all of us, but also one of us. One who has been through all that we see on a daily basis, he has found the Way.

"I speak of the prophet. The man who has walked the same path as us, the one who has risen above and ascended. But brothers and sisters he knows what it is like out there. He has been there when the rest of the people, the ones that call themselves society, have turned away from us. Like all of us, he has felt the scorn that this society places on us."

The preacher spoke the word "society" like it was a disease.

"This society doesn't know about pain, about the suffering we have to endure. They don't know what it takes to survive on the streets. The horrible things we have seen and, yes brothers and sisters, the horrible things we have had to do, just to live. They don't know this, and why? Because this society takes care of its own.

"Now, I know what you are going to say. You're going to say, but they do try to help, what about the missions? What about the soup lines? Well I say these are nothing but salves for their guilt. They help just enough to keep us alive so they can look down at us from their high places and say, well thank God I am not one of *them*.

"Let me ask you brothers, how many of you have been on a job interview recently?"

A handful of people raised their hands and Silas noticed that most of them were the shills he had identified earlier.

"And none of you got the job did you?" The preacher asked.

A few cries of "not me" or even "I was laughed out the place" came out of the crowd again, mostly from the shills. Silas stopped listening. It was the same old spiel used to spur every revolution since the beginning of time. But Silas was beginning to put together Webb's method.

"First find your army, unite them against the enemy, then give them the ability to fight," Silas whispered to Abigail. "Standard revolution planning. Most revolutions fail because of step three," Silas said quietly to Abigail.

"That's where the catalyst comes in. At some point he transforms them into beings that can fight," she murmured back.

"Right. The question is why exactly? He's got to know that even if he transformed all the homeless in New York into these monsters he still can't stand against, say the U. S. Military. All he is going to accomplish is raising the Pale from the mainstream and hasten the end of the world. Even if he doesn't know about the balance, there is no end game for him. As nasty as these creatures are, they can't stand against a united humanity."

"Unless he truly is crazy, then none of this really matters," Abigail said.

"If this is just madness, then we are really fucked. Nothing is going to stop him from destroying the world."

There was a burst of activity from the crowd and the preacher spoke up.

"And how is the Prophet going to accomplish all this? How is he going to help us all rise above the streets and tunnels we dwell in? Why with the elixir. The Blood of the Wyrm."

As he spoke, several men walked through the crowd carrying silver trays with small shot glasses. In the glasses was a red liquid. As the servers walked by, hesitant and nervous hands reached out to pick them up.

"Don't worry brothers and sisters. This is just a taste of the elixir the Prophet has created. There is nothing dangerous in it, just the blessing of a man that understands and loves us. I know many of you have polluted yourselves with drugs and alcohol before; in fact, I bet most of you have something impure floating through your veins even now. But this is different; this blessed drink will burn the impurities out of you and replace them with natural euphoria--the natural high of understanding.

"Take one, but only one, my brothers. This is but a taste of the power and the strength awaiting you if you are ready to take the next step. We no longer have to be the ones at the bottom, feeding on the refuse from society."

Silas watched as people began drinking the liquid. Most winced like it was strong liquor. Soon smiles appeared on faces, and people who only moments before seemed little more than drug addled zombies began to show life and energy. Somebody laughed out loud and others joined him. People that before had ticks or lame feet shook them off. From his perch on the stage the street preacher watched on with a smile.

A tray appeared in front of Silas, and the red liquor gleamed with malice in the low light.

"Oh no, thanks, I'm more a bourbon man," Silas said.

The large man holding the tray raised an eyebrow. Silas had the feeling that any members of this congregation that didn't drink would quickly find themselves reevaluated as unworthy. Not that Silas was against taking drugs—hell, he was pretty sure he had a vial of coke in his jacket pocket, but this was different. This drug was magical, from an unknown source, and in fact, might be responsible for transforming humans into deadly monsters. There was no telling what it would do to him or how permanent it would be. From the corner of his eye he could see Abigail eying the tray with the same concern.

"Take the drink, brother. Show your dedication; trust me you'll like it," the server said. Silas could see the telltale shine of silver scales on the backs of his wrists. He took a glass, but did not drink. The server chuckled. "It looks like little brother is eager."

Silas saw that Michael was putting an empty glass on a server tray. *Uh oh.*

There was a commotion from the stage and Silas looked up to see another of the preacher's handlers step up to him and whisper in his ear. The preacher listened for a second then nodded.

"I have just been informed that we have newcomers in our group," the preacher said and looked directly at Silas.

As if on cue, the crowed parted around them leaving only the men serving the drinks near them. It looked as though they have become the focus of the party. Several more thugs stepped closer to them.

"Drink new brother and sister, drink and understand," the preacher said.

"I am pretty sure that's what Jim Jones said too," Silas said.

The smile left the preacher's face. Several people, holdouts that hadn't drunk yet, paused with their glasses halfway to their lips. Of course many more had ignored him and were trying to snatch another glass off a passing tray.

"It is not death that waits you at the bottom of the glass, but a new life. One filled with purpose and strength," the preacher said and then sighed theatrically. "But you did not come here for that did you? No I think you came with your heathen heart and blasphemous ways to tear asunder what my master has built."

The last few words of the rant ended with spittle flying from his lips as his face tightened in fury.

"Now hold on there, Jim Jones," Silas began.

"Kill them," the preacher said.

Silas didn't know what was in the glasses, but from what he could smell with his demonic nose it was a volatile substance. Before the thug nearest him could react, Silas waved his hand over the tray of red liquid and flame erupted from the glasses. With his other hand he slapped the flaming tray into the stunned face of the thug.

The monster screamed as the burning liquid reacted like napalm, sticking to his face and shoulders. But Silas didn't have long to admire his handiwork, another thug was on him. This one threw a punch, but it was slower than the other creatures they had fought, and when it connected with Silas stomach it lacked the force of other monsters. A mortal would have been thrown back. Silas just smiled and dropped the transmogrification. There was no point in keeping up the charade.

Silas enjoyed the look on the man's face when he saw that he wasn't fighting some drunken old homeless man, but instead had just punched a drunken demon. Silas took his turn and punched him in the face, feeling the man-creature's jaw snap as his fist crushed bone. It staggered back, screaming from a ruined mouth.

A few feet away Abigail had just dispatched one of the thugs, leaving him on the ground bleeding from multiple slices and stabs. The rest of the man-creatures stayed back, wary of these deadly strangers. Silas heard a noise behind him and turned to see the preacher abandoning the stage and making a break for the open garage door. They needed that preacher. Abigail could take care of the low level thugs here.

Silas let lose his demonic fury, and felt it infuse his mortal limbs and bones. With three strides he leaped over one of the thugs, who watched his airborne acrobatics with a stunned expression, and landed in the midst of the homeless congregation, taking three of them down with him. Others scattered and screamed as they struggled to get away from Silas.

With a second leap he landed on top of the stage. Pallets shattered from the force and sent wood pieces flying in all direction, but the main structure held. He sprung again and caught the preacher just as he was entering the back of the truck. Together they hit the ground and slid into the container.

Silas had him pinned. He grabbed the man's collar and pulled him close so there would be no doubt that the preacher could see the demon in him.

"What is Webb up to? Why is he making these monsters?" Silas yelled at the preacher.

Subtle interrogation had never been his strong suit. The preacher looked confused again.

"My master, he has left me," the preacher said.

"Your Master? You mean Webb?"

"It will be an army the likes of which this world has never seen," the preacher whispered and his eyes became maniacal, darting left and right. "Monster soldiers to cleanse this world."

Silas shook him to try to make him focus. "How? How is he doing this?"

"Blood of the Wyrm, blood of the Wyrm is the stuff, the juice that gives a kick to his blessing. Precious stuff, must protect it. Jeremy did a bad thing, you never steal the blood."

Silas didn't know who Jeremy was and didn't really give a shit. He didn't have much time before the preacher's handlers reached them.

"When is he planning this war?" Silas asked.

"Soon. Soon. Because of you. Must act quickly. Must cleanse this world. We wanted to wait, build our strength, but not now. Now we must cleanse this world..."

"Yeah yeah, cleanse the world blah, blah, blah. When, dammit?"

"Sunset on the morrow. The sun goes down and the Children of the Wyrm will rise."

"Where is he doing this?"

"Down, down, down underground," the preacher hissed.

He heard someone enter the trailer behind him. He turned to see Abigail standing just inside the door, blood dripping from her daggers.

"Where underground?" Silas asked, shaking him again.

"Under, Undercity... deep down, down with the worms..."

They were losing him. The preachers eyes became distant, engrossed in his own mind. A hiss and growl came from the front of the shipping container. Now that he was in the dark of the trailer he could see clearly with his demonic sight. Against the front wall of the compartment stood a group of the lizard creatures. They were of the larger variety.

There was a grunt of surprise from behind and Abigail fell to the ground next to him with three of the thugs from the congregation on her. She sliced one open and threw another off instantly. Then the door to the container closed with a bang and the engine started. It almost seemed like this was some sort of trap.

Frankly, Silas was disappointed.

He grabbed the last thug struggling with Abigail and threw him at the cluster of lizard creatures. The truck lurched under his feet and his aim was off, but still the flying body knocked down a couple of the creatures. Unfortunately, there were still many standing and they charged forward.

In the near pitch-black of the container the only one at a disadvantage was Abigail...which meant he was outnumbered.

"Silas this is no good," Abigail said. She crouched, blades out, virtually blind.

"Here they come," Silas said as the first one struck.

It sliced at his face with a clawed hand. Silas dodged back then kicked it in the gut, sending it flying back into its friends, claws flailing about. Another stepped up to take its place and kicked his side. He caught the foot and with a well-placed twist, broke its leg. The creature screamed.

Their one advantage was that only a few could attack at once in the narrow confines of the shipping container, but there were at least a dozen creatures to step up as soon as they removed one. A battle of attrition won't work when you are this badly outnumbered, and to top it off Silas had to dodge the deadly blades of his blind partner. It was time to let some light in.

To buy some time Silas summoned flame to the palm of his hand and flared it while holding his arm up. The sudden, albeit small, burst of flame momentarily stunned the creatures and they fell back. Silas wouldn't be able to maintain the fire for long.

Silas grabbed the creature with the broken leg at his feet. With one hand he gripped the scaly collar bone, digging into the hard flesh as best he could and with the other he grabbed its groin, not bothering to douse the flame. The creature screamed even louder. Silas felt claws slicing the skin on his arm and chest, and blows like a sledge hammer rained down on his torso and the thing struggled. He heaved it towards the ceiling as hard as he could, then slammed his fist into another of the creatures that had come close as he brought his arms down.

The creature's lizard shaped head with bony protrusions and hard scaled skin made a good can opener. It burst through the metal ceiling of the shipping container, stopping wedged halfway through hole. Its taloned feet flailed about.

With the light extinguished the creatures were moving forward again. Being careful of the powerful legs sweeping the sharp talons back and forth, Silas jumped up and pulled the creature down upon its fellow monsters. The violent motion ripped the creature from the hole and made it larger. Lights from the city streets outside cast some illumination into the shipping container, but it wasn't going to be enough.

The creatures kept coming and while it appeared Abigail could now see better it was still very limited. Her stilettos zipped around like deadly stingers sometimes glancing off scales, but more often slicing skin. Silas struck out with fist and foot crushing bones, but it was like punching a knight in armor. More and more a claw, talon or shark like bites got through his defenses. They were still going to lose, they had to get out of this death trap.

"Abigail! Up!" Silas cried

He positioned himself under the hole in the roof and flared his palm fire again. Knowing it would be less effective this time as their eyes adjusted to the little light from above, he kicked the nearest one into its friends at the same time and then knelt. He hoped she could figure out what he was doing.

She did. He felt her boots dig into his side and shoulders as she used him as a step ladder. He would have to tell her to wear tennis shoes from now on.

She ran up his back and he leaped to his feet, propelling her through the hole. She caught the edge and pulled herself through. Great, now he just had to get through it. He jumped as the remaining creatures surged at him. His hand caught the edge of the opening, leaving his lower body exposed to claws and teeth.

I swear if one of those sons of a bitches goes for my junk... Silas thought as claws and teeth sunk into his legs and abdomen. With a curse he heaved himself through the jagged opening, lifting three of the creatures that had a hold of him. They fell away as he cleared the opening.

On top of the moving truck the street light zipped by and the sounds and smell of traffic were all around him.

"They have Michael," Abigail said.

Silas looked behind them, but the warehouse was nowhere in sight. The truck was speeding down the road. He and Abigail crouched low on the swaying of the vehicle.

"Now what?" Abigail asked.

Silas looked over the edge. They would have to jump, and the truck was moving at almost fifty miles an hour. There was a screeching, metal-twisting sound. Silas looked down and saw one of the creatures rip open the side of the shipping container with its clawed hand. He saw another hand punch through farther down the side of the truck.

"Here they come," Silas said.

Like ants hunting for a meal they began cutting through the shipping container and crawling up the side. They were trying to come through the hole in the roof, but Abigail's blades were keeping them at bay. Although the truck swayed, Silas remained upright with little effort. He had once possessed a ballet dancer with excellent balance, but he didn't like to talk about that.

He saw a clawed hand come over the edge. As soon as the head came over he gave it a swift kick, sending the beast flailing back onto the street below. Another popped up on the other side, and Silas stepped over and kicked that one as well. Even as he did, two more sets of claws and heads started crawling over the edge. While he liked whack-a-mole just as much as the next guy, this was not going to work.

Silas kicked another lizard face as it appeared over the edge. Just as his foot connected with its head, the truck lurched to the side, throwing him over the edge. He caught the edge of the container and his body slammed against the steel side, but he held on. His feet dangled above the fast moving asphalt. Silas had to lift his legs to avoid smashing into an SUV as the truck sideswiped it.

Abigail's face appeared over the side of the container.

"Need some help?" She asked and grabbed his arm.

She pulled with her supernatural strength, and he was soon up and over. But they had lost valuable time. Some of the creatures had been able to climb on top, and more were coming over the side and though the hole in the ceiling.

"Friend of yours?" Abigail asked.

She was looking behind him. Silas turned and saw the large lizard-man he had fought in the alley and had tried to fight in the bar. *Coth*, Silas thought Webb had called him. He stood at the end of the shipping container just behind the cab of the semi-truck; he must have climbed up from the passenger seat.

Eight or nine of the creatures climbed up behind them, Coth in front. Silas didn't like the odds.

"No retreat this time," the Coth rumbled with a smile. He put his claws out to his side, and the three inch talons at the end of this fingers gleamed in the flashing, chaotic lights of the city racing by.

"Hey Silas!" A voice cried from over the edge of the truck.

Silas glance over the edge and saw the limo driving alongside the truck. The large sunroof was open, and Michael was hanging out of it waving his arms. Steve was swerving the limo back and forth, trying to keep from being smashed by the truck's maneuvers.

"I like to think of it as a strategic advance to the rear," Silas said to Coth, then grabbed Abigail. "Jump!"

Abigail half jumped and was half tossed towards the weaving limo. Silas didn't wait to see if she landed in the sunroof before he jumped, leaving Coth roaring behind him in fury. Abigail landed in the sunroof head first, but Silas missed, catching the lip with one hand, just barely saving himself from skidding off the roof and onto the cement.

With a roar Coth jumped. Steve slammed on the breaks. The limo started skidding, but the sudden decrease in speed caused Coth to misjudge his jump, and he landed on the ground in front of the sliding vehicle. Silas flew over the sunroof as he lost his grip, sliding across the roof and windshield until he could catch himself on the lip of the hood just below the wipers.

He had just found his grip when the limo slammed into Coth. The force of the crash sent a stunned Coth flying into the parked cars along the side of the road. Silas almost lost his grip, but managed to hold on as the limo decelerated to a stop.

Coth burst from the wrecked cars with the sound of twisted metal and shattering glass. Steve put the car into reverse. The tires screeched and they were backing away from the enraged lizard-man. Coth began running and Steve sped up. Amazingly Coth kept up; the powerful beast was fast.

Dedicated son of a bitch, ain't he? Thought Silas. Now the question was how fast this limo could go in reverse.

The limo began swerving in traffic, going backwards the wrong way down a one way street. Blaring horns and squealing tires surrounded them. Silas swayed back and forth on the hood, but held on. Soon they were leaving Coth behind.

With some distance between them Steve stopped the limo and turned down a side street finally moving in the right direction. Silas looked down at his feet. The front of the limo was crushed from where it had hit Coth, but it was running fine. He climbed back on the roof and slid into the sunroof.

"Wow, Mr. Silas! That was amazing. What the hell was that thing?" Steve called from the front.

Silas ignored him and looked at Michael. "We saw you drink that liquid. How are you feeling?"

"Nah, I didn't drink it. Just poured it out real quick when they weren't looking. I played along because it looked like they weren't going to take no for an answer."

Silas nodded and Abigail pulled Michael into a hug.

"I thought they had you," she said.

"Nope, I took off during the commotion. They were way more concerned about you two than a kid like me. I saw you guys go into the truck, so I got out the back and found Steve."

"Luckily I was passing by at the moment and saw Michael come running out," Steve said.

"I heard the truck and figured out what was happening. So I had Steve chase the truck."

Silas pulled the extra bottle of whiskey out from under the seat. Damn, he needed a drink.

"What now?" Michael asked.

"We are getting a good picture of what's going on here. Webb is building an army, luring the homeless and mentally ill into the Undercity, then using this Blood of the Wyrm stuff as a catalyst, he is transforming them into these monsters. Apparently we have until sunset tomorrow night to find where he is building this army and stop him."

"What will happen if we don't?" Michael asked.

"Well the world will watch as New York is overrun by lizard monsters and wake up to the fact that all their superstitions and fairy tales might have some truth to them. Then down will come the Veil of the Pale and the supernatural will have free rein in the mortal world. Your basic end of the world scenario. Drink?"

Silas offered Michael the bottle, but then pulled it back at the glare from St. Abigail.

"The only thing I am really puzzled by is this Blood of the Wyrm. To transform that many people and hold it, make it almost permanent, takes a huge amount of power."

"He has to be working with someone or something that has that power. I'm with you--no mortal man could do this," Abigail said.

"There have been a few mortal sorcerers with this type of power, but even they would need a catalyst. Merlin for one. Alistair Crowley, maybe. The secret rests with the potion, this Blood of the Wyrm."

"Again I have to ask, what now?" Michael asked.

"We follow the only lead we have left. We find this grad student Lily. The Undercity is a huge place, almost as big as the upper city. Without a guide we wouldn't have a chance of finding where he is even if he is sitting on an army. This chick can tell us where the writing Father Delentante spoke of is. That will give us a starting point. But *you* go back to the mission. No arguments. We can't tell Father Deluca where were going. If we don't return by tomorrow night, you will have to tell him to get word to the Vatican and Moreales."

"So where do we look for her? We have her home and office on campus," Abigail asked.

"She's in college and it's a Friday night. She won't be in either of those places; she'll be out partying. At least that's what I would be doing," Silas said, smiled and took a big swig from his bottle.

11

S ilas was disappointed. In the end they found her at her office. He was hoping to find her at a huge party. The woman that opened the office door at their knock was not the bookworm Silas had expected.

She was short, especially standing next to St. Abigail, and she had long brown hair that hung straight, parting only slightly around her face and small glasses. She was, Silas decided, cute. Faint dark rings were starting to appear under her eyes, speaking of long nights and little sleep.

"Yes?" Lily asked, holding the door only partway open. Beyond her shoulder Silas could see a desk covered with books and papers. A chair in the corner was also covered by documents and books.

"Hello, my name is Abigail Lee and this is my partner Silas Robb," St. Abigail said. "We were wondering if we could ask you a few questions about somebody you worked with--Doug Perkins."

"Partner? Are you guys cops? Thank god, you guys are finally doing something about that missing person report I filed; it's been days. Come in, come in," she said and stepped away from the door. "Don't mind the mess; I was just doing a little research."

Now that they were inside the office Silas could see that it wasn't just her desk and chair that were covered by books and documents. Every square inch of table top and furniture was covered. Whatever she was researching, it seemed to be consuming her office little by little.

"Actually we aren't cops," Abigail said.

Silas frowned. Leave it to Abigail to ruin a perfectly good cover. It's not as if they lied to her; she'd come to the conclusion herself.

"Oh?" Lily said and paused in her cleaning off the documents from the couch. "Then who are you?"

"We are agents with the Vatican. Doug was with a priest when he... disappeared. We have been instructed to look into the incident."

"Agents with the Vatican? I didn't even know they had those. So you're a priest and a nun?" She asked.

Silas chuckled. Abigail gave him a sharp look.

"No we are not ordained, just trained to work on certain matters for the Catholic Church," Abigail said.

She nodded as though this was a good enough explanation, then sat behind her desk. "Should have guessed; you guys don't look like you work for the cops. Then again you don't really look like you should be working for a bunch of priests either. What do you want to know?"

"Well for starters can you recap everything you told the police?"

Abigail started the interrogation. This seemed more her speed anyway; if they had to rough her up he could step in. He was more interested in the books and documents scattered about. Most of them seemed related to Native American culture.

"Well," Lily began. "We had been doing a lot of urban exploring under New York; we belong to a club where we sneak into all the sewers and tunnels under this city."

"Sounds like loads of fun, walking through sewers and muddy utility access tunnels," Silas said and received an elbow jab from Abigail.

"You would be surprised at the amazing things you find down

there; it's not just sewers and muddy tunnels. We've found abandoned subway stations, natural caverns and countless underground streams. And we haven't even explored the half of it yet."

"Not even close," Silas said quietly.

"What?" Lily asked with frown.

"You were saying?" Abigail asked.

After giving Silas a puzzled look, she turned back to Abigail.

"We'd been doing a lot of exploring, and at one point we were deeper than we had ever been. In what we took as a natural cavern Doug saw some carvings on the wall. We thought they might have been pre-colonial Native American carvings. This was, of course, an amazing discovery. Nothing like this had ever been found in the area. Doug was really excited. He said he had a friend, a priest, who was a scholar in this area and wanted to share it with him. His name was Father Delentante.

"The first day the father was free I had to teach class, so Doug went with Father Delentante. Funny, I was so pissed he wouldn't wait for me."

"I guess you were lucky," Silas said.

"Yeah luck. When Doug didn't come back that evening, I called the church and asked to speak with Father Delentante. I was told he was away on sabbatical in Rome. He had just left. I assume you talked to him? Care to let me know what happened?"

"We did speak with him, but before we go into that, did you ever try going back to that spot. Back to where you saw the carving?"

"No, I've been so busy I haven't had a chance to go back down there."

"So it was a great discovery and perhaps the last known whereabouts of your friend, but you never went back?" Silas interjected. She was lying about something.

"Yes. I mean, I called the police and told them everything I knew, although it didn't even seem like they cared. They told me he was a grown man and could take off anytime he chooses. I knew the priest had made it back, so I didn't think Doug would still be there."

"Interesting books you have here," Silas said picking up the nearest copy.

"Yes, most of them are on the Lenape culture. As I said the carvings were Native American, so I've been reading up on them." She stood as though to show them the door, "Now if you will excuse me I have..."

"But we haven't even told you about the priest. You said you tried to get a hold of him. Don't you want to know what happened?" Silas asked.

"Of course, yes what did Delentante say?" Lily asked. She was flustered, and Silas was sure what she wanted most was for them to leave.

"He's dead," Silas said. "Murdered."

The blood drained from her face.

"Doug is dead too, murdered in the same cavern the carvings were found."

She fell back into the chair eyes wide in shock. "No," She said in a whisper.

"Yes. These books are on Native American culture alright, but they are not really all scholarly works, are they? I think many of these you could find in your local new age shop. They're all about Native American shamanism and occult."

She sat there, stunned. "I didn't want to think he was dead, and since the priest was alive I thought there was a chance."

Silas grabbed one of the chairs, pun it around and sat on it, folding his arms across the back.

"I think Lily--can I call you Lily?--I think, Lily, that you did go back down there, and I think you saw something that made you think there might be some truth to these silly little new age stories," Silas said. "Abigail, I think the Pale might be lifting from this one too."

Abigail put her hand on Silas' arm then said to Lily, "I know this is hard Lily, but we need you to tell us the truth. You have to trust that no matter what you say, we will believe you."

"Yeah, and we are probably the only ones," Silas said.

Abigail squeezed his arm hard. "Gently, Silas."

"The next day, when he had not come back I went down there. I thought maybe he was hurt, it is not always safe down there; he might have broken a leg or something," Her voice was shaking and she looked up at them. "I saw the blood--blood everywhere. There was so much of it. I didn't know what to do. I didn't see Doug anywhere, just blood. So I panicked and ran. Blindly at first, and I ran down some tunnels I had never seen. That's when I saw them."

"Them?" Abigail asked, but Silas was pretty sure he knew who 'them' was.

Lily nodded. "I noticed moving light ahead so I slowed down and I don't know why, but I turned off my flashlight. Maybe it was all the blood, but it just didn't feel right so I turned it off just in case. When I turned the corner a saw a large, open cavern filled with... with..."

"Overgrown iguanas?" Silas offered.

"You've seen them too?"

"Yes we have, and we can tell you more, but please continue with what you saw," Abigail said.

"Well there were hundreds of these things just sort of wandering around the cavern. It might have been feeding time because it looked like many were eating raw meat, and I saw dogs and other animals being brought in cages," Lily said with shudder. "There was only a little light, mostly from torches and flashlights that the few humans amongst them carried. I'm not even sure they were humans since some of them looked as if they were in the beginning stages of trans-forming into one of the creatures."

"They didn't see you?" Abigail asked.

"No. When I saw those demons, I took off. I'd been running blindly, but I found my way back to somewhere familiar then I got the hell out of there. I haven't been back since. I couldn't tell the police the truth about the monsters, they would have thought I was crazy and never even try to find Doug, so I told them that I had seen some large wild animals down there. Unfortunately, I think that accomplished the same thing. When I mentioned it, they sort of shut off and stopped taking notes. That's also why I didn't tell you. I just assumed you would think I was crazy."

"So you've been trying to research this on your own ever since?" Silas asked.

"There has to be a connection. Lenape artwork, monsters underground that could easily be interpreted as evil underworld spirits. It seemed like Shamanism might be involved. The Lenape and Native American cultures have a strong connection with the underworld, and there are some ancient Lenape stories that speak of a great monster trapped under the earth."

"Not to burst your bubble, but we have reason to believe that these creatures are a recent addition to the sewers of New York," Silas said.

"But there is that Native American who showed up at the bar, and Delentante spoke of one being there when he was attacked. There might be some other connection," Abigail said.

"Native American?" Lily asked confused.

Silas sighed, "Go ahead and tell her. She knows a lot already."

Abigail began telling her what had happened with Delentante, setting the interrogation in the real world rather than the otherworld. No point in confusing her any more than she already was.

"And then Delentante was killed by one of these lizard things?" Lily asked.

"Yes, shortly after we left the room," Silas lied.

"Is there any way you could draw up a map to the location you saw the carvings or this cave full of the creatures?" Abigail asked.

"You guys are going down there?" Lily asked.

"Yes, we have to. It's only a matter of time before these things get out of the Undercity and start terrorizing people. There have already been some encounters up here. Those humans you saw are the leaders organizing them. That is one of the reasons we were asked to investigate."

"But you don't understand, these things were monsters--claws, sharp teeth--the whole nine yards! They already killed Doug. If the

Vatican has evidence we need to call the police, hell the National Guard. There was an army of those things down there."

"We know. We can't call the government because we don't have any real evidence other than the three of us as witnesses," Abigail said.

"So the two of you are going down there and try to stop them yourselves?"

"Yep. That's the way we roll," Silas said. "So if you could just whip up a quick map or directions, we can be on our way."

Lily leaned back in her chair, the shock and sadness gone from her face. She glanced around at all the books and papers sprawled around her office and seemed to come to a decision.

"No. I want you to take me with you," she said.

"What? Hell no! This is going to be extremely dangerous! You saw those things. The last thing we need is to be babysitting a civilian," Silas said.

"You said it yourself--Silas, was it? You said it was the discovery of a lifetime. My specialty is not Native American culture, but a chance like this, to find a real link between stories of the underworld and reality? This is the type of things academics live for. I can't pass up this chance."

"Fine, but only as far as the carvings. Then you go topside when we continue," Abigail said.

"Now wait a minute..." Silas began.

"Deal," Lily said. "When are you planning this journey?"

"This is crazy Abigail..." Silas tried again.

"Immediately. We have to stop them before sunset tomorrow," Abigail said, and when Lily raised a questioning eyebrow, she reluctantly continued. "We have reason to believe that they are planning on coming to the surface to attack the city tomorrow night."

"I think there's a lot more you're not telling me," Lily said.

"We will tell you more in the limo, but we need to get moving,"

"A limo?"

"We ride in style, one of the perks of saving the world," Silas said, giving in.

"Give me a moment and I'll meet you outside."

They left her leafing through a few folders on her desk. As they exited the building, Silas couldn't help but feel that bringing her along was a bad idea.

SILAS DROPPED through the manhole first. The small tunnel was lined with pipes and electrical conduit. The air smelled musty and cool. A breeze was moving through the tunnel carrying the faint scent of sewage. He was again surprised by how much the sights, sounds, and smells of New York could remind him of home.

"All clear," he called up to Abigail. Although they hadn't expected any trouble this close to the surface, there might have been a city worker checking the tunnels. They did not want to have to explain what they were doing skulking around in darkness.

He heard Abigail drop down silently behind him. There was a click and light filled the tunnel from her head lamp. The head lamps had been Lily's idea. She had come out of the building carrying a large duffel bag full of what she called "urban exploring gear". In the limo she had pulled out the pieces of equipment one by one and explained how they worked. They tried to divvy it up three ways, but Silas refused to wear or carry the gear, especially not those ridiculous head lamps.

"I can see just fine in the dark," he had said.

"It will be pitch-black down there; no human can see in that kind of inky darkness," Lily had said.

"I agree," Silas had said and looked away. Now would probably not be a good time to tell her that he was a demon. She would learn soon enough. She had shrugged, and the ladies had separated the gear two ways.

Now under the streets, the bobbing light threw off his dark vision. Great.

Lily dropped down less gracefully than Abigail.

The only gear he had agreed to wear was the small ear piece and tracking pin that Mort had given each of them. It allowed communication with Mort, as well as each other, if they should become separated. They were sophisticated, and Mort assured him they would work through the tunnels despite the large amounts of concrete and dirt between them and the surface.

"Mort, you hear me?" Silas asked.

"Yep. Loud and clear. I have disabled the few security cameras in your tunnel and will turn them off as you guys move, but I won't be able to alter any unknown or magical security. The tracking devices are working great too."

Silas frowned at that. He hated having to wear the tracking device; it made him feel like Big Brother was watching. At first he had refused, but Abigail convinced him it was more for them than him. So they could locate him if they became separated.

Silas stepped aside and let Lily take the lead. "We have to go deep. We follow this tunnel to where it meets with a larger access tunnel; then from there we enter the subways."

Silas looked around as they walked, but he didn't recognize the area. He had been to the Undercity many times in his stay here in New York. Of all the areas of the city, it was perhaps the closest to the Pale. Many supernatural entities and groups called this realm home. The humans-- "mole people" as they are referred to by other humans--that live down here walk a fine line between the normal world and the world where things go bump in the night. Many of them interacted with the supernatural daily.

It also hosted the Bazaar, an area deep in the underground that served as a sort of black market for the supernatural. Alchemy, magic, occult services, really good chow mein--all could be found in the grand Bazaar. But that visit would be for another adventure; for now he had to keep Lily away from the more radical areas of the Undercity.

Occasionally they came across a small group of homeless people living along one wall in a particularly large tunnel. In these upper areas many of the homeless did not know of the other world around them. They were the most recent additions who believed that poverty and hunger were as bad as it got and for many that was the truth.

They passed through several more tunnels, leaving the homeless behind, then down stairs, that led them deeper into the Undercity. The tunnel opened into a large, abandoned subway station.

"Do you hear that?" Abigail asked.

Silas did, and he also thought he knew what it was.

"Like a rattling sound." Lily said.

There was indeed a rattle sound coming from a side passage, but Silas didn't think it was a threat. And he was right. A light appeared at the end of the tunnel and was soon followed by a woman pushing a shopping cart. She turned as she left the tunnel oblivious to them standing there.

"An alchemy merchant, I suspect, heading to the Bazaar,"

"Bazaar?" Lily asked.

"Merchant," Silas called to the woman. "Do you have any Molcaen dust?"

She stopped and looked back, squinting in puzzlement.

"And who be you?"

"A customer, if you have what I'm looking for."

"And what do you be wanting with Molcaen dust? Trying to poison a werewolf, or perhaps turn yourself into a woman?"

"What?" Silas said. He knew about use of it to poison a werewolf, but not about the sex change thing. "No, no. Neither of those, I just have my uses."

"And I wouldn't be an ethical apothecary if I didn't ask the intent of my more potent ingredients," she said.

He almost laughed. "I have cash," he said instead.

"And then I have what you need. Come closer. I have it here in my basket. How much you be needing?"

"All that you have."

That made her pause.

"And that will be expensive; I have at least six ounces," she said eying him again cautiously as he approached.

Silas pulled a money roll from his pocket. "Last time I checked Molcaen dust was going for two hundred an ounce. Is that still the rate?"

Her mouth widened into a great smile. "And yes it is. Still be quite rare; if it had more uses it would be a lot more expensive."

Silas peeled off a few bills and handed her the money. She pulled a small pouch out from her bags.

"And I throw in the leather bag for free, because that is the kind of merchant Helatia is." She looked up into his face and frowned.

"And are you the one they are calling Silas?"

Silas was caught off guard, "Yes."

"And Phil be looking for you. I'd stay away from the Bazaar if I were you," She said.

"Ah he must still be mad after that incident years ago. Can't believe he's still upset about that."

"And they be saying you killed his five children."

"Well yes. But they were all assholes," Silas said.

"And that is true. I best be going now. Like I said, stay away from the Bazaar. And if you come, watch your back."

She pushed her cart and wandered off down a side tunnel.

"Who the hell are you guys?" Lily asked. "Did you really kill some guy's kids?"

"Yes, but they were adults at the time," Silas said. "And they were trying to kill me."

They had told her as much as they could on the ride over, but in the grand scheme of things that wasn't much. She knew that there was something dangerous and not really of this world lurking beneath the city streets. Some of their vague answers had pissed her off. She didn't believe most of it, which they had expected, but since she had seen evidence of the monsters with her own eyes she was convinced at least some of what they said was true. If she decided to bolt now they would be in trouble without a map.

"What did you need that dust for?" Abigail asked.

"I'm hoping we don't need it, actually."

"I am serious. I want to find out what's going on, but this is crazy! Who the hell are you?" Lily asked, angrily this time.

"We told you we are agents for the Vatican investigating unexplained phenomena and the murder of one of our priests..." said Abigail.

"Yeah, yeah. You said that all before, but this is bullshit. I want to know WHO you are right now, or I don't go another step and you can find the carvings all by yourselves."

"I'm a demon summoned from hell. This is St. Abigail. She's a Saint returned from the outskirts of heaven. We work for the Holy Roman Inquisition and are humanity's greatest, and perhaps only, hope for survival as we approach the coming apocalypse. Our primary job is protecting humans from evil, supernatural entities that grow stronger by the day. Oh yeah, and I'm also a singer in a rock and roll band that plays in a bar off Thirty-eighth," Silas said.

Lily said nothing, her mouth wide open.

Silas smelled something rancid just before hearing the faint scurrying sound. "Quick, get into the tunnel."

"Why?" Abigail asked. Lily was still looking stunned.

"Goblins. A lot of them."

"Goblins? This close to the surface?"

"Yep. I would know that smell anywhere," Silas said and grabbed Lily's arm, pulling her toward the tunnel.

"Goblins?" Lily squeaked.

"Yeah. Disgusting little creatures, but vicious as hell. If they see us it would be like walking into a family of honey badgers," Silas said.

Abigail jumped down into the train tunnel and Silas followed, dragging Lily with him. He switched off Lily's head lamp just as the goblins rounded the corner. It was a small tribe, maybe ten or twelve carrying torches. They stood about four or five feet tall with skin pulled tight against their heads and bony joints. Each carried a large knife or sharpened piece of rusty metal at its side. With their long arms and short, stocky torsos they looked like green, emaciated monkeys.

Lily was about to scream, so Silas pulled her close and covered her mouth with this hand. She screamed into it and began to struggle. He clamped down tighter and held her still with his arm wrapped around her body.

"Quiet, or you're dead," he whispered into her ear. He could probably take on the whole tribe and survive, although it would not be pleasant, but they were quick and he wasn't so sure he and Abigail could keep Lily from being torn to shreds in the process.

Lily grew quiet in his arms.

The last goblin in the group paused and looked around as the rest headed off down a side tunnel. He peered down the dark train tunnel. Goblins' vision in the dark was almost as good as Silas', but he hoped they were well concealed behind the concrete wall.

The creature sniffed the air a few times and took a handful of steps in their direction. Silas prepared himself to make it quick; he didn't want to risk the rest of the tribe hearing their friend and come running back. But the creature just sniffed a few more times before running to catch up with its friends. It was probably confused by the smells at this level. Goblins usually roam much deeper where there are fewer human civilians roaming about.

Abigail waited a few minutes to make sure the goblin was gone before speaking. "Goblins this close to the surface--that can't be good."

"My guess is the lizard creatures our friend is making might be driving some of the deeper denizens of the Undercity out of their usual lairs. Yet another reason we have to stop him fast," Silas said.

Abigail nodded towards Lily. Silas realized he was still holding her with his hand over her mouth. She was glaring up at him.

"Oh, sorry," Silas said, and let her go.

She stepped back a few feet from them. "I don't know what exactly is going on here, but I want out. Now."

"I know this is a lot to take in, but we have told you the truth. If we don't find Webb and his army there won't be a New York to go back too," Abigail said. "You've seen enough to know this is true."

Lily looked down, but Silas saw she was not buying it. Time to work in his forte--temptation and greed.

"Look at it this way, Lily. You're an academic right? Aren't you the least bit intrigued by the little glimpse of this new world that we've shown you? I mean, think about it. You've seen goblins and lizard creatures and are talking with a real saint and a handsome devil. Even if you don't fully believe we are who we say we are, you know we aren't your average, run-of-the-mill agents," Silas said.

Silas could tell that gave her pause, so he plowed on.

"You're an anthropologist? Think about the potential for the mythological cultures that you can now be introduced to. Think of the books you could write!"

"And you'd do this? If I help you, you would help me understand this new world? This Veil and this Pale you talked about in the limo ride over, I know you didn't tell me everything, but it is real? There's a whole world of the supernatural around us?"

For a grad student at a prestigious university, she was kind of slow on the uptake. "Yes, there's no going back now. The Veil has been lifted from you. Help us, and we can give you some pointers; leave and you're on your own in this new world."

She chewed her bottom lip as she thought about it. Abigail pulled him aside and they stepped a little way from Lily.

"You know Moreales would never let a credible book be release about this."

"Of course, and even if he did, no one would give it any credibility. They'd laugh her right out of any university she worked at. The important thing is that she doesn't know that, or at least the greed for this knowledge won't let her think it through. Besides, it's not as if she'll get nothing from it. She gets to learn about fairy tales and fantasy and all that bullshit. You tell someone like her that all that stuff is real, and her curiosity will never let her put it down again."

"Okay, I'll do it. The deal is back on," Lily said.

"Great! Let's get going," Silas said, avoiding Abigail's disapproving look.

Lily led them off down the subway tunnel. They cut through three more side tunnels, each looking more unused than the last. Finally, it opened into a larger space and they could hear voices ahead, many voices as though in conversation.

"Must be one of the side markets," Silas said to them. "The Bazaar area is like the central hub of the Undercity; it's where all the inhabitants and many foreigners from topside go to find whatever they need. It makes the markets in the Middle East look tame and ordinary. Almost anything can be found in the Bazaar. But like any place with money flowing through it, the area has those who are in control, and setting up shop there comes with price. Those who can't afford to pay set up shop here, on the outskirts."

"When you say control, you don't mean in a strictly legal sense, do you?" Lily asked.

"There is no formal law here. More like an agreed upon list of rules that can change from time to time..You just hope you're the rule changer and not the one caught with their pants down. It's more like a collection of mob bosses running the show rather that any sort of official government."

"Like this Phil guy that wants you bad," Abigail said.

"Yep. Like Phil. And they're pretty much all assholes."

"I'm surprised you don't spend more time down here. Sounds like your kind of place," Abigail said.

"Yeah sometimes I do sort of miss it. But really there's so much more going on up top. Not much call for a rock and roll band down here."

As they got closer, the talking became louder and he could smell liquor. "Looks like it might be a bar, new place. I don't remember it being here before."

Light from hanging lanterns appeared ahead. Lily and Abigail switched off their head lamps. Soon they saw a doorway in the wall with lamps to either side of it. Above the door was a sign that read "First and Last Chance Saloon".

"I guess it depends on which direction you're traveling," Silas said.

Near the door a small group of people stood, talking loudly. It looked as if they might have just been kicked out. From inside Silas could hear loud conversation and even some music from an old juke box. On the other side of the door a man leaned up against the wall. Silas reached out a hand to stop them.

"A Bone Gnawer," he said quietly. He heard Mort whistle softly in his ear piece.

The man leaning against the wall was no man at all, but a Bone Gnawer. It stood a little over six feet tall, but appeared stocky and squat because of the layers of muscle under its worn leather clothes. Its face was the wrinkled black mask of a long-dead corpse surrounding small beady eyes. Large teeth, sharpened to points, lined its small mouth. It wore its species' traditional black leather clothes, which functioned as armor, and a belt that held as assortment of weapons, including sharpened blades and a large pistol.

"Whatever you do, stay away from it Silas," Mort said through the ear piece.

"They're mercenaries, usually working for those who control the Bazaar, but always open to the highest bidder. When they're around it can only mean trouble," Silas said.

"Funny, that's what Mort said about you," Abigail said.

"True, but they also like to eat people, and I never really developed a taste for human flesh. My point is, they're usually working for someone, and until we know who it is, let's avoid them. They rarely work alone, so there's probably more nearby. Just walk on by the bar."

They walked on the far side of the tunnel. It pissed Silas off that he had to slink on by; if it hadn't been for Lily, he would have busted that Bone Gnawer's face just for the hell of it. Of course, if there were a few of his friends nearby it might have been more challenging.

"You there."

The sound of the Bone Gnawer's voice sounded old and unused. They spoke little, somehow communicating silently. In fact, they did everything silently, which made them the most dangerous hunters and assassins in the Undercity. Silas turned to him.

"Who are you?"

"Who do you want me to be? Tell you what. I'm somebody who doesn't answer to a wrinkly shit like you," Silas said. Well, everybody said he couldn't control his tongue. He felt his demonic fury rising.

The Bone Gnawer laughed, at least Silas thought he did, though it sounded more like a growl. "I think you be the one they call Silas. I can smell Hell on you."

Silas turned and gestured for the women to walk in front of him then turned to ignore the Gnawer.

"Phil is looking for you," the Gnawer said.

Silas turned, ready to fight if the Gnawer attacked. If its friends were not around, it would be quick. But the Bone Gnawer did not move from the wall. It raised its hands in a placating gesture.

"I no work for Phil," the Gnawer said. "I just wanted to warn."

Silas doubted that. Bone Gnawers never helped without something in it for them. Silas turned his back on him and they continued.

"I don't understand. I've used this path a few times and never seen a bar or a... what did you call that thing?" Lily asked.

"A Bone Gnawer," Silas said.

"Right, I mean with this whole world that exists down here--I should have seen something right?"

"The mind protects itself. You did see something I am sure. You would probably have seen a group of drunken homeless men sitting by the side of the tunnel or whatever your mind would dream up to protect you from what lies behind the Pale. Come here enough times though, and your mind might have started to see the truth. Or perhaps one of the denizens would have attacked you. It is far more dangerous down here than any normal human really knows," Abigail said.

"What about this Bazaar? Surely that can't be so easily hidden from normal humans."

"That is different. It hides itself from civilians. If you came close to discovering it you would find yourself veering off subconsciously, trying other routes. If, somehow, you could have overcome that subconscious impulse, you would have found your way blocked. It is hard to find the otherworld if you do not already have the Veil lifted," Abigail said.

"Now, of course, you're fucked. You'll see everything and everything will see you. You're on the other side now, and fair game," Silas said. "My advice is never come down here again, assuming you survive this trip."

"As tactful as ever, Silas," Abigail said.

"Here," Lily said and pointed at a crack in the tunnel. "We go down that."

"Tight fit," Silas said.

They stooped and squeezed through the crack. It only went about twenty feet before spitting them out into an even less used sewer tunnel. Water ran along the bottom of the passage, about two feet deep. Lily dropped her pack and pulled out knee-high rubber boots. Abigail also had a pair on loan, Silas assumed, from Lily. Silas looked at the water and grimaced. He did not usually travel via used sewer lines when in the Undercity.

"The water is mostly run off from above. You won't find much sewer sludge in this part of the sewers; they aren't really used anymore. What you're seeing is the remnants of an underground stream; further down it meets with some others to form a river," Lily said.

"A river under New York?" Abigail asked.

"Yeah, there are actually a few. When the city was being built not much care was given to creeks and streams. They were simply rerouted away from whatever they were building. This caused a lot of artificial rivers to form. Some are fast-moving, complete with rapids-- and in at least one case, a significant water fall. Oh great," Lily said.

Silas followed her gaze. A small archway off the sewer was blocked by a pile of rubble.

"This wasn't there the last time I came through," Lily said.

"Could it have collapsed recently?" Abigail asked.

"Possibly, but unlikely. Believe it or not, everything is pretty stable down here. Besides, look at the ceiling; it still looks intact. No. I think someone purposefully blocked this off."

"Webb and his followers. After you and Doug stumbled upon their little hiding place they probably wanted to close up some of their back doors," Silas said. "The question is, which way now?"

"I can't help you much right now. You're off the map that I have of the sewer system. I can see if I can find an alternate way, but not knowing the destination makes it a pain in the ass," Mort said.

"I know another way around, but it involves a large stream and that waterfall I mentioned," Lily said.

"Do we have much choice?" Silas asked.

"No I suppose not. I'm just glad I brought all that gear."

She led them off down the sewer. They made a few more twists and turns and the water became deeper. Silas could no longer avoid getting in the water, the current tugged at his legs.

"That's a strong current," Silas said.

"Like I said, it builds up. We're close to the waterfall."

Silas could hear the roar of water further up the tunnel. It did indeed sound like a waterfall. Another five minutes of walking brought them to it. They stood at the mouth of a tunnel and the water spilled past into a part man-made, part-natural cavern. The water fell twenty five feet to a large pool below. A river continued beyond the cavern. On one side there was a shore of dry land with several other passages leading off.

Lily began pulling out rope and other climbing equipment.

"Can't we just jump?" Silas asked.

"You can, but I don't know how deep that pool is. Besides, it's pretty gross water. We can repel down and get to that spit of dry land against the corner there."

Silas nodded and then jumped. He landed in the water, but it only came up to waist height. Good thing Lily had not jumped; she might have broken a leg. He looked up and saw her fastening two ropes to large pieces of concrete rubble.

"I'm doing at least two ropes at a time in case we're in a hurry coming back and can't wait to take turns," Lily said.

Silas nodded. That made sense; they didn't know how quickly they would be returning or what might be chasing them. When she had the ropes secured, she and Abigail started repelling down.

As they left the top of the waterfall, Silas saw movement in the darkness and two Bone Gnawers appeared at the top.

"Look out," Silas cried.

But it was too late. Knives flashed out and sliced neatly through both ropes. Lily and Abigail fell to the pool below. To Silas' right more Bone Gnawers spilled into the cavern from the side tunnel. It was a trap and Silas was pissed at himself for not seeing it coming. He turned to the group of Bone Gnawers on the dry land.

The water erupted around him and something strong gripped his calf from below. He didn't even have time to cry out before he was pulled under. Tendrils like iron bands wrapped around him under the murky water. Silas reached out to grab at whatever had a hold of him--he doubted it was another Bone Gnawer--but his hands came away with nothing. The bands around his body grew stronger.

A Water Elemental, it had to be. It was almost impossible to defeat a Water Elemental in its own environment. He began to pull at the only thing he could find, the solid tendrils of water around him. Even as he pulled, the tendril would disappear and another would take its place. It was like trying to catch the wind. An Elemental would not be here naturally; a sorcerer had to be involved, and Silas was pretty sure he knew who it was. It was a trap all the way around, and they had fallen into it nicely.

His feet found the ground and he heaved himself above the water, pulling the tendril with him. The only chance he had was to get to shore, and to do that he needed to get as much of his body out of the water as possible. Of course, the shore was crawling with Bone Gnawers, but he would have to deal with that when he got there.

He shoved again with his feet and pushed himself a little more out of the water, then fell back in, but a little closer to the shore this time. He could see that both Lily and Abigail were also caught up in the Elemental. The Bone Gnawers above were watching with smiles on their small, teeth-filled mouths.

The tendrils lifted him out of the water and slammed him down against the shore, but they did not let go. He felt one of his ribs crack and his breath left him in one large whoosh, but he clawed into the earth trying to hold onto the shore. The tendrils pulled at him, dragging him back to the churning water and certain death for his mortal form. His fingers carved gouges in the stone shore of the river as he tried to slow himself.

Then a Bone Gnawer slipped a black iron band around his wrist. Instantly his demonic fury left him, like a door had been slammed shut on it. Silas cried out in surprise as he felt his strength dissipate. A second iron band was quickly slipped on his other wrist. And with the click of the band closing, everything that made him better than a mortal, everything that made him a demon, was gone. He was left a simple mortal husk.

He gasped in shock and despair. The Water Elemental was no longer trying to drag him back to the water. But it didn't matter, it was over. He tried to reach inside himself, to find his demonic spark. Nothing. Just an emptiness that seemed to go on forever.

The watery tendrils receded, their job done, but Silas lay there unsure of what to do next. Lily and Abigail were deposited on the ground near him. They were unconscious and he hoped they weren't dead. Without his demonic senses he couldn't tell.

Bone Gnawers stepped aside as a handful of the lizard creatures stalked into the room, followed by Mr. Webb.

"Well, well Mr. Robb, it seems we finally get a chance to meet in a less hectic setting," he said.

Silas rolled onto his knees and tried to sit up. His ribs screamed in pain and what he could have ignored moments ago, now almost brought tears to his eyes. He felt weak and feeble and, for the first time, what he thought might be fear. He looked down at the black bands around his wrists and realized what they must be.

"Demon manacles," Webb said, and with a gesture the black bands pulled themselves together, effectively becoming handcuffs.

Silas knew of them and had even seen a pair a few times, but they were rare. Their creation was a closely guarded secret and involved the risk of almost certain death for the creator. On mortals they would be nothing more than ugly bracelets, but when placed on a demon they effectively rendered him mortal. It cut the demons off from their fury, the part of them that made them demons. Short of permanent confinement to the Void, there was nothing worse you could do to a demon.

And Silas knew of only one person who might have had access to demon manacles.

"I have to admit, I would never have known what exactly you were without a little help," Webb said, a greasy smile under his aviator sunglasses.

From the passage the huge bulk of Mephisto appeared. "Hello Silas. Fancy meeting you here."

Silas glared at him.

"That was a merry chase you led my hounds on." He walked over until he was only a few feet from Silas. "After you left without paying my price, I got to thinking. That Saint would make a great trophy to present to my demonic superiors. Might even be enough to gain back some of my dominion stripped from me decades ago."

Silas tried to stager to his feet and lunge at Mephisto. Out of the darkness stepped the giant, Coth, a massive, clawed hand swung and smashed into Silas' face. He flew through the air and landed on the ground inches from the water. Pain throbbed through his head. His jaw wasn't broken, but it had come close. His vision swam and the room spun.

"Not quite the same is it? Being mortal that is," Mephisto said.

"You know what those bracelets are don't you? They are quite rare; in fact, I know of only three pairs in existence. They don't really make you mortal--you will always be hell spawn--but they make you as weak as one. All that demonic fury that powers our existence... poof! Gone.

"You are a fool, Mephisto, for joining him."

"The deal was simple," Webb interrupted. "Mephisto approached me, and since I knew him from a long time ago, we let bygones be bygones. I allowed him to find me."

Mephisto harrumphed, but Webb went on.

"He told me what you were and that you were going to try to stop me. Since you had proved very hard to kill so far, Mephisto's advice was appreciated. I agreed to stage the ambush, and he gave me the means to defeat you. In return he gets the Saint."

"Don't worry. I will treat her great right--up until the time I kill her, painfully," Mephisto said and gestured for the Bone Gnawers to take Abigail. Two came forward and lifted her up, carrying her like sack of potatoes. "Of course she can't really be killed, so I will have to settle for destroying her mortal form and condemning her to hell for eternity. But you take what you can get." Mephisto looked at Silas quizzically.

"What are you going to do with him?" Mephisto asked Webb.

"I have never seen what my transformation would do to a super-natural being. I think it will be fun to experiment, of course, after he is more pliable. I think Coth is eager to help with that." Webb said.

Coth chuckled deep in his throat.

"And the mortal girl?"

Lily was coming to and moaned softly.

"I'll do the same. I will convert her. She will see the light, or I will dispose of her. Perhaps she can be used to control Silas."

Mephisto laughed. "Good luck with that. Demonic nature suppressed or not, he will not be an easy one to control."

"We shall see," Webb said.

12

They pulled Silas through the caves; most of the manmade tunnels were left behind. He stumbled a few times, cursing his now mortal weakness. His body was bruised and ached from the battle he just had with the Elemental. He now he had to endure it like a human. It made him sick.

Occasionally Coth would strike out with his hand and hit Silas in the back of the head or his back. Each blow was like a hammer. He was sure he had a concussion and a severe headache to prove it. Each time Coth struck his back he thought his spine might shatter. But what really pissed Silas off was that he knew Coth was holding back.

"When we get you to your cell I will show you the price for defying the will of the father. This pain you feel is nothing compared to that," Coth rumbled behind him.

Silas couldn't understand why Mephisto had done it. What Webb had planned was much worse than the trophy of a Saint. When the infernal ranks discovered that he precipitated the end of the world and the final judgment, they wouldn't care if he dropped the Pope, Jesus Christ, and the Dali Lama off on their doorstep. They will tear him to pieces. It just didn't make any sense.

Coth slammed him up against the rough wall of the cave. Silas grunted in pain and Coth chuckled again.

Unless... unless Mephisto thought he could take care of Webb himself and planned some sort of double cross for his new partner.

Silas moaned, and not from the pain in his body. Mephisto had no clue what he had gotten into. He probably thought Webb had a small handful of these creatures hidden away, not the army of blood thirsty lizard creatures he and Abigail had discovered. Mephisto had some clout in hell, but there was no way he could raise a sizable demonic army. He probably thought he could deal with Webb using just his henchmen, some Screamers and maybe a small group of Bone Gnawers. Silas didn't know exactly what Webb had down here, but from everything they had learned he had a feeling they would be no match for Webb. Besides, Mephisto was an idiot.

"Silas are you there?"

The voice was so loud that Silas almost jumped. It was like somebody speaking directly into his ear. Then he realized somebody was. Mort. He almost answered in surprise, but caught himself. Apparently, they had not noticed the small device in his ear. Tiny and flesh colored, in the pervasive dark of the Undercity it would hardly be noticed.

"Silas, what happened? I heard you mention Mephisto. Is he down there?"

Silas wished he could make use of this fact.

"I see that your signals have become separated. Have you split up? Dammit Silas, answer me."

They stopped abruptly at a line of doors. They had not gone far, perhaps only a few hundred feet from the river where they had been ambushed. A lizard creature opened one of the doors and dragged Lily inside. Coth opened the next door and threw Silas in the room beyond. He tried to stand, but Coth's fist met him on the way up, slamming into his gut. Silas doubled over and would have thrown up if he had any food in his gut.

"Are you okay Silas? You sound like you might be sick," Mort said in his ear.

Being mortal or not, if he got out of this the first thing he was going to do was strangle Mort.

"Not now, Coth. Time enough for that later; we need to prepare for this evening," Webb said.

Coth grunted and reluctantly backed away. Webb knelt near Silas. With a wave of his hand the manacles separated, and they were back to being bracelets. "You should feel privileged, Mr. Robb. You will witness the birth of a new race tonight. It won't be easy and there will be much bloodshed, but in the end we will prevail and the weaker races, the scum that think they are so important, the ones that think they rule this modern world, will be crushed and exterminated like ants. I know you don't believe we can accomplish this, and that is alright. You will understand."

"All I understand is that you are a spoiled little brat who thinks the whole world is against him, and so instead of just manning up, you are throwing a tantrum," Silas said, his face aching with each word.

Webb didn't take the bait. He smiled and dabbed at the blood seeping from beneath his sunglasses. "I am not mad at you for those words, my child. You just don't understand, but you will. You will see our glory with your own eyes. I know you think that the mortals with their military will defeat us. But we have a surprise, an ace in the hole so to speak."

He stood and walked toward the door. "Tonight Mr. Robb, tonight you will see the truth, and it will be beautiful."

He left with his words ringing down the hall. Coth gave one swift kick to Silas before he followed Webb. The kick connected with Silas' ribs, and he heard a crunch as pain shot up his side. He cried out. When Coth left, he eased himself onto his back and stared at the ceiling wondering what the fuck he was going to do now.

"Whatever happens, whatever he says, don't open that door." Silas heard Coth say to a guard outside.

Surprisingly, he still could see in the dark; it seemed his demonic vision was still a part of him. It was a small thing, but for some reason it made him feel better.

"We're fucked Mort," he whispered; he was not sure he could have spoken above a whisper even if head wanted to.

"Silas! You're there! Thank fucking God! Did you get separated? I see you and Lily close by each other, but Abigail is moving away in another direction."

Mort would need the story for his report. Quickly Silas told him about what had happened all the way to where he now lay on the ground staring at the ceiling.

"You can't just give up. I can send for reinforcements. I have your location," Mort said, but Silas knew he was grasping at straws.

"What reinforcements Mort? To get the resources to handle Webb would require days, even weeks unless you have another powerful supernatural agent of the Inquisition at your disposal. You don't have the time, none of you humans do."

Mort was quiet.

"You know what I'll miss the most Mort? The music. I really think that is humanity's greatest achievement. I mean sex, drugs, alcohol... those are all up there, but the music is what really.."

"Coward," Mort said. He said it quietly, but it boomed in Silas' ear.

"What?" Silas was not sure if he had heard him right.

"You, Silas, are a fucking coward. A little pussy."

"Watch it Mort. I told you it was all over. Without my demonic side I can't stop them, I'm just... just..."

"Mortal. Well boo-fucking-hoo. I live with that handicap every day; billions of us do, and we outnumber the demonic and angelic and every other supernatural creature. We rule the God-damn world. We created fucking rock and roll as you so aptly put it."

"This is not the same Mort, I'm Silas Robb the..."

"The pussy. Yes, Silas I know," Mort interrupted again. "You are demonstrating that perfectly. Curl up in a ball until Coth comes to make you his bitch."

"Fuck you, Mort! What the hell am I supposed to do? I'm locked in a cell, fuck knows where, my powers gone, I just got the shit kicked out of me by an overgrown lizard gorilla thing."

"I got news for you Silas. Brace yourself, this is going to come as a shock. You know why the Inquisition chose you? I read your file, I know exactly why. They had the names of several demons, they had their pick and you know why they picked you? It wasn't because you are a bad ass; it wasn't because you are one of the strong ones. It was because you have possessed more people than the entire demonic host put together. You have thousands of lifetimes of experience inside you. Yes Silas, believe it or not, they picked you for your brains. That is your greatest strength."

Silas looked around the room. It looked natural, like it was carved out of the rock. The Undercity was honeycombed with natural caved and manmade tunnels. From the look of the natural walls they were pretty deep underground. He slowly and carefully got to his feet, his cracked rib shooting pain through his side at each movement.

The door and door frame were makeshift, but sturdy. He put his shoulder against the door and pushed. Even without his demonic fury he was a big guy, but the door didn't budge. A small slit was cut in it about head height. He looked through and saw a torch lit hall-way. Against the far wall stood a man, a guard Silas guessed. Although Silas could see the telltale glint of emerging scales on the man's forearms, he was only at the beginning of the transformation.

I guess they don't consider me much of a threat anymore. For some reason that pissed him off even more than Mort's little speech.

"Silas? You still there?" Mort asked.

"Quiet, I'm thinking," Silas said.

He examined the lock. He had once possessed a locksmith who had also happened to be a thief. One of the best lock picks in the business. Unfortunately, this wasn't much of a lock. There was no key hole, at least on this side, and from the small crack between the door and the frame it looked like it was some simple bolt mechanism. He did, however, think he recognized the manufacturer.

He ran through the specifications he pulled from the locksmith's memories. He was pretty sure he knew how the mechanism worked. Now if he only had a tool to get inside the box around it.

He went through his pockets; they had not searched him properly as evidenced by them missing the ear piece. His fingers found the leather bag of Molcaen dust. He would rather have had a pick or screwdriver even, but an idea started to form.

"Hold on Mort, we are getting out of here," Silas said.

"What are you talking about? I'm up here in a van drinking a beer; you're the one stuck in the sewers with a psychotic sorcerer," Mort said.

Yep. Mort was definitely going to die after this one.

Silas pulled the bag out and carefully poured the powder on top of the lock case directly above where the latch mechanism would be under the eighth-inch of steel. He was careful not to drop any on the floor; he would need as much as he could get on top of the metal. He had purchased the Molcaen dust because of its unique property to burn very brightly. He had thought it would come in useful when fighting the lizard creatures, who seemed sensitive to light. It also burned at a very high temperature as he had learned when he had possessed an alchemist in the middle ages, quite by accident really when he had tried to corner the market on the stuff. Most alchemists were unaware of the property because you needed a large quantity to make it work and the stuff was very rare. He hoped the amount in the bag would be enough to do the job.

When he had the pile placed as accurately as possible, he pulled a small cigar case out of his jacket pocket. He opened the case, hoping it was as water proof as the manufactured claimed it was. This was his only chance since he couldn't summon fire. Inside the case the cigars were dry; he breathed a sigh of relief.

"Hey buddy, can I get a light?" Silas called to the guard outside.

The guard looked at him coldly and didn't move.

"Come on, give a condemned man one last smoke. I have another. You can have it if I can get a light. It's Cuban."

The guard looked at the torch and then back at Silas. He shrugged and pulled the torch from the wall sconce. He held the torch back while holding out his hand. Silas knew what he wanted and slipped the cigar through the slit. The guard took it and lit his with the torch while staring at Silas through the slit. Silas stuck the other cigar in his mouth and shoved the end through the slit.

For a moment Silas thought he was going to walk away and was preparing a list of ancient curses to spew at the son of a bitch when the guard lifted the torch to the window. Silas stuck the cigar in and coaxed a strong red glow from the tip. He stepped back and lifted the cigar.

"Thanks buddy, hope you enjoy," Silas said.

The guard grunted and placed the torch back in the sconce. Silas stepped back from the door and took a few puffs on the cigar, getting the ember nice and hot. He set it down so the burning tip touched the pile of dust, then stepped back and turned away.

Similar to magnesium, it took a moment to light, but when it caught the light would be blinding. He saw the back of the room light up like a spot light had turned on behind him and heard the loud hiss of the dust igniting.

"What the hell is going on in there?" The guard called from outside.

"Ah, ah, ah, Coth said not to open the door, no matter what," Silas said.

The guard had taken the words literally; he didn't open the door. The dust burned out quickly and Silas reached into the hole created by it. The twisted metal on the outside was hot, but he ignored the burns with a few hisses and winces as his fingers sought the release latch. He found it and the door lock released.

With a violent kick he opened the door, counting on the guard being just on the other side. He wasn't disappointed. The guard fell back into the hallway with a satisfying grunt. He recovered quickly and charged at Silas as he stepped through the door. If the guard had been one of the more advanced lizard creatures Silas, stripped of his power, would not have stood a chance, but he was a big guy and had possessed several martial arts masters over his lifetime, including an aikido master in the nineteen-thirties. Personally Silas had never been a fan of aikido because it usually did not involve enough pain, but it worked surprisingly well against big, charging idiots.

Silas stepped aside, grabbed the guard's arm and redirected him into the wall. His head connected with stone, and he went down with a wet crunch. Pain flared from Silas' cracked rib, but he managed to stay standing.

I guess aikido ain't half bad, Silas thought.

There was noise from down the tunnel and two lizard creatures appeared out of the dark. Now he was fucked. He had not counted on this in his grand jail break plan. The creatures growled and stalked toward him.

Behind them Silas caught movement followed by a bright flash and a thud. One of the creatures went down, and behind him stood the Indian, holding a glowing, ornate club. The other creature turned in surprise. The Indian chanted a few words then struck out again with the club. He hit the creature's gaping mouth and it howled before falling to the ground dead.

As Silas watched, the Indian lowered the club, then fell against the wall, sliding down as though he too was hurt. Taking no chances, Silas approached him cautiously. The Indian was breathing hard, and Silas could see he was old. He could have been in his eighties, and it had taken all his strength to defeat those two creatures.

"Who are you?" Silas asked.

"The last of my kind," he said.

"Last of the Lenape?"

"No," the man shook his head. "The last of the Guardians. My name is Leonard. We don't have much time."

"What is your part in all this? What are you the last Guardian of?" Silas asked.

"It is a long story and we have no time, but I will tell you what I can. Many years ago, maybe a thousand, my people did battle with an ancient evil spirit that called itself the Wyrm. It almost killed off my people, but with the help of shamans from many tribes we created a weapon that would allow us to defeat it. This is that weapon."

Leonard held up the club he had been carrying.

"The club is the traditional weapon of my people, the Lenape; you were right about that. With this weapon and the courage of many warriors they were able to trap the evil below the earth in a cave, but even with this weapon they could not kill it completely. They wounded it enough that it fell into a deep sleep.

"Knowing that it would still live and someday awake, the shamans got together and formed a secret group within my people called the Nataepu."

"Silas is that you?" Lily said from behind the door next to his cell.

He had almost forgotten Lily. He opened the door to her cell and let her out.

"What the hell happened? I remember those things cutting our lines and us falling into the water; then something grabbed me, something in the water. Next thing I know I wake up lying on the ground in that room," she said, then to Leonard, "And who the hell are you?"

Silas quickly filled her in on what had happened while she was unconscious, leaving out the part where he had almost given up.

"You're hurt," she said and squatted next to Leonard.

"It's the club. It uses the strength of the wielder and well... I'm getting too old for this shit," Leonard said with a smile. Then he grew serious and forced himself to stand with the help of Lily. "We cannot stay here. Come, let's go. I will tell you the rest at a safe distance."

He took the torch from its sconce and walked down tunnel. Silas and Lily fell in behind him after grabbing her pack of gear from the floor in the hall. A few more twists and turns down the tunnel, and he started talking again.

"The purpose of the Nataepu was to remember what had

happened and to guard against the time when the Wyrm woke again," he said.

"So there are others like you?" Lily asked.

"No. That is the problem, I am the last. And now that it might wake I am too weak to do anything about it."

"This is all very interesting, but we need to get going. We have to find Abigail and stop an army."

Leonard turned to him and held the torch up close to Silas.

"You don't understand mahtan'tu, Webb and his army are waking the Wyrm. Your goal and mine are the same. We must stop him, but we must not wake the Wyrm."

"So you've been skulking around down here watching Webb trying to figure out what to do?" Silas asked.

"Yes. After I saved the priest I started following Webb and his lieutenant, Coth, who seems to have a personal vendetta against you. They led me to your bar. When I saw them attack you I thought perhaps we could be allies,"

"The enemy of my enemy is my friend?"

"Yes, but I watched you from afar and tried to figure out what part you played in this."

"The name you called me a moment ago, you know what I am don't you?"

"Mahtan'tu. Yes it means Devil," Leonard said pausing in his fast walk to look at Silas. "You are an evil spirit."

"Then what makes you think you can trust me?"

"Just because you are mahtan'tu that doesn't mean you are all bad," Leonard said and starting walking again.

"What? That doesn't make sense," Silas said.

"Sure it does. It means you are an asshole, but deep down you really care about humanity and its survival," Leonard said with a shrug. "Believe me, you would not be my first choice as an ally, but I am too weak and time is too short to keep looking for something better. So I have to settle for you."

"You really know how to inspire confidence," Silas said. "Besides, I am not going to be much help with these on."

He held up his arms to display the manacles. Leonard turned to look at them critically.

"These were made in the underworld?" He asked.

"Straight from the pits of hell, so the story goes."

Leonard grasped both bracelets in his hands. "I am a shaman and have traveled the underworld many times. I have an understanding of it. Let me see what I can do."

Leonard held Silas arms with his eyes closed for a moment. Then he started chanting. Silas did not recognize the words, but he did feel the pulse of magic in the air. The bracelets on his arm grew warm and began to vibrate angrily. Leonard frowned and chanted louder. Silas glanced up the tunnel. Leonard was loud; hopefully none of Webb's soldiers were nearby.

Silas felt a sharp pain in his wrists. He gritted his teeth as the pain grew. Just as it felt like his wrists would break, there was a clinking sound and the bracelets fell off. He gasped in relief and immediately reached for the part of him that had been stolen. He felt it, but it was still out of his reach.

"It's not working, my demon self is still gone," Silas said in frustration.

Leonard nodded. "I could remove the device causing the damage, but it is up to you to heal the damage done. It will heal, but I don't know when. Could be hours, could be days."

"Don't start pitying yourself again," Mort said in his ear. Lily had been updating Mort as he and Leonard talked.

Mort was right, although Silas would never tell him that; there was nothing he could do about it, he would just have to wait. Unfortunately, Silas was not very good at waiting.

"We have to go rescue Abigail. Mort, do you still have a fix on her location?"

"Silas," Leonard said sadness in his eyes. "We don't have the time.

Saint Abigail is a good being, but if we don't stop Webb, millions of people are in danger. Abigail wouldn't have wanted us to wait."

"Leonard is right, we don't have much time, and you and I both know there could be more at stake than millions of people. I don't like this anymore than you, but it's the right call. It's the call Abigail would have wanted you to make," Mort said.

"We can go after her once we have stopped Webb," Leonard said, but his eyes shifted down when he spoke.

He and Silas knew the same thing. They might not be able to stop Webb; in fact, the odds were against them. And then they would not be able to save Abigail. He, more than any of them, knew what was awaiting her in Hell if Mephisto dragged her there. He could not let her suffer like that.

"You don't think we should go after her, Mort?" Silas asked.

Mort paused then said, "Not until we have stopped Webb."

"And what would Moreales say? What would be his direction?"

Again Mort paused, probably because Silas had never asked what Moreales would want. "Yes, he would want you to stop Webb first."

"So everybody agrees we go after Webb first?"

They nodded. Silas reached down and picked up the open bracelets and slipped them into his pocket. He couldn't have these just lying around.

"Well, what good is rock and roll without a little rebellion? I go after Abigail."

"Silas..." Mort started.

"No. Discussion done. I go after Abigail, but I will be able to save her a lot faster with a little help."

"Silas, I am too weak to go after Webb myself. We need you," Leonard said.

"Sounds like a personal problem old man. Thanks for helping me with the manacles, but I got to go see a demon about a girl."

Silas started to walk away.

"Mort where is she?" He asked.

"Silas..." Mort began.

"Mort, don't try it. If you don't tell me, I won't go after Webb. I will come up to your van and use your equipment to find her for myself. If you get in my way, I will kill you."

Mort sighed, "I will try to get a location give me one moment."

Lily grabbed his hand and pulled him to a stop. "We will go with you and try to help."

Leonard nodded behind her, "But we do this quick and then stop Webb."

"Sure old timer, whatever you say."

"Um, Silas," Mort said into his ear. "I think I know where she is, and you aren't going to like it. According to the most recent maps I have, she is somewhere in the Bazaar."

"Great," said Silas. "So much for keeping a low profile. Well guys, it looks as though we are going to the big city. Hope you've both had all your shots."

13

———————

Silas could here noise ahead. They were reaching the outskirts of the bazaar.

"So when did you fall in love with Abigail?" Lily asked next to him.

"What?" Silas said. Lily was looking at him with a smile. "What the hell are you talking about?"

"Oh come on, you're risking the world to save her. I'm pretty sure that might be the definition of love."

She was actually smirking.

"I'm a demon. We are physically incapable of love, we're made to hate," he said. "Look, I've come to appreciate her as a partner, which I'll admit surprises me as much as anybody, and she has helped me in some situations lately. So you could say I owe her--but love? No, I don't think so."

Lily didn't say anything, but the smirk remained on her face. She wasn't buying it.

"We're just partners. Like buddy cops in the movies; we make good partners."

"Uh huh. I think she likes you too," Lily said.

"What makes you say that..." Silas started.

"We are close, Silas," Leonard said. "I know of this Bazaar, but have only been to the fringe a few times. What can we expect?"

"Think of it as a middle eastern bazaar on steroids. It sprawls across several large caverns, and some shops spill out into nearby tunnels like the bar we passed. There's everything from small booths to grand shops and houses. Keep in mind, by grand I mean compared to the rest of the hovels you see the homeless living in down here."

"I still don't know how something that big could exist down here and never be found?" Lily said.

"You're chasing after a saint captured by a demon with another demon and a real life shaman, then we are going to fight a sorcerer and his lizard creature army and you are surprised a city can be hidden under New York? The truth is that while it's hidden by the Pale, it's the repository of the refuse from the world above both the human rejects and its trash. Frankly, nobody up there *wants* to know this place exists. Just like no one really wants to go hang out at the local junk yard. The Bazaar is protected by humanity's apathy, and that works better than any camouflage.

"When we get there, keep your eyes down and don't talk to anyone. You might be tempted, intrigued or even seduced by what you see, but keep in mind this can also be the most dangerous place on earth."

"Silas," Mort said in his ear. "I can't get an exact location on Abigail; there is too much rock in the way and interference from the Bazaar."

"I need an exact location. The place is too big to do a search."

"Sorry Silas, all I have is somewhere in the Bazaar. I will keep trying."

"Great. Searching that place would be like looking for a needle in a haystack," Silas said.

"Is there some place that it would make sense to start looking for her? Some way we can narrow it down?" Lily asked.

"No, I don't know why Mephisto would even come here. He can carry Abigail away to hell at any time... wait," Silas said.

Silas felt a coldness growing inside him as he realized why Mephisto was at the Bazaar. The cold anger became heat as his demonic fury reacted. Lily and Leonard took a few steps back from him. He slammed his fist into the tunnel wall, sending shards of rock flying in every direction.

"Looks like you are getting your mojo back," Leonard said.

"Abaddon, lord of the pit," Silas growled.

"Who is that?" Lily asked.

"Abaddon is one of the most powerful of demons and guardian of one of the entrances to hell. And the entrance he guards is not one you would like to use if you were trying to get there. If hell is like a septic tank, then going through Abaddon would be like going through the garbage disposal first on your way there."

"If Mephisto can send her to hell anywhere, why would he take her here?" Leonard asked.

"So she would suffer even more," Silas said and punched the wall again, sending another shower of rock flying.

"Jesus, Silas can you watch it?" Lily said as she dodged small rocks.

"Also, it's a way for him to brag. If he displays her for Abaddon and then casts her in, he will get more attention from the Infernal Host."

"So it is just a PR stunt?"

"Exactly."

"Do you know where this pit is?" Lily asked.

"Yes, it's on the outskirts, but on the opposite side from us. Come on, we have to hurry. If Mort still has a signal then that means she hasn't been thrown in, but we don't have much time."

He took a right turn and they were confronted by the sights and sounds of the Bazaar. He had not been exaggerating when he had described it. Even though he had been here many times before, it never ceased to amaze him. He walked from quiet, deserted tunnels to a bustling medieval metropolis. The cavern opened up, revealing row after row of shanty structures and streets thronged with people and non-people moving from shop to shop mostly ignoring the hawkers trying to get their attention. This was still the edge so most structures were shoddily constructed lean-tos and booths, but in the distance you could almost make out some of the larger structures. Lights of all types hung from shops and makeshift street poles. Gas, electric, even some running on magic caused a strong enough glow to illuminate the streets like the city above.

"Oh my God," Lily said.

"Yeah, it stinks doesn't it?" Silas asked. The smell of many unwashed bodies wafted over them. "They're also not really concerned with sanitation down here."

"No. I mean this is amazing. To think this has been under my feet nearly all my life and I never knew it."

"Come on," Silas said and began to shoulder his way through the crowd. Vendors called to Lily and Leonard trying to entice them to see their wares, most of which were pieces of refuse and other semi-usable objects. The true wonders of this place were deeper in, but the vendors could smell fresh meat. Silas pulled Lily after him knowing how easy it could be to get distracted for the first time.

He wove in and out of alleys and shops to avoid any areas where he might be recognized. Even so, he had to pause occasionally to get his bearings. The Bazaar was fluid and ever changing as people came and went. He led them down paths that lead to the darker parts of the Bazaar where people were scarce and looked at them with suspicion, and in some cases, open malice.

He stopped outside a booth selling various metal jewelry, charms, and metal decoration. It was all pretty beat up and dirty. Silas didn't want to know where it came from.

"Wait here, and don't talk to anybody. I have an idea."

He slipped inside the small hovel that served as the store. Moments later he emerged with two bracelets on his wrists. He held them up for the others to see.

Leonard knew what he was up to. "They look pretty good, but you can tell they are different if you look close."

He was right; these were black, but with a green tint and one was darker than the other, but it was the closest match he could find. Silas had possessed several accomplished poker players over the years, and he knew that the secret to a good bluff was all attitude. Silas was good at attitude.

"Is any of your strength coming back?" Leonard asked.

It had come to him back at the tunnel, but only in a trickle and now it seemed to elude him again. "I think it's getting better, but still inconsistent."

"Is this Abaddon stronger than you?" Lily asked.

"Sort of. He is an Incarnate. Most demons, like me, have to possess a human body to walk this world which means we are trapped by the confines of this world and we have to limit our powers."

Silas grabbed Lily's hand and started walking quickly; they had to reach Abaddon before Abigail was thrown in.

"A demon incarnate would have immense power; it would be like dropping a nuclear bomb. Obviously a destructive force like that would not go unnoticed and upset the balance, so it is forbidden for demons to incarnate on earth."

"But you said Abaddon was an Incarnate?" Lily asked.

"Yes, but he is confined to the gate he guards."

"So he is like a contained nuclear reaction at a power plant," Lily said.

Silas paused, "Yes, yes exactly. Mort, are you still reading Abby?"

"Yes there has been no movement for a while. I think they have reached their destination," Mort said, his voice breaking up. The depth must be affecting their communication devices, regardless of what Mort had said.

"They had quite a head start, but I suspect Mephisto made some stops along the way to brag and display her," Silas said.

Silas took them out of the main cavern and down a side tunnel.

Immediately the smell got worse. People were sitting against the wall, some in their own filth. Others looked through hooded eyes, red from drugs. One reached out to touch Lily. Silas punched him in the gut-- no demonic fury there, just good old fashioned biker muscles. He doubled over and started retching.

"You didn't think the lord of the pit to hell would live in the nice part of town did you?"

As they moved away from the Bazaar, the people disappeared and the passage they took slanted up. After a few more turns he stopped them.

"We have almost reached the Pit. This area is honeycombed with tunnels and passages and a lot of them lead to the chamber of the Pit. I am going to enter from one of the upper entrances because I don't think it's the one that Mephisto would have used. He'll most likely be on the ground next to the pit summoning Abaddon. This will give me a chance to look around."

"Do you have a plan?" Leonard asked.

"Yeah, I just told it to you. That's as good as it gets. I have some ideas for the rest, but for the most part I'll just be winging it."

"You really know how to inspire confidence," Lily said.

Silas grunted. "You two will stay here. No arguments. I need to move quietly."

"I wasn't going to argue, I have no desire to see a pit to hell."

"I'm with her," Leonard said. "Not really a prime tourist attraction is it? More your element anyway."

"Great, so much for Indian braves," Silas grumbled and headed up the passage.

He reached an opening and peered around the edge of the doorway, being careful to stay behind cover as much as possible.

The room that housed the Pit was large, with a dome-shaped ceiling. It had once been a large sewer junction long since abandoned, but appropriate for a pit to hell. The junction itself was about forty feet across. The bulk of the room was taken up by a large pit that dropped away into darkness. Around the edge was a ten-foot wide lip.

Channels were cut into the lip in four directions as foul water running from old sewers lines poured in.

About twenty feet above the floor an old, rusting platform circled the room with two sets of stairs to the lip below. The doorway Silas was looking through opened onto this platform. Silas eyed it critically. He wondered how well it would support his weight.

Bellow, Mephisto stood looking at his watch and tapping his foot impatiently. His great bulk took up a large portion of the floor. Three Bone Gnawers stood against one wall, looking nervous. Silas guessed they knew what was coming and he didn't blame them, a demon incarnate was enough to make anyone nervous.

Abigail was on the floor propped against the wall. Steel cable wrapped her body in three places. No magic manacles for her; steel cables would hold her just as securely. She moved her head slightly and Silas could see she was awake.

He had no idea how long Mephisto had been waiting, but by the way he kept checking his watch he appeared impatient, which meant the demon could show up at any minute. As he watched, Mephisto waved his hand over the pit and spoke the summoning words. He spoke them loudly, again a sign of impatience. It was probably not the first time he had tried.

Abigail was seated near another passage. The Bone Gnawers had their eyes on the Pit. He might be able to sneak through that back passage and grab her. It was the only plan he had.

He ducked back through the passage he had come and circled around, trying to remember which tunnel would connect with the one closest to her. He felt a rumbling vibration coming through the rock. Abaddon was coming, he had to hurry. When he thought he was in the right one, he poked his head through the doorway. Abigail sat off to his right close to the passage. Mephisto and the Bone Gnawers had their backs to them as they watched the show in the Pit.

It started as a small vibration then whispers of a thousand suffering voices began echoing out of the pit. There was the sound of rushing wind, then screaming voices in the distance. They grew louder, and a banging started shaking the room as though something was crawling up through the hole in the floor. And something was.

Black shadow mist spilled from the Pit like an overflowing septic. The screams grew louder as a liquid-like tar bubbled up from below. It churned and leaped as though boiling, but there was no heat. It was as though the mist stole the heat from the room, dropping it to below freezing almost instantly.

Abaddon always did know how to make an entrance.

The boiling of the tar subsided and a shape began to take form in the shiny goop. It stretched and flowed, slowly transforming into a demonic visage. The Bone Gnawers took a step back. Silas, who by now was out in the room a few feet from Abigail, paused, hoping they wouldn't decide to turn and run. If they did, they would run right into him. Abigail was also looking at the pit in horrid fascination, so she didn't see him.

A large head had formed above the black pool. A black mouth filled with glistening teeth smiled at them; above the mouth two big sloped eyes stared. The whole head was maybe ten feet across.

Silas had to move fast. He reached a hand around Abigail's mouth and clamped down, stifling any surprised screams and found she was already gagged. She must have been giving them an earful. For a moment he felt sorry for them, then he leaned her back so she could see it was him. Her eyes widened in surprise.

"Why have you summoned me Mephisto?" Abaddon said his voice low and slow, vibrating through the walls.

"I have come to deliver a tribute to the entire infernal realm, a Saint. I thought it fitting to deliver her to hell through your gate."

And that was when all eyes turned to look at Abigail and Silas as he investigated her cables.

"What..." Mephisto stuttered in surprise and then recovered with a smile. "Well Silas, I am not sure how you escaped Webb, but I guess the more the merrier."

"Just don't throw your man boobs at us again," Silas said as the Bone Gnawers surrounded him. He reached for his demonic fury again and it was there, but only a whisper, his touch slid passed it. Damn.

"Always the sarcastic one, even when you should be begging for mercy. I know giving you over to Abaddon and the Pit will not kill you, but you will suffer as you never have until you are finally spit out at home."

Silas lowered his eyes as though concerned and thinking. He gathered all the skills of every liar, con man, and card shark he had ever possessed.

"Look at you Silas. Striped of your demon essence--I can see you still have the manacles--and trying to save a Saint? Really? Look what this indenture to the Vatican has cost you. You are their lackey, already trained to save their precious packages. It is making you foolish and stupid. Throwing you into the Pit will be a great lesson, and I know in ten years or so when you get out you will thank me for it."

Silas staggered a little as if stunned. He took a few steps toward Mephisto before falling to his knees, tears in his eyes.

"Silas sheds tears?" Grumbled Abaddon. "I suppose there are still a few surprises left for someone as ancient as me. Give me the Saint, Mephisto. I would taste her soul."

"Please," Silas whispered.

"What was that?" Mephisto asked. "Did I hear Silas Robb say please?"

He took a few steps closer and leaned over.

"Come on Silas, beg. Beg and I can finally say I have seen it all. I can spend the rest of eternity knowing I made Silas Robb beg."

"Please, just take off the manacles. Don't send me into the Pit with these on."

Silas thrust out his hands towards Mephisto letting them shine in the light of the lamps the Bone Gnawers carried.

"Oh yes! Silas begging. That is better than any music to my—wait let me see those," Mephisto said with a sudden frown. He stepped forward and grabbed both of Silas's wrists.

In the nineteen twenties Silas had possessed a fellow named Ralph Melnish. He was a small time hood that dealt in card tricks and shell games. He was a pitiful little man who died at thirty three, and Silas could honestly say the most exciting event of his life was being possessed by a demon. As well as being very good at sleight of hand--maybe the best there ever was--there was one trick in particular that he had mastered. When a cop tried to put cuffs on Ralph, the officer would usually find that somehow the hand cuffs had found their way onto to officer's own hands. It was a trick that he was so famous for, police would usually knock him unconscious before handcuffing him. That was back when cops could beat up a guy for no reason at all, especially a small time hood.

With a quick movement, the demon manacles closed on Mephisto's wrists with a click. Mephisto stepped backed as though he had been slapped. "What? No, no what is this?"

Before the Bone Gnawers could react, Silas ripped the bracelets off and showed them. They hesitated, unsure of who held the power now.

"No Silas, wait, how did you... we can make a deal," Mephisto said, holding up his now shackled arms. "I have connections! You know I didn't mean what I was saying..."

He staggered a little. With his demon strength gone he was not used to supporting his own huge weight

"Give me the Saint," cried Abaddon.

"Sorry Abaddon, no Saint for you today. How about roast pork instead?" Silas said and then slammed his shoulder into Mephisto, sending his already unstable body over the side.

The blackness in the Pit reacted as Mephisto went in, bubbling and spiting. Abaddon let out a small sigh of pleasure, but Silas doubted he would be satisfied until he had Abigail too.

"Now Silas, give me the Saint. Give us the Saint. Think of the glory. I will personally commend you to the infernal host," Abaddon said.

"Sorry, never really been one for caring what people think," Silas said.

The Bone Gnawers were looking at each other as though trying to decide what to do. Silas showed them his unadorned wrist and tried to look menacing. Another bluff, and he did not think it would last long. Unfortunately, they had blocked the door and he was not sure if his bluff would hold if he charged them. Stalemate.

The only way out appeared to be the steps going up to the rusty platform above. He gestured for Abigail to stand. Her arms were bound to her torso, but her legs were free to move. She tottered to her feet. Silas stepped toward the Bone Gnawers, but they didn't flinch. Time to go, they were gaining their courage. Silas turned, threw Abigail over his shoulder with a muffled squawk from her and a wince from him as his bruised ribs sent a stab of pain into his side, and ran toward the stairs. The Bone Gnawers chased after him.

He was three steps up the stairs when rust started falling from above and the metal started moaning in protest. The stairs lurched as the bolts securing it to the concrete wall came loose. He had no choice but to keep moving and hope it would hold; a Bone Gnawer was already on the stairs behind him. He heard Abaddon chuckle at the show.

Letting out a final shudder and screech, the catwalk pulled away from the wall completely. With the sound of metal sheering, it swung out over the pit. Silas fell, and the catwalk sunk out from beneath his feet and sloped toward the black tar below. With one hand holding the steel cable binding Abigail, he caught the railing with the other to stop their slide.

The Bone Gnawer was less lucky. The railing it grabbed tore away from its hands in a shower of rust. He slid down the bent metal of what was left of the stairs. Abaddon had moved its head to the bottom of the stairs, widening it already huge mouth. The Bone Gnawer slid off the metal stairs and into the waiting mouth lined with teeth. He disappeared with a gulp.

"And now the Saint," Abaddon called up. "Drop her Silas and I will let you crawl away unharmed. There is no other choice, the metal won't hold much longer. It is old, so old." He chuckled that low baritone rumble again.

The catwalk lurched and Silas looked down at Abigail. She nodded at him. He ignored her as a Saint becoming a martyr was a little too dramatic for his tastes. He looked around desperately trying to figure out a way up as the metal catwalk careened even further over the Pit. In moments it would drop in. He could not let go of the railing with his hand to try to climb, the moment he did they would both slide into Abaddon's maw.

A rope hit him in the face. He looked up and there, just inside an upper passage, was Lily; the rope went past her to the tunnel beyond. Silas assumed Leonard was at the other end, hopefully securing it somewhere because he doubted Leonard could hold his and Abigail's weight by himself. The catwalk lurched again, and Silas let go of the railing and reached for the rope. He grabbed it and immediately started sliding, the rope burning through his hand. He reached for his demonic fury and it was there, at least a part. He clamped down on the rope, ignoring the pain and they stopped their slide.

The other Bone Gnawers near the Pit had disappeared. Probably decided with their employer gone the job had gone to hell, literally, and it was time to get out while they still could.

He felt the rope tug and then they were moving back up, slowly. Silas found purchase with his feet in the metal grate and helped move them along.

"No! No!" Abaddon moaned as he saw his pray escaping. "Give me the Saint. Let me taste her flesh, please I beg you."

Foot by foot they made it back to the passage as Abaddon screamed his rage louder and louder. When they reached the top, Lily helped pull them into the passage. Silas was feeling his demonic essence flowing through him once again. Instantly his injuries started healing. He grabbed the cable around Abigail and pulled them apart with a massive tug.

"Looks like you're back to your old self," Leonard said.

Silas smiled and flexed his hands feeling the strength returning.

Abigail pulled the gag out of her mouth. "What the hell happened? The last thing I remember was falling into the river, and then I woke up surrounded by Mephisto and those things in that room. They took my radio, so I couldn't hear you."

Lily quickly filled her in, including what Leonard had told them so far while Silas basked in the feeling of his returning fury. Abigail cast a quick glance at him when Lily mentioned that he had gone after her instead of stopping Webb right then and there, but she didn't interrupt.

"No thanks necessary," Silas said when Lily was done.

Abigail ignored him. "Ask Mort how much time we have before sunset?"

Lily relayed the question.

"A little over an hour until the sun goes down," Mort said.

"A little over an hour," Lily relayed.

"Thank God we still have a little time. I hope it will be enough. We should go," Abigail said.

"Okay, maybe a little thanks would be nice," Silas said with a frown.

"Thanks for what? Saving me or risking the end of the world?" Abigail said and stalked off down the passage. Lily looked up at Silas for a moment then ran ahead to catch up with Abigail.

Silas looked at Leonard and shrugged, "I've been around for millennia and I don't ever think I'll understand women."

"That's okay; I'm pretty sure the Creator didn't have any idea what he was doing when he made them anyway," Leonard said.

They followed after the ladies.

14

L eonard and Lily were able to guide them to the spot of the carvings once Silas got them to a point they recognized.

"I know of it and I have seen Webb's people, but I am unsure of the location of this large cavern that you mentioned Lily," Leonard said. He looked uncomfortable for a moment. "It has been so long, my people have forgotten how to find the cavern of the Wyrm. I have been trying to protect it and I don't even know exactly where it is. Lily, I believe it might have been the cavern you saw or at least near there."

Silas examined the carvings on the wall. He saw the depiction of the hunters subduing the beast underground. Across from the carving were the modern words in paint.

"I assume this is your work?" Silas asked and pointed at the writing.

"Yes, I was not sure I would be able to stop Webb, so I tried to write a warning. I know it is cryptic, but I planned to add more."

"Can you tell us more about your people, the Nataepu I mean?" Abigail asked.

Leonard nodded wearily. "As I said, the shamans got together and formed a group secret even to the tribes. The Nataepu were required to learn as much as possible about the shamanic arts, to study as much as possible so we could protect the tribe when the Wyrm woke. All our teachings were handed down from generation to generation."

"But it didn't quite work out?" Abigail asked.

"No," Leonard sighed; he was looking a little gray in the flashlight's glare. "This was before the coming of the colonists and others. The original Nataepu could never guess how our world would change. With each generation more of the young ones grew disinterested or even refused to believe the tales. As science took over the world around us, our beliefs became the superstitions of savages. Now I am the last and left with only a scrap of the original teachings. My father was a great man, but even he had little to pass down."

"I think I can lead us to the large cavern where I saw the creatures," Lily said. "Are you going to make it? Do you need to rest?"

Leonard shook his head. "I have to see this through. If Webb does wake the Wyrm though, I am not sure I will have the strength to fight it, even with the sacred weapon."

"Well, I guess we'll have to stop him before he wakes it. Let's go," Silas said and gestured for Lily to lead the way.

She led them through several passages, pausing occasionally to get her bearings. The last time she had been here she had been running in fear. It wasn't until he smelled a familiar scent that he stopped them.

"What?" Abigail asked.

Silas held up his hand to silence her. Then they all heard it--many footsteps, but also strange clicking sounds, and then the rough sound of something slithering on rock. Silas ushered them into a side passage and quickly took them down it several feet, turning off their lights before coming back to look at the tunnel they had just evacuated. Abigail took up position behind him.

Down the hallway came the troupe of demons, walking, slithering, and clawing along like the world's most grotesque menagerie. They were all low-level demons, more grunt soldiers than demons of any significance. Silas ducked back up the passage as they passed. He counted no more than a few dozen. This had to be Mephisto's plan to double cross Webb by sending his own demon force.

Unfortunately, Mephisto had grossly underestimated Webb. It would not work; Silas guessed that by sheer number Webb's army would defeat this haphazard demon force. It even looked as though they weren't even all demons; some had been minor devils most likely forced into servitude by Mephisto, sort of like a demonic draft.

But maybe they could use this to their advantage. He and Abigail went back to the others after they had passed.

"I think we just saw Mephisto's solution to Webb. A very small demon army," he said.

"Do you think it will work?" Abigail asked.

"No. We've fought those lizard creatures and those demons were fairly low level grunts from hell. If Webb has any number of soldiers at all, these demons don't stand a chance. But I do think it might work as a distraction. While the bulk of Webb's people are fighting we might be able to get to him more easily."

They followed the demonic platoon. It was not hard to follow the trail of foul smelling sludge and fecal spore left behind.

"I thought you said demons had to possess somebody to take form in this world. These things were monsters right?" Lily asked.

"Yeah. I'm using the term demon loosely. They are more like demonic pets than true demons. They were created by other true demons and have a form all unto themselves. Their primary use is to terrorize souls in hell, but they are also the frontline troops of demon armies. They are vicious and powerful fighters, but they have no real demonic essence or nature."

Lily stopped them at a side passage. "This is where I headed to find the cavern, but the demon trail heads that direction."

"Most likely Mephisto knew of another entrance to the cavern, probably the main entrance as that would be what Webb would have shown him. It looks like they're going to knock on the front door, another reason this army will have little effect--no sense of strategy. We go your way, maybe we can avoid the chaos."

Lily nodded and took them down the passage. They were getting close so they moved slowly. Eventually, Lily stopped them again and whispered.

"That turn ahead is the last one. Around it is where the opening to the large cavern is."

Silas could smell and hear it now, the smell of unwashed bodies and poor sanitation washed over them. And blood, the smell of lots and lots of blood. Sounds, animal and human, came from down the tunnel.

A lizard creature stepped around the corner, surprised to find them standing there. Abigail's stilettos were a blur, but the punctures they made in the creature's throat and chest were enough to kill it almost instantly. It tumbled forward onto the ground.

"Jesus," Lily said. "That's faster than the chefs at those Japanese steak houses."

"Yep almost as fast as me," Silas said with a wink.

Abigail raised an eyebrow at him. "It must have been a guard; we have to be ready for more. It seems we were lucky to get this far without encountering one." Abigail put away her knives and they crept forward slowly until they could see into the cavern beyond.

It was just as Lily had described, several hundred of the lizard creatures roamed the floor below. They moved around snapping and biting and talking among themselves. They were arranged in groups with the strongest and most transformed at one end of the cavern near a raised dais while the back group was mostly human. Full humans did walk among them organizing-- talking and handing out makeshift equipment and a few weapons. It was a war party, and they were preparing for battle.

The raised dais had been constructed at one end against a large gray boulder. A table had been set up against the rock with various chalices, and what looked like a spigot had been driven into the side of the rock.

"That's no rock," said Silas as he pulled the others away from the opening. "That's a goddamn dragon out there."

He looked at Leonard and jabbed a finger at him. "Is that your Wyrm? A dragon?" Silas leaned back against the wall covering his eyes with hands.

"It must be, but I have never seen the Wyrm," Leonard said.

"It looks like he is draining the blood from it," Abigail said. "That must be the catalyst. The Blood of the Wyrm."

"With that kind of catalyst he could transform most of the city. No wonder he had so many soldiers. Dammit! Why didn't I see this before? Even the creatures he's creating I thought were some sort of lizard monsters. But no, he's transforming humans into some kind of dragon hybrids."

"Is this bad? It looked like the dragon was still sleeping; what happens if it wakes?" Lily asked.

"You ever watch those old Godzilla movies?" Silas asked. "There's a reason they were hunted to extinction years ago. If that things wakes, bye-bye city."

"Hello Armageddon," St. Abigail said.

Silas crawled back to the opening and looked again, this time knowing what he was actually seeing. The dragon was massive, not quite as big as Godzilla, that had been a little exaggeration, but it had much more destructive power. They were also almost impossible to kill, as the Lenape had discovered when they fought it. He could only see its back as it was curled away from him, but on the other side he could see a horn sticking up, most likely where its head was.

"Mort are you there?" Silas whispered.

No answer. Mort had faded away as they had gotten closer to this cavern. Silas suspected they were too deep for effective communication; so no information from the Vatican database on dragons, if they had any at all. They were one of the rarest of supernatural creatures, right up there with unicorns. The best they could hope for was that it did not wake. He heard the rest of the group come up behind him to get another look.

The crowd grew hushed and in a moment Silas saw why. Webb was making his way into the chamber followed by that draconian creature Coth. He walked through the crowd like a celebrity--no, like a prophet--touching his followers and pausing to talk to some. No smile on his face this time though; this was a war party. He had the same large aviator glasses on and constantly wiped at the blood trickling down his face. Silas wondered if that was for show, maybe make him seem more mysterious. Eventually, he made it to the dais and walked up with an entourage.

The fucker loves this, thought Silas.

He raised his hands and the crowd cheered; it came out more as growls and hoarse calls, but it was obvious they loved him. The cheering noise stopped.

"Brothers, my children thank you. I love you too. We have been through a lot, and tonight we will finally taste victory over the oppressors above," Webb said, his voice ringing out across the throng without the need for a microphone.

His followers cheered again.

"Tonight we will end their rule with blood and claw, we will rend their pathetic little hearts, we will..." Webb drifted off as a commotion at the back of the cavern caught his attention.

The darkness at the back of the cavern exploded out as the demon army made their entrance. The screaming, churning mass of demonic creatures fell upon the rear of the chamber like a black shadow. It would have been impressive if Silas had not known the inevitable outcome. They were outnumbered, and the fight would be over soon. If Silas and his friends were going to take advantage of this diversion, they had to move now.

"Destroy them!" cried Webb from the dais and the loyal ranks of draconian warriors surged forward at the demonic force.

Silas turned to the others. "Now's our chance. Let's go down there and stop Webb."

"What's the plan?" Abigail asked.

Silas looked at her and spoke a little slower, "Let's go down there and stop Webb. That's the plan, baby."

He turned and jumped through the opening, sliding down the sloped wall of the cavern to the floor. The opening through which they looked had been about thirty feet up so it only took moments. A few stragglers from the main force had not charged to the other end of the cavern yet and saw him. He headed straight for them, letting his demonic fury have full reign. It felt wondrous.

He laughed as he fell into them, fists swinging. One went down with a massive blow, another he grabbed and swung like a baseball bat into a third. He felt, rather than saw Abigail by his side with her stilettos snaking out and dispatching two more who came at them. There were only a handful between him and the dais. Webb and company were so engrossed with what was happening at the other end they did not even see the doom heading toward them.

From the corner of his eye he could see the demonic horde swarming into the cavern. They were hopelessly outnumbered, but they still had the advantage of surprise on their side. Silas dodged to the side as a dragon creature lunged at him and slammed a fist into its jaw. He was rewarded with a satisfying crunch and the creature went down.

The carapace of a large demonic spider slammed into him and knocked him a few feet off course. The main battle had spread quickly and demon horde fought dragon hybrids not more than twenty feet from them. A group of creatures charged toward Abigail. Silas turned to help when he saw that they had been spotted.

Coth leaped from the dais and landed in front of Silas. He was grinning.

"I'm glad you escaped. This is the way I wanted it," he growled.

"Yeah, I always suspected you had the hots for me," Silas said. Behind Coth, Silas could see that Webb had taken his eyes off the battle to watch them.

Coth swung a massive clawed fist at Silas. Silas dodged to the right and brought his arm up, but the force of the blow was enough to stagger him. Silas used his momentum and brought his foot up to kick Coth's stomach. He connected with a nice thunk, and Coth took two steps back.

Coth charged with a roar, catching Silas in the torso and lifting him up and over the bony protrusion across his shoulders and back. Bone and scaly plates dug into him as Silas went over. It was like sliding down a rocky mountain face first. When he hit the ground he tried to roll to his feet, but Coth had turned and his clawed foot kicked into his side like a bar of steel. Silas rolled a few feet and tried to regain his feet.

Damn this guy was tough! But then *he* was Silas-mother-fucking-Robb.

Silas jumped and kicked Coth in the face with his steel-toed boot. Coth brought his hands up to his face in surprise. Silas didn't hesitate and rammed his fist into Coth's solar plexus, one of the few unarmored places on his body. The breath went out of Coth's lungs in a great whoosh and he double over. Silas' knee was there to meet his face. There was a satisfying crunch, and Coth dropped to the ground.

Silas turned and ran for the dais as Webb, perhaps sensing a turn of fortune for himself, tried to flee in the other direction. Silas caught him and spun him back toward the center of the dais. He fell to his knees, glasses flying from his face. Silas grabbed him by the lapels and hoisted him up.

The whites of Webb's eyes were stained pink with blood. It seeped out of his eyelids as though he had a permanent brain hemorrhage. It ran in rivulets down his face, giving his face a red, cracked look like broken marble.

"Please, please. It's gone," Webb whispered.

Even with his eyes filled with blood Silas could see the madness. His pupils were black pinpoints in the pink flesh of his eyeballs.

"Silas!"

Silas turned to see that the battle was all but over. There was still fighting at the rear of the chamber, but for the most part it had subsided. Now there was a very angry army of dragon creatures staring at him. Hundreds remained standing while the remnants of the demon army consisted of black rotting corpses spread throughout the room.

Coth stood at the front of them holding Abigail. They were surrounded by a pile of dead dragon men, so Silas was sure she had put up a good fight. But now Coth held her by both arms pinning them to her body, her stilettos were on the ground at her sides. Three of the other dragon creatures held Leonard and Lily, walking them to the front of the dais so Silas could see them.

"Let him go Silas," Coth rumbled.

"Yes, yes that is what you should do. It's gone now, it has abandoned me. I am a nobody," Webb babbled.

Something was different. Gone was the confidence he had seen in Webb. He had been a religious leader, now he was a sniveling weakling. Silas saw nothing but fear and madness in him now. The blood in the eyes, the hemorrhage, the sudden shift in personality--he was beginning to get a picture of what was going on here.

"You cannot kill all of us Silas," Coth said. "Let the Father go. The purification will continue tonight as planned."

"But I don't have to kill all of you, that ain't how the magic works."

And with that Silas snapped Webb's neck, killing him instantly.

Coth roared in rage and bent Abigail's arms back, her face contorted in pain; but then it was Coth's eyes widening in pain, and he dropped her arms. Moans came from the dragon army as they began falling to their knees and writhing in pain. Coth remained standing, but only barely, wobbling across the floor to the dais. His skin began to pulsate and bubble.

As Silas watched, the soldiers' draconian features softened, and they changed back into the human flesh and bone they once were. It was a painful process and not without its share of scarring. Some, those who were most draconian, did not survive the transformation back and fell to the ground in death throes.

In front of him Coth melted into a tall, well-built young man. He looked at his hands, seeing that they had returned to simple flesh and fingers. Tears were in his eyes.

"Gone, it's all gone. What have you done? What of the new world?" He gasped.

"Welcome to the new world kid, same as the old one," Silas said.

Coth looked up at him, and his eyes grew big in terror. They were human eyes so Silas could see it quite clearly. Lily and Leonard both stared at him, faces pale. Even Abigail, who had regained her knives, seemed unsteady and shocked.

"Let me guess," Silas said calmly. "There's a large dragon behind me and he is awake."

They nodded in unison. Silas dove off the dais and the others broke and ran for cover as a roar of flame engulfed the spot he had just been standing.

Silas felt the heat blast his body, but he avoided the direct flame. From the amount of screaming it didn't sound like many of the recently restored humans made it out of the way.

The dragon stretched its neck and spread its wings, then arched its body as though stretching like a cat. It was a magnificent creature; silver and gray scales glistened a rainbow of colors reflecting the light from the lamps and fires its breath had created. Its head alone was twice the size of Silas; with its wings spread it could easily reach from one side of the cavern to the other. It let out a roar that shook the rock walls of the cavern.

Yep, they were screwed.

The others had taken cover behind a large rock near the passage they had come through. Silas ran to the others while the dragon was waking.

"So much for not waking the dragon," Abigail said.

"It had always been awake, at least its mind was," Silas said.

"What do you mean?"

"Remember when Mephisto said he didn't think Webb had the skill to pull this off. That he was small time?"

"Yeah he said he would need help. I thought he was talking about the catalyst."

"No, dragon's blood was the catalyst that transformed his army, but it was more than that."

Silas turned to Leonard. "Your Wyrm was controlling Webb this whole time. That's why his eyes bled. The force of the dragon's mind in his own was causing a hemorrhage. And that damage is why when the dragon left him he was left deranged. It was using him."

"So this army was the dragon's idea? He wanted to attack the city?" Abigail asked.

"Yep, that's my guess and with a dragon behind them, they would have been a much greater threat to humanity above. With the Pale torn asunder and a dragon as the leader, many other supernatural creatures that hate humanity would have rallied. It would be all-out war and humans wouldn't stand a chance."

The dragon finished stretching and eyed the newly restored humans scrambling around the cavern, climbing over each other to get out. It reared back and then let loose a great billow of flame washing across the former dragon army.

"My God we can't let him just cook those people," Abigail said.

"Those people wanted to destroy New York just moments ago," Silas said.

Abigail glared at him. "They were confused. We can't just let them be cooked."

"And what are supposed to do? Did you see the size of that thing?"

"I don't know, but we have to figure something out."

Leonard crawled closer to them, his face ashen. "It is my duty to stop the Wyrm, but I am weak and I don't know if I am able fight it." He held the club out toward Silas, it was glowing softly. "It draws its strength from the wielder, I can't think of anybody stronger than you to use it."

Silas held the club in his hand. In vibrated angrily.

"It doesn't seem to like me," he said.

"Of course not, you are mahtan'tu," Leonard said without expression.

"So let me get this straight, you want me to fight a fifty-ton fire-breathing dragon with a stick that doesn't like me?"

Leonard just stared at him.

"Well I've been in worse situations. How does it work?"

"You hit the dragon really hard. I suggest on the head."

Silas considered hitting Leonard over the head. "I know how to use a club. I mean how to activate its magic."

"Oh," Leonard said and scratched his head. "I am not sure. That part of the teachings has been lost for centuries. All I know is that's the weapon used to stop it originally. Do you know any Lenape chants by any chance?"

There was another blast of flame and new screams from those unfortunate enough not to have made it out of the cavern.

"We have to do something now," Abigail said and grabbed a hold of Silas' arm.

"Okay, okay."

Silas stepped out from behind the boulder, doing what he did best; winging it. He hid the club behind his back. The dragon had turned away from the fleeing people and charred remains at its feet. It was examining the cavern walls, and particularly the ceiling, looking for a way out. Based on its size and strength, Silas doubted it would have any problem digging its way up to a large subway tunnel or station.

One massive claw scraped the ceiling. Rocks and dirt rained down as it used its second claw to rake the dirt and rock. It was going to cause a cave-in for the rest of the cavern.

"Hey dragon!" Silas called.

It did not seem to hear him, but continued digging at the walls and ceiling some more. Rocks fell from the other side of the cavern. Silas reached for his demonic fury and let it add fuel to his voice.

"DRAGON!"

His voice shook the ground and caused even more rocks and dirt to fall, but it got the dragons' attention. It spun away from the back of the cavern, its neck snaking around to the same level as Silas.

"Ssssiiiiilllllaaasss," the dragon hissed.

Of course it knew him. It had been in Webb's head all along. Silas charged at the head, bringing the club up as he ran. The dragon's eye ridges came together in a frown, but it did not move. He was a mere twenty feet from the dragon's head when a bus hit him.

Silas was thrown across the cavern and smashed into a rocky wall. He managed to hold the club as he fell to the ground, but just barely. He was stunned, but didn't black out,. His fury burned through him, keeping him conscious. The dragon's tail whipped back and forth in front of it. That must have been what hit him. He staggered back to his feet, a whole new set of injuries screaming pain at him.

The dragon saw him and tilted its head like a puzzled dog, probably wondering how he was still standing. Hell, *he* was wondering how he was still standing. Another blow like that, and he could kiss this mortal form good-bye. He started moving toward the dragon, wary of the tail this time.

The dragon reared back its head to breath fire. Silas looked around; there was no cover, nothing to protect him. He held up the club, hoping it would do something. He didn't know any Lenape chants, so he did the next best thing. He spoke a minor spell to protect from heat, but he didn't have a sympathetic link to the magic, so he doubted it would do much good. The dragon let loose its breath.

Flame surrounded him like walls of heat, but he didn't burn. The flame had parted where it met the club leaving him singed, but unharmed. He felt the words of his spell being sucked into the club as well as some of his strength, just a trickle, but enough for him to be creeped out by it. Now he knew what Leonard meant by using the wielder's strength.

The dragon saw that he was unharmed and roared in rage. It thrashed about in a tantrum, sending more of the ceiling falling to the ground below. Then it charged.

Silas had no time to move before the huge creature was on him; a gigantic claw snatched him off the ground and brought him up toward the beast's mouth. He wouldn't be able to get a good angle for a blow this way. The massive jaws lined with three-foot teeth opened in front of him. Well, if he could survive the chewing maybe, he could give it a nasty case of heartburn. He was going to miss this world.

Suddenly, the dragon howled and whipped its head around. Behind it Abigail was stabbing its tail with her stilettos and screaming. Leonard and Lily were pounding ineffectively on it with rocks, and even Coth had found a knife and was stabbing at it. The dragon shook its tail, sending them all flying. Abigail and Lily landed in a heap near the passage they had come through; Leonard hit a rock head first leaving a red streak; and Coth was flung onto the remnants of a large, demonic war blade. He was killed instantly as the blade erupted through his chest.

This was his only chance. Silas swung the club down at the claw that held him. The club flared and the dragon roared again in pain. The claw went slack and Silas leaped with all the strength he had right into the face of the dragon as it opened its jaws to rip him in two. The club connected with the dragon's head just above the eye socket in a fiery burst. The dragon fell back as though hit by a great blow, and Silas went spinning to the ground.

Ignoring his cracked ribs and countless other injuries, he jumped to his feet and charged again at the dragon as it writhed in pain. This time he didn't bother going for the head; instead, he swung at the soft underbelly just below the neck. Again there was a flare, and Silas felt a tug on his strength. The dragon fell back against the wall, shaking the cavern.

The dragon's head spun around looking through its one good eye for Silas. It found him and opened its mouth to breath flame. Silas jumped and brought the club down on its head just as the flame boiled out from its mouth. There was an explosion. The jaw snapped shut and flames shot out in all direction and through its nostrils as its head slammed into the ground.

Silas hit the ground and got to his feet for one last blow. Blood was dripping from numerous slices and gouges covering his body. In places his skin felt charred and crispy, but he ignored the pain and approached the beast. The dragon eyed him helplessly through its eye, too exhausted to fight. It growled at him.

"In rock and roll it's all about the stamina, bitch."

He swung with his last strength, hitting the dragon right in the center of its head. Light burst out and the ground shook. Silas collapsed, dropping the club.

WHEN SILAS AWOKE, the ceiling was moving. It took him a moment to realize the ceiling wasn't moving, he was. Somebody was dragging him by his jacket. Scratch that, two somebodies.

Abigail saw that he was awake. "Thank God. There was no way we were going to carry you out of this cavern."

Silas tried to sit up and winced; the world spun briefly, and it took a moment for him to get his bearings. They were still in the cavern. The dragon lay in a heap in the middle of the room; rocks and dirt were falling from the ceiling, and the whole cavern shook. He must have been out for just moments.

"The dragon--is it dead, or just unconscious?" he asked.

"I don't know, but we don't have time to find out. The cavern is about to collapse. We have to get out of here."

"Leonard?"

"Dead," Lily said. "I would take him to be buried, but I don't think we can take the time."

Silas could see tears in her eyes. The ground shook again, and Silas crawled to his feet gingerly. Demonic fury or not, he was in a lot of pain. With one last look at Leonard, they crawled out through the passage, moving as fast as they could, but none of them were in any shape for running. They had made it several hundred feet up the tunnel when they heard a large crashing noise and felt a debris cloud billow up from behind them.

"That's it then. The chamber just collapsed, burying the beast forever. If it wasn't dead before, it sure is now," Lily said.

Silas looked down at the club tucked into his belt and wondered.

15

It was almost midnight, and Silas was nowhere near drunk enough. It had only been a few hours since they had climbed out of the sewer after having saved the world... again. He healed fast, but he was still in a lot of pain. The liquor was medicinal. The waitress brought over another two shots and a beer, which he downed almost immediately. He looked up at the deserted stage. No show tonight. The band was cool with that; they all could use a night off. But tomorrow they would be rocking the house once again. He smiled at the thought. Then he looked at Mort and the smile disappeared.

"So that's everything? You've told me everything that happened down there?"

"Yep. Have you talked to the others? It should match up. Should make a nice little report for Moreales. And I am expecting a nice little deposit in my account for all this."

"Well, there is the little matter of burning an apartment building to the ground," Mort said.

"Now wait a minute..."

As he spoke, the door opened and Lily walked in followed by Michael, and Steve. Mort had Steve take Lily home to clean up and then bring her back. There was some unfinished business. Mort had been making a lot of calls as Silas tried to drink himself into a stupor.

"So the dragon is dead?" Mort asked.

"I don't think so," Silas said.

"There is no way anything could survive all that rock covering it, even a monster that big," Lily said.

They had all seen the news of a giant sink hole opening up in the middle of Columbus Park. Still, Silas didn't think it was that easy.

"I don't know. When I used that club I kind of got to know it, and I don't think it was ever intended to kill. In fact, I think that's why it hated me, because it's in my nature to kill and destroy."

"Does that mean we have to somehow get down there and check?" Lily asked. "I don't think that's possible; the tunnels have all collapsed. We might be able to find a new route, but the actual cavern is probably gone."

Silas smiled--that was what he was hoping to hear. "No Lily, we can't go back down. I have another solution." He pulled the club out of his belt and handed it to her. He could feel it grow warm as she gripped it. "Nataepu."

She looked up at him, confusion on her face.

"Leonard is gone, but the dragon might still live. There needs to be a new guardian, one who understands the danger and can pass it down to other generations."

"Me? But I don't know anything about the Lenape, I mean other than what I read in those books."

"This isn't about the Lenape anymore. You heard what he said; they had mostly forgotten. He was the last. This is about guarding against a great threat to all humans. Somebody needs to take over the job. And frankly I hate humans, so I don't think that would work out."

She stared at the club as it glowed once and then faded in her hands. It seemed the club approved.

"Well now, that's settled. I just want to tell you how happy Moreales is about the team you have assembled—"

"Whoa, whoa! Team? No, I work alone."

"Nonsense. Steve here now works for the Inquisition Project; going forward he will be your driver. We will, of course, outfit a new limo with some enhancements appropriate for your line of work."

"What about my bike?" Silas asked. He did not like where this was going.

"Michael here will be staying with Father Deluca, but he has proved to be a great resource for intel on the streets, so he will stick close to you."

Michael was grinning ear to ear. His brother had been one of the reluctant converts in the back of the cavern. When the demon horde had invaded, he had been able to escape. Of course, as a half-formed monster he didn't know where to go. When Webb died, though, he had changed back and had enough of his humanity to make it back to his brother; he had been one of the few lucky ones. More than half the transformed humans had been killed by demonic soldiers or burned to death. He had said it was the knowledge that he had to find Michael that had helped him retain his sanity. He was currently resting in a bed at the mission.

"And Lily here, well you already named her Nataepu. She has already requested to be part of the Inquisition Project."

Silas slammed back another shot and put his head in his hands. A kid, a moron, and a bookworm, just great. He thought of something and looked up at Mort.

"Speaking of teams, where's Abigail?"

Mort pursed his lips and looked down at his hands.

"Mort? Where is Abby? She's late."

"Silas, she's gone," Mort said.

"What? Why? What do you mean she's gone?"

"She wasn't assigned permanently Silas. This was always just a one-shot deal for her. Moreales wanted her to help temper your methods, give you some subtly. She served her purpose."

Just like that she was gone. Silas sat back in his chair as the others began talking about the new arrangement. Mort was talking briefly about the training they would all have to go through. They just faded away for Silas. He took another drink.

"Silas," Lily said and nodded to the door.

He looked over and saw Abigail in the doorway. She smiled at him and then ducked out. He got up from the table, ignoring the others and followed her. She was leaning up against the building.

"Mort said you'd left."

"Yeah, I have my orders. I'm supposed to head back to Europe right away."

"Look Abby, I know we didn't always see eye to eye, but there was something between us right? I mean we work well together."

"Yes Silas, yes we did."

"So, what now? You just head out and we never see each other again? Is that how this is going to work?" Silas asked.

"You never know what the future is going to bring. We both still work for Moreales. Who knows what is in store for us?"

"You can't just leave. I mean you're the one who corrupted me with your aura, made me feel compassion and icky stuff like that. Now you are just going to go? Leave me all fucked up?"

Abigail looked confused for a second and then smiled. "Silas, I, like you, exude an aura. Where yours is of menace and anger, mine is peace and compassion, but you have no control over yours. Mine only goes where I direct. And Silas, I never directed it at you. Whatever you felt at those times was your own."

That couldn't be true. She was just trying to deflect the questions.

"So this is good-bye." It was a statement not a question.

"Except for one thing," she said stepping close to him. "My flight doesn't leave until tomorrow."

"Oh?"

"Don't you live a couple of blocks away?"

"Oh!"

She stepped in and kissed him, and it was like fire and ice. He put his arm around her, pulled her close and together they walked home.

"So it looks as though he succeeded," Father Moreales said.

"Yes sir," said Christopher, but Moreales heard reluctance in his voice.

"It seems with a little help our Silas can be efficient and maybe even subtle."

Moreales turned from the stack of reports on his desk and looked at his secretary. They had worked together for almost five years now, and he was a good man. Christopher went to the table that held the tea he had just brought in and poured two cups. He brought one to Moreales.

"I just don't feel that an uncouth demon is a good champion of humanity," Christopher said finally.

Moreales sipped from his tea as he gazed down into the courtyard. Some of the new recruits for the Project were down there practicing hand to hand combat. A minimal amount of combat training was required for all members of the Project whether they were agents or not.

"It's funny, I see it a little differently," Moreales said. "We are on the side of heaven; we fight to prepare mortals to ascend to heaven when judgment day comes. The Infernal host, they just want whatever they can get and will drag as much of humanity down on that day as they can. Silas doesn't want heaven or hell to win. He is the only one fighting for humans to stay human and do their own thing."

Moreales paused and took a sip of his tea. "I think that makes him humanity's greatest champion."

ALSO BY ERIK LYND

NOVELS

Asylum

The Collection

THE HAND OF PERDITION SERIES:

Book and Blade

Eater of Souls

The Demon Collector

Rise of the Soulless

SILAS ROBB SERIES:

Silas Robb: Of Saints and Sinners

Silas Robb: Hell Hath No Fury

COLLECTIONS AND SHORTER WORKS

The Long Fall Into Midnight Vol. 1

The Hanging Tree

Dark on the Water

His Devil

Dreams

Siege of the Bone Children

In the Pit

ABOUT THE AUTHOR

Erik Lynd writes novels and short stories primarily in the horror, dark fantasy, and urban fantasy genres. Currently he is in the middle of two ongoing urban fantasy series; Silas Robb and The Hand of Perdition series. He also writes the occasional horror novel such as Asylum and The Collection. He lives in the Pacific Northwest where yes it does rain a lot and no he does not mind it.

For more information...
www.eriklynd.com
erik@eriklynd.com

Printed in Great Britain
by Amazon